KILLER
COCKTAIL

Also by Sheryl J. Anderson

Killer Heels

Sheryl J. Anderson

KILLER

COCKTAIL

 St. Martin's Minotaur
New York

www.minotaurbooks.com

Library of Congress Cataloging-in-Publication Data

Anderson, Sheryl J., 1958–
    Killer cocktail / Sheryl J. Anderson.—1st ed.
        p. cm.
    ISBN 0-312-31944-4
    EAN 978-0-312-31944-1
    1. Women journalists—Fiction. 2. Young women—Crimes against—Fiction. 3. Advice columnists—Fiction. 4. Hamptons (N.Y.)—Fiction. I. Title.

PS3551.N3947K547 2005
813'.54—dc22

                                                                2004066448

First Edition: August 2005

10 9 8 7 6 5 4 3 2 1

To my husband,
Mark Edward Parrott,
the unsung hero

Acknowledgments

I am delighted to have another opportunity to thank my amazing husband, Mark, and our beautiful children, Sean and Sara, who are my constant joy and inspiration; they make everything I do possible and wonderful. I also thank our families for their love and support, especially my parents, Alden and June Anderson, and brother and sister-in-law, Eric and Allison Anderson, for an amazing stay at the Algonquin, and Mark's parents, Bob and Iva Parrott, for liking this book even more than the first one. A special tip of the hat goes to my uncle, Donald McLean, for teaching me about Johnny Mercer, "snark," and other vital facts. Thanks also to our agent, Andy Zack, and to Kelley Ragland, Carly Einstein, Rachel Ekstrom, and all the fine folks at St. Martin's for their hard work. Special thanks to all of the wonderful friends (what a blessing that they are too numerous to name here) who sustain us with their prayers, encouragement, and enthusiasm, and who, as soon as they finished *Killer Heels,* started asking, "When's the next one coming out?"

KILLER

COCKTAIL

1

Solving a murder is a lot like falling in love. The first time, you do it without thinking about it, certainly before you've analyzed the consequences, weighed the possible outcomes, or thought about how badly you might get hurt. You get caught up in the momentum, the intoxication of "It has to be right," and you hurtle along, powered by instinct, adrenaline, and naïveté.

And then—*boom*. It's over. Before you know it. Before you're prepared for it. And you suddenly find yourself cleaning up, sorting things out, trying to make sense of everything, and thanking your lucky stars you weren't hurt any worse than you were.

So then you vow, "Never again." And you stick to that vow, change your ways, and live a quiet, sane life while your wounds heal and you regain some perspective on the world.

Until the little voice in your head says, "Well, maybe just one more time."

Actually, it wasn't a voice in my head. It was in person. The person of Tricia Vincent, one of my two best friends. And that's the most dangerous thing about friends. They can talk you into doing things that you would never consider doing on your own. Like going out with someone. Or tracking down a killer.

She didn't try to strong-arm me. She was lovely and polite because Tricia would be lovely and polite in the middle of an alien abduction and probing; she's just wired that way. She just said, "Molly, I need you to figure out who killed her."

I hadn't gone to the Hamptons intending to get involved in this sort of thing. I'd actually gone to get away from it, or from the fallout, at least. But there I was, on the rebound as it were, and there was Tricia, asking me to take the plunge again. Naturally, I'm always willing to do anything I can to help Tricia, but, just as we have to ask ourselves after a devastating breakup if we're ready to plunge back into the potentially horrifying world of emotional entanglements, I had to ask myself if I was ready to deal with another murder.

There was a time in my life when the only dead bodies I'd seen were in open caskets in funeral homes. And I hadn't even seen very many of those because the Forrester family thankfully has pretty good genes in the longevity department and those who had passed away did so with the lid down. (Probably the first time some of the Forrester men had ever left the lid down.)

But Teddy Reynolds moved me to a whole new level of dead body contact. Teddy was the advertising director at *Zeitgeist,* the magazine where I work here in New York City. I tripped over his body and wound up trying to solve his murder with some help from Tricia and my other best friend, Cassady, and despite the protests of a seriously hot homicide detective named Kyle Edwards. This all came from my brilliant idea that I could not only solve the murder before Kyle did, but could write an amazing feature article about it and redirect my career.

What's that saying about people making plans and God laughing? To be fair, I did solve Teddy's murder. I wrote the article and Garrett Wilson published it in *Manhattan* magazine, a top-flight credit in my circle. I got that far and I have a mounted, laminated copy of the article and a bullet scar on my left shoulder to prove it. But after the dust settled, so did the rest of my plans. The lovingly imagined transformation from advice columnist to crusading girl reporter didn't happen. My article created a nice buzz, but not enough to get anyone to take me seriously as a full-time feature writer. We got a new editor at *Zeitgeist,* because our old editor . . . never mind, that's another story. Though you can order my article from *Manhattan*'s archives through their Web site if you're interested.

Anyway, now we had a new boss at our magazine, an ice-blooded horror who took great delight in shooting down every idea I had outside my column. And my relationship with Kyle Edwards continued to defy description, classification, and reason. So I hadn't been planning on hunting down another killer any time too soon.

But this was Tricia. Crying and asking me to dive in all over again. I've never been very good at turning down a friend, especially a friend who's also in tears. I always thought "A friend in need is a friend indeed" deserved a corollary: "A friend in need needs a friend in deed." Besides, I knew Tricia's plea for help was heartfelt and based on her own judgment of how I—excuse me, we—had handled the first murder. Despite some initial hesitation, she and Cassady had been quite supportive, on both the emotional and investigative levels, so she knew what she was getting into. Or assumed she did.

But if good intentions pave the road to hell, assumptions

form the median strip. Not that I expect life to lay itself out neatly, with easy-to-follow directions and shiny game pieces and fun prizes. I know that part of life's beauty is its unexpected twists and turns. But wouldn't it be nice if life occasionally turned in the right direction?

"What's the fun in that?" Cassady asked when I ran the theory by my two best friends one afternoon, a couple of days before Tricia's tearful plea. We were having lunch at 'Wichcraft, an amazing sandwich place in the Flatiron District, and I was doing my best to make sure the tomato relish stayed on my meat loaf sandwich and didn't wind up all down the front of my brand-new white James Perse crewneck tee. My chest is a natural tomato magnet, especially when I'm wearing white. Or maybe it's the size of my breasts; the tomatoes think they've found kindred spirits.

Tricia was quiet and thoughtful, which is not that unusual. She has an innate sparkle, but she keeps it contained and unleashes it only after careful consideration. People make the mistake of assuming that she's malleable because she's quiet and darkly delicate, but she's just coiled. Her emotional outbursts carry far more impact, because of their rarity, than mine do because of their appalling regularity.

While Tricia often idles, Cassady goes full throttle. Today, Cassady was in fix-your-life mode, to the point that the counterman, a buff beauty of a boy, was flirting with her and she hadn't noticed. Cassady's stunning, with that if-she-weren't-so-much-fun-you-might-hate-her combination of long legs, auburn curls, green eyes, and great body. Men flirt with her all the time, and she generally manages to acknowledge, if not participate, but right now she was completely zeroed in on me.

"It's not about fun, it's about satisfaction," I countered, quickly licking up the relish that was dripping down my thumb before it could leap onto my shirt and introduce itself to my breasts.

"Those aren't mutually exclusive. In fact, they should be required to be inclusive." Cassady's an intellectual properties lawyer and I've often accused her of deliberately choosing a profession in which she gets paid to manipulate both the language and the people who use it. She's never disagreed, she's just pointed out that she's very good at doing both, so it makes sense that she's turned that into a career. Satisfaction and fun, a case in point.

"What about 'grim satisfaction'?" I volleyed.

"That's like 'gallows humor,'" Cassady explained. "You concede the direness of the situation, but still admit there's an element of fun or pleasure in the result. C'mon, Molly. Didn't you feel grim satisfaction when you caught Teddy's killer?"

"I felt huge relief," Tricia said. Tricia's an event planner, which fulfills her need to make people happy. It also appeals to her desire for order, organization, and a smooth flow of foreseen incidents. Being part of a murder investigation had been very trying for her.

"As did we all," Cassady admitted. "But now, with some emotional distance . . ."

"Okay. Grim satisfaction. And maybe, actually, not all that grim. What is grim is the fact that I don't know what to do next."

"Concerning the career or the boyfriend?"

"Neither one is where it should be."

Tricia sighed in disagreement. "Isn't it more of a case of 'where you want it to be'?"

I shrugged. "Well, as the philosopher said, 'You can't always get what you want.'"

"Don't start quoting the ancients." Cassady leaned in.

"Listen, I know you thought this whole Teddy Reynolds thing was going to change your life and you think it's failed to do so. I contend it has changed your life and will continue to change it, but more gradually and insidiously than you're comfortable with right now."

I looked to Tricia for backup, but she was nodding in support of Cassady's theory. "Patience has never been your strong suit."

"What's this, tag-team therapy?"

"We want you to be happy," Tricia said firmly.

"I am happy."

Cassady arched her eyebrow so perfectly, no makeup artist could have painted it on better. She and Tricia had personally observed many of the ups and downs of my relationship with Kyle and had heard my recitations of most of the others. After all, you can only discuss your problems with a man with that man to a certain point. Then you need to get some genuine perspective, which means asking your best girlfriends what they think.

They thought he was delightful. And sexy. And charming. All of which I was in agreement with. But they hadn't learned to relax around him completely. I was struggling with that, too. He was a pretty intense individual in an incredibly intense profession. He'd always make a point of asking how things were going at the magazine, but how could advising some lovesick public relations exec that it was time to ask her boyfriend to move in with her, even though it meant learning to understand fantasy football, ever compare to solving a murder? My work paled next to his because his changed the world. And, truth be told, I was jealous.

Dating any man is a challenge and, with the column, I have a front-row seat at the dizzying parade of complications that trying to synchronize two lives can bring, especially in the areas of emotional baggage and outstanding commitments. But when you date a man sworn to uphold the public good, the stakes increase dramatically. Now you're not just competing for his attention with the ex-girlfriend, the ex-wife, the hockey buddies, or the doting mother, you're competing with a higher calling at all hours of the day and night. Even if you're very high-minded and secure in your place in the universe, it can be difficult to find your footing in a relationship that's constantly hitting the hold button because his cell phone is ringing again, and never with good news.

Kyle and I had tried taking time off from each other, but we couldn't stay apart. We'd even tried starting over again from the beginning, with proper dates and plans, but we'd been through so much together by that point that it felt artificial. So we went back to this odd in-between space of being intensely close and still not knowing each other as well as we wanted to.

"I'm just not as happy as I'd like to be," I confessed to Tricia and Cassady as a blob of tomato relish evaded my thumb and threw itself at my cleavage. Such as it is.

"That's the human condition," Tricia offered, immediately dipping her napkin in her water glass and handing it to me.

"Exactly. So I'm learning to live with it and I'm changing the subject. Is it rub, not dab or dab, not rub?" I asked, damp napkin poised above the relish stain.

"Maybe we could get the chef to lick it off for you," Cassady suggested.

"Dab," Tricia said. I dabbed.

Cassady's perfectly arched eyebrow slanted unhappily. "None of this is about the career. It's about the man."

"The Man keeps us all down. You, of all people, should have learned that at your parents' knee." Cassady's parents currently run an educational foundation promoting literacy in inner-city schools, but they met as Eastern Studies majors at Berkeley in the late sixties. Cassady's named after Neal Cassady. (As Tricia's named after Tricia Nixon, they make quite a pair.) Cassady refers to her parents as "evolved hippies." They're intensely cool, but never call attention to it. Which is where Cassady gets it from.

"When's the last time you talked to Kyle?" Cassady persisted.

"I don't remember."

"You remember the date, the time, and what you were wearing. Or not wearing, as the case might be."

"He called yesterday." I tried to leave it at that, but Cassady shook her head to let me know I couldn't get away with it. "Last night. Eleven-fifteen. There was a slight breeze from the southeast and I was wearing jeans and a sweatshirt because I was lying on the couch, watching *The Daily Show*."

"You turned Jon Stewart off for him?" Tricia asked.

"Yes."

"I'm impressed."

"What did you talk about?" Cassady asked.

"Movies. Politics. We veered perilously close to the weather, but all sorts of internal alarms went off and I brought up football instead."

"How very high school of you," Cassady said.

"Thank you."

"How long were you on the phone?" Tricia was driving at something, but I couldn't get a sense of the direction yet.

"About an hour."

"And you hung up without a date being scheduled?" Cassady asked, probably pulling an eyebrow muscle or two to get them to arch so high. "I withdraw the snarky high school comment."

"Thank you."

"In its place, I now say 'junior high.' "

"He's in the middle of a case," I attempted, not sure which of us I was defending more.

"You need to get out of town," Tricia pronounced. "Remind him what he's missing."

Cassady pursed her lips doubtfully. "What guarantee do we have that she won't wind up missing him?"

"None, but the Hamptons are known for their ability to distract. That's why we're going to Southampton. This weekend."

I winced. Weekend getaways had contributed heavily to my current state of romantic frustration, so it wasn't a favorite concept at the moment.

Kyle and I met in October. Things had lurched along reasonably well until right before Christmas, when he'd taken me to the precinct holiday party. Kyle was their most eligible bachelor, which meant I was under intense scrutiny by all the wives and girlfriends present. While I'd been spared an interrogation, I had managed to wear, say, and do the wrong thing all in one evening, a feat even for me. My dress had been too low, too short, and too black. I'd trashed the weepy tearjerker they'd all just finished loving in their book club. But my crowning achievement had been to slip on the plastic snow scattered cheerily around the dance floor and spill my eggnog on the commissioner on the way down.

Kyle wasn't bothered by any of it; the eggnog incident actually amused him. But I expected Santa to drop a scarlet *A* down my chimney and let me guess what it stood for. I was so sure I didn't fit into his world, maybe it was becoming a self-fulfilling prophecy. He'd had to work on New Year's Eve, so I'd extended my vacation in Virginia. In January, he'd caught a really heavy case and we'd only seen each other twice, so I boldly invited him to my place for dinner on Valentine's Day. He accepted and it was wonderful. In March, we'd gone to a charity dinner Cassady's group was cosponsoring and Kyle had been charming to everyone, though his impatience with the politics of the evening had been apparent to me.

After that, we'd finally seemed to gain some momentum as a couple. That's why ten days ago, I'd suggested we go somewhere for a weekend, just the two of us. He hadn't said anything for a long time and then had said, "We'll see." I could hear the squeal of brakes and feel the whiplash. Since then, we'd had a couple of vaguely unsatisfying phone calls. Clearly, I'd made him uncomfortable. How uncomfortable was the question.

But perhaps it was a question best pondered somewhere out of town in the company of my two best friends. I tried to remember the balance on my credit card. "It's the first week of May. When does the season start?"

"Doesn't matter. We're going to my aunt's house."

Cassady and I exchanged a look, confirming that we were troubled by the same thought. "Aunt Cynthia?" I asked.

"Yes."

"Aunt Cynthia of the ever-fluctuating last will and testament?" Cassady asked.

"The same."

"The Aunt Cynthia who got drunk at your grandfather's funeral and stood on the dining room table and sang 'We'll Meet Again,'" I continued, just to make sure that we were all, in fact, talking about a woman we had heard Tricia vow she would never speak to again unless under court order.

"That's her."

Cassady and I wavered, uncertain of the etiquette involved in saying the next thing. I took the plunge. "But you hate her."

"Yes, but she has a great house," Tricia insisted, a little too brightly.

"Oh, I get it. She's going away and you've bribed the housekeeper to slip you the keys for the weekend," Cassady said.

"No. She's going to be there. The whole family's going to be there." Tricia's smile stretched to the point where I feared it might permanently torque her small face like a bad facelift. "And if you guys don't come with me, I could very well wind up being the one singing on the dining room table."

Cassady shrugged. "Well, I can't miss that. Count me in."

"What's going on?" I asked.

"That's Molly's way of saying that she'd love to come, too," Cassady teased.

"Well, of course I'd love to, but I don't get it. If Aunt Cynthia's doing the whole black sheep thing, why's the entire family trooping down there and why don't you just plead heavy workload and not go?"

Tricia's smile faltered. "It's David's engagement party."

The Vincents are a fascinating family. New England bluebloods, super-Republican, the closest thing to aristocracy I've ever met. Tricia jokes that her ancestors came over on the advance ship *before* the *Mayflower*, to make sure the Colonies were suitable and that everything had been set up properly; planning and controlling are in her blood. Her parents live in Connecticut, but they also keep an apartment in the city because they're constantly coming in for some function or another. They've always been lovely to Cassady and me. Tricia's crazy about them, but they also make her crazy. Her favorite brother, David, is a case in point. She adores him, would walk out on the president to take a call from him, but David acts first and thinks second and usually calls Tricia to clean up third.

"They got engaged?" Cassady asked.

Tricia's smile disappeared altogether. "Her parents are throwing some huge party in L.A., but Mother and Dad decided to up the ante and throw them a proper engagement party here first. Mother doesn't think those show people on the Left Coast respect social ritual. But Mother and Dad's little project turned into a whole weekend that turned into too many people for the house in Connecticut. Obviously, someone didn't put the scotch away soon enough and got on the phone with Aunt Cynthia, and you guys have to come because I don't know how I'll get through it otherwise." The fingernail of her right index finger dug into the cuticle of her right thumb, Tricia's classic sign of distress.

"Of course we'll be there," I assured her, taking her hand in mine to stop the digging.

Then, because it is Cassady's gift, she said the thing we were all thinking. "He's really going to marry that bitch?"

For just a moment, I thought that glow beneath Tricia's Dresden doll exterior was going to reveal itself to be molten lava and we were going to watch it erupt. But ever the lady, Tricia struggled to keep it all inside and lifted her glass instead. "To my brothers and their god-awful taste in women," she toasted.

We clinked glasses in assent. In all the years we'd known Tricia (the three of us met as college freshmen thirteen years ago, but please don't do the math), David and Richard Vincent had excelled at involvements with nightmarish women. Richard had gone so far as to marry Rebecca Somerset two years ago. Rebecca's mom was electronics money, her dad was shipping money, and Rebecca was an heiress *cum* designer *cum* disaster. She was famous in a large number of nonintersecting social circles for consistently inappropriate and boorish behavior. I'd had the pleasure of seeing her in action at a fundraiser where she sat next to the Chilean consul's wife at the head table of a five-k-a-plate banquet, loudly critiqued the poor woman's dress and jewelry all through dinner—holding up the Chilean consul's mistress as a paragon of style—then tried to redo her hair during the keynote address.

After a very public romance, Richard and Rebecca eloped to Jamaica and Tricia's mother literally took to her bed for a week. Richard and Rebecca had made it a whole thirteen months before splitting up—a full trip around the rocky cape of the calendar so they could ruin every holiday once, was Tricia's theory—and the Vincent family was still reverberating, six months into the separation.

And now David was apparently engaged to Lisbet Mc-Candless, one of the few women in America capable of making Rebecca look good by comparison. Lisbet was second-generation Hollywood, the spawn of a movie direc-tor and a studio executive, both famous for their tempers and sexual flexibility. Lisbet had been a sitcom star as a child; as a teenager, she drifted into a series of films quickly for-gotten despite Lisbet's willingness to do nudity.

Now in her twenties, Lisbet had worked her way back on to television, basic cable at least (rumor was, her mother was having an affair with the network executive who ordered the show). She played a rocket scientist who stumbles upon a government cover-up of life on Venus—the only thing that was covered up on the show. It was a huge hit, thanks mainly to the plunging necklines on Lisbet's costumes, and the success put Lisbet back on top of the tabloid heap. Lately, she'd gotten into so many public brawls with other starlets that her father had shipped her out to do off-Broadway during hiatus as career rehab. David had met her shortly after her arrival in New York and they'd been pa-parazzi fodder ever since. And now they were engaged.

I put on my most optimistic expression. "So, your parents are throwing them a huge party. They must be pleased about the whole thing."

Tricia scrunched up her face. "Mother's terrorizing the staff and Dad's taking way too many meetings. They're not happy."

"Then why the big party?"

Tricia sighed. "Apparently, Rebecca and Richard have one common belief left, which is that my parents were opposed to their marriage and undermined it from Day One."

"Smart parents," Cassady said.

"But in their shell shock, Mother and Dad apparently feel that if they make a big show of supporting David and Lisbet, those two won't be able to accuse them of the same thing when their marriage blows up." Tricia's eyes narrowed. "And blow up, it will."

"If it's a big family thing, do you really want us there?" I asked.

"You're more family to me than some of the piranhas in my gene pool. Besides, if you don't come, who will join me as I sit with my bottle of champagne in the corner and sip and snipe?"

"Sounds like my kind of weekend. Count me in," Cassady volunteered.

"Could be fascinating," I had to admit.

"Thank you. I feel so much better about going now." Tricia smiled genuinely and did seem immensely relieved.

Which is why, that Friday, I was overpacking my overnight bag and wondering when—possibly even, if—I should call Kyle and tell him I was going away. He was trying to wrap up a case so I had no expectation of spending the weekend with him. When we'd last spoken, he'd said he didn't know when we'd be able to get together. So if I called him now and told him I was going away for the weekend, would it seem like I was forcing him to revisit the subject of our going away? I didn't want to seem punitive. Or worse, clingy. Fortunately, I was spared the agony of examining this ethical dilemma by the fact that Kyle chose that moment to call me.

"Hey." He said it warmly, but gave me no indication of whether he was standing in the middle of his office or in the middle of a pool of blood. "This a bad time?"

I opted for the breezy, no-big-deal approach. "No, actually good timing. I'm on my way out. What should I bring you back from Southampton?"

There was a pause. Brief, but still discernible. The Pause is risky, more for the recipient than for the pauser. Resist all you want, you're still going to read something into the Pause, a problem that can feed on itself when the pauser realizes he's paused and starts wondering about what you're reading into his pause. You're on one end of the phone, thinking he's bracing himself to tell you bad news, to get his lie in proper order, to struggle against his desire to declare undying love. And he's on his end, perhaps doing any one of those things, but maybe just stifling a sneeze or being momentarily distracted by some slut in an exceptionally tight T-shirt and gaudy belly ring.

Communication is the foundation of any good relationship, God help us.

"The weekend?"

I made sure I didn't pause. "Uh-huh."

"Going alone?"

"Does that affect your request?"

"Among other things."

I liked that answer, and did my best to detect jealousy lurking around the edges. "Tricia's family's having a thing and she wants Cassady and me to come along and protect her."

"Hazardous duty."

"Only for my liver."

"One of *those* weekends."

"With any luck."

"So you're hoping to get lucky this weekend?"

"Ah. You can take the boy out of the interrogation room, but you can't take the interrogation room out of the boy."

"Or evasion out of the girl."

"I'm going down to keep Tricia from telling her aunt what she really thinks of her. My sole mission."

"Aunt's a piece of work?"

"Putting it nicely. You may have heard of her. Cynthia Malinkov."

"Any relation to Lev Malinkov, the developer?"

"Ex, with an emphasis on big alimony."

"You're a good friend."

"It's my only shot at heaven."

He laughed. It was a great sound, especially because he didn't do it very often. I stayed quiet, which I don't do very often. It didn't really constitute a Pause, because I was giving him the opportunity to say something in addition to the laugh. I was also realizing that he hadn't said why he called.

"You underestimate yourself," he said, and I could tell he was still smiling.

"Chronically."

"Have a great time."

"You haven't answered my question. Or told me why you called."

"You sure you didn't call me?"

Now I laughed. "Not really."

"I don't want anything. Just call me when you get back."

"But why'd you call?"

"Tell you then. Stay out of trouble."

"I'll do my best."

He sighed and I knew he was remembering the circumstances of our first meeting. "Try harder."

In retrospect, he gets to look all brilliant and psychic, which isn't entirely fair. Of course, if any of us had realized how the weekend would end, we would have all stayed in Manhattan, even if we did nothing more exciting than sit in my apartment eating cold Chinese takeout and playing cribbage. But life is never that simple. Thankfully.

2

Maybe there's something in the air, something in the water, some magical portal you pass through as you drive out Route 27—but the Hamptons are a different world. And it's more than the fact that there's so much accumulated wealth in the area that you smell newly minted money rather than cut grass when the gardeners are at work. It's beautiful, engaging, and not quite real. Even appalling, soul-numbing traffic on the drive there can't diminish the beauty once you arrive. The water, the sweeping expanses of green, the jaw-dropping homes, it's all pretty amazing.

Aunt Cynthia lives in Southampton in what Tricia calls a "large house," which befits Aunt Cynthia, a woman of large reputation and even larger holdings. Apparently, her greatest talent is structuring her own divorce settlements, which she has done four times. I don't know whether it speaks to how happy the men were before things went south or how happy they were to get out alive once things headed that way that she consistently emerged with the social standing, the friends, and fifty-one percent of the assets. Always leave them taking more, I guess.

Currently, her massive portfolio included astute real estate holdings, a Broadway show that was actually making money, and underwriting a stepdaughter who's *the* hot housewares designer of the moment. According to Tricia, her aunt was deplorably lacking in basic humanity, but she seemed to have a pretty good eye for business.

Tricia pulled up to the wrought-iron gate at the foot of a driveway that would have run the entire length of the subdivision I grew up in. She poked the button on the intercom and a gruff male voice responded, "Lap dancers are supposed to use the service entrance."

"Jokes are supposed to be funny," Tricia retorted.

"I must advise you to retreat now, before your troops are fired upon," another male voice, less rumbly but pleasantly deep, continued.

"Can't you guys find something better to play with than the intercom?"

"Not until you bring Molly and Cassady into the house."

"And who's keeping me from doing that?"

"It's Richard's fault," the first voice assured her.

"Everything's Richard's fault. Open the gate, Davey."

"Did you bring me a present?"

"I brought you Molly and Cassady."

"Excellent. Advance."

There was a discreet hum and the great gates swung back with mechanical grace. "My brothers obviously opened the bar early," Tricia sighed as she drove up to the house.

Cassady and I declined to comment because we were busy gaping. It was a magnificent Georgian mansion and looked like something out of a British miniseries, one of those gray stone country houses where important people hid during World War II, having tea and rationed milk in between discreet affairs. Tricia parked in front of the massive double front door and hopped out of the car, heading straight for the front steps. Cassady and I scrambled after her and I pointed to the trunk of the car. "Shouldn't we bring our stuff in?"

"Nelson will take care of that," Tricia explained over her shoulder.

Cassady and I looked at each other in delight. "Nelson," Cassady repeated.

"He'll get the bags," I returned.

We managed not to giggle as we followed Tricia inside. Which was just as impressive as the outside and sparkled a great deal more. Tricia introduced us to Nelson, who was less Anthony Hopkins and more Mel Gibson than I'd anticipated. He greeted us with a warm formality and informed Tricia that most of the family was already dressing for dinner since the guests would be arriving soon. When she inquired about her brothers, Nelson rolled his eyes in the most respectful manner possible and said they, too, had gone to dress. He suggested we go up to our rooms and he would bring up our things.

Cassady watched him as he walked out the front door. "Nice to have a man around the house," she offered.

Tricia sighed. "I'd rather not consider all the ways Aunt Cynthia might keep him busy." She called out for her brothers, but there was no answer, though I swore I heard an echo. Tricia checked her watch and hurried us upstairs where, without benefit of a compass or trail of bread crumbs, she was able to find the room where she always stayed. Cassady and I had been assigned the room next door.

It was going to be an eclectic mix of people all weekend, which would be a source of entertainment unto itself. The relatives—plus Cassady and I—were staying here, with the rest of the guests scattered around the area at their family manses or friends' palaces. Most of the guests were David and Lisbet's social set, but there were friends and associates of Mr. and Mrs. Vincent on hand, as well as some friends of Aunt Cynthia's whom she told Tricia she'd invited to make sure things stayed interesting.

Our room was massive and yet welcoming, furnished with pieces to make a museum director drool, and soft, elegant fabrics that made you want to curl up in a wing chair or drape yourself over one of the two double beds, which I did immediately.

Nelson arrived moments later with our bags and a plump young woman named Marguerite who wore a classic black-and-white maid's uniform and carried three flutes of champagne on a silver tray. Nelson and Marguerite left their goodies and withdrew, leaving us to freshen up, toss back the champagne, and slip on our party finery. My Elie Tahari floral silk dress had had the good manners not to wrinkle, so once my Edmundo Castillo black patent sandals were buckled (the huge buckles were what sold me, even more than the three-and-a-half-inch heels), I was ready to go.

Cassady, on the other hand, uncharacteristically chose to fuss with her hair. "Most people go out of town to let their hair down," I pointed out as Cassady piled her auburn locks on top of her head.

Tricia stood near the door, wearing a Dolce & Gabbana fitted paisley dress, draining her champagne and trying not to tap her Ashley Dearborn–framed toes. "Cassady, you're more stunning than mortal eye can bear. Let's go."

Cassady pursed her lips at her reflection in the bureau mirror. She was wearing a strapless Stella McCartney and looked fabulous, of course. "I just want to make a good impression. For your sake, Tricia."

"Gild by association?" I had to ask.

Tricia walked over and tugged on the front of Cassady's

dress. "Sweetheart, no one's going to realize you even have a head. Aunt Cynthia likes punctuality. Let's go."

We followed Tricia through another maze of gently illuminated hallways, down a staircase wide enough for the Giants offensive line to descend in formation, and out to the backyard. I doubt, though, they use that word in Southampton. The south lawn, perhaps. The back forty. The adjacent county, even. On the vivid expanse of lawn there was a gently billowing tent lit by gauzy globes. Within the tent, people were finding their way to their tables while waitresses of the aspiring model/actress/trophy wife variety stood off to the side, ready to serve. This was evidence of Cassady's theory that the Hamptons are the only true example of trickle-down economics: All the excess cash in Manhattan has trickled down to the Hamptons where it then trickles down to all the waitresses and lifeguards and dog walkers who pool that cash to move to . . . Manhattan.

It was twilight and the lighting inside the tent had that indirect glow that makes everyone look fabulous, but keeps you from being absolutely sure that what's on your plate is cooked thoroughly. And then there were the people. I've been to a lot of society functions in New York City, but there's usually an undercurrent of nouveau riche that cuts the headiness of lots of old money being in one place. But here, you could sense the trust funds in the rustle of designer clothing, hear the boarding schools in the practiced laughter. Apparently, life is a Ralph Lauren ad after all.

Tricia, being the high priestess of protocol that she is and a dutiful daughter to boot, led us straight to her parents, who were just about to leave their greeting post to go to their table.

The Vincents are the definition of a handsome couple. Tricia gets her penetrating eyes from her father, Paul, a commanding, broad-shouldered man with a jazz disc jockey's voice and an intimidating handshake, but most of her looks come from her mother, Claire, a slim, elegant woman whom I suspect of wearing pearls to bed.

Mr. Vincent hugged us all enthusiastically, planting a large kiss on Tricia's forehead. Mrs. Vincent was a little more restrained in her embraces, offering her cheek to each of us. It didn't bother me but alerted Tricia to something amiss.

"Mother?" she asked with a leading lilt to the word.

"I'm fine, dear. You're sitting with some of Davey's chums. Go keep an eye on them. We can't throw off Cynthia's timetable."

"Mother," Tricia repeated.

Mrs. Vincent summoned up a polite smile and asked, "Did you see who came with Richard?"

All three of us turned and looked out across the guests at the same time. Richard is a tall, sculpted hottie and even in this shining crowd, he was easy to spot. We just weren't prepared for who was on his arm.

"Rebecca?" Tricia gasped.

There was a moment I thought Tricia was wrong, that Richard was unfortunately dating a new woman who looked uncannily like the old one. But then I realized Tricia was right. It was Rebecca, just with radical changes. The platinum marcel with rose highlights had become a soft cinnamon page boy. Pearl studs had replaced the retro oversized hoops. Courtney Love had morphed into Courtney Cox.

"What's with the extreme makeover?" Cassady muttered in my ear.

"At least she's started wearing a bra," I whispered back. The dresses Rebecca designs are actually quite pretty.

They're clingy and sheer and brightly colored—three potent reasons why Rebecca, who is not as svelte as she thinks she is, was often her own worst advertisement. But tonight, not only did she seem properly strapped down, she looked like she'd been working out.

"Richard's trying to annoy us," Mr. Vincent said with the stiff upper lip of a practiced politico. "He must be bored."

"This couldn't have been his idea." Tricia looked like she was having trouble breathing and I wondered if there was a special Heimlich maneuver for someone choking on bad news.

"It's hardly a discussion to have right here where everyone can see us." Mrs. Vincent's smile didn't waver as she patted Tricia's cheek reassuringly, then gestured to the tables. "Have a seat and we'll talk after the meal."

Tricia inherited her mother's distaste for public awkwardness, so she politely followed instructions. Cassady and I trailed behind her to a table occupied by a young turk on a cell phone and a couple who were either kissing or licking pâté off each other; the lanterns made it impossible to determine which. Tricia slid into her chair, eyes still fixed on Richard and Rebecca, and we stationed ourselves to her right. Our tablemates didn't even register our presence.

"I don't see Lisbet and Davey," Tricia said.

"Stop staring at your other brother and look around a little," Cassady suggested. She pointed across the tent and both Tricia and I turned to see the guests of honor huddled with Aunt Cynthia beside the bar. At first glance, I thought David and Lisbet were getting a lecture, the way their heads were bowed and they were leaning in to Aunt Cynthia as though to listen earnestly. Then I realized Aunt Cynthia was pouring into three shot glasses she grasped expertly in one hand. David and Lisbet were poised to take and toss the moment she stopped.

Aunt Cynthia is a tall, angular woman with cheekbones as sharp as her business sense. David takes after his aunt more than his father would like. He's a little gaunt, a little loud, but his charm and his smarts keep you from staying too mad at him for too long. It remained to be seen whether his matrimonial track record would be anything like hers.

Lisbet is a lithe, sloe-eyed vamp with annoyingly good legs. Her neckline plunged, as usual, its openness emphasized by an emerald necklace that commanded the eye even from the other side of the tent.

"Amazing necklace," I noted.

"What's amazing is, she's wearing it. It's a family piece of Dad's. Richard wanted Rebecca to wear it to some premiere early on and Mother and Dad said no. I got to wear it for my debut and haven't asked since." Tricia looked from Lisbet to her parents. "They're trying so hard, they're going to hurt themselves."

The trio did their shots, then Aunt Cynthia handed the bottle back to the bartender and strode to the platform where a jazz combo was quietly playing "Moonlight in Vermont." Aunt Cynthia yanked at one of the tiers of her silk tornado of a dress and grabbed the microphone from the keyboard player's stand. "Good evening and thank you all for coming."

The combo and conversation stopped immediately. Aunt Cynthia gestured to where the Vincents were seated. "On behalf of my brother, Paul, and his lovely wife, I'd like to welcome you to this gathering. We're going to have a lot of fun this weekend, celebrating the engagement of two fabulous young people, my nephew David and his marvelous Lisbet."

The guests applauded and a few people whooped, Arsenio Hall's enduring contribution to Western civilization. David and Lisbet waved to everyone while they made their way over to join Mr. and Mrs. Vincent at their table. Lisbet already had the slow blink that comes with a good buzz, and dinner hadn't even been served.

"But before we eat, we must hear from the man himself. Paul?"

Mr. Vincent, smooth and practiced, was already making his way up to the bandstand. He took the microphone from his sister. "My sister's generosity is legendary, but she's outdone herself. Thank you, Cynthia."

Aunt Cynthia flapped her hands in mock annoyance at the applause, sending her armful of gold bangles bouncing up and down, but the smile she gave Mr. Vincent seemed genuine. They were very different, but they were still brother and sister.

"This weekend, we celebrate the addition of a glowing jewel to the Vincent family crown," Mr. Vincent continued. "David and Lisbet honor us by sharing their happiness with us. Congratulations and best wishes to them and *bon appétit* to us all."

Tricia seemed surprised. "That's actually sentimental, coming from my father."

Mr. Vincent handed the microphone back to Aunt Cynthia. She tossed it to the startled keyboard player and stepped off the bandstand with her brother. But as he returned to his table, she made a beeline for ours.

"Incoming. Brace yourselves for impact," Tricia warned, but Cassady and I weren't in any danger. Tricia was the one enveloped in the silk tornado and crushed to the bony bosom. I worried for a moment that Tricia might be squeezed into the rib cage and be entrapped there forever, but after a moment, Aunt Cynthia released her and parked herself in the next chair.

"Well." Aunt Cynthia thumped the table, her bangles jangling noisily. The impact was enough to separate the kissing couple and get the young turk off the phone, but Aunt Cynthia didn't seem to notice. She was too busy frowning at Tricia.

"Aunt Cynthia. You remember Cassady and Molly," Tricia said.

"Nice to see you, girls. Is my niece behaving herself?"

"A lady never tells," Tricia answered for herself.

"Except in a deposition. Have you spoken to either of your brothers? I'm not sure which one of them is demonstrating the greater lack of character."

"Whose idea was the necklace?" Tricia asked.

Aunt Cynthia flipped her hands skyward in dismissal. "I'm sure David was trying to make a point to Richard. They'll never outgrow that. Have a nice meal and we'll talk again later." Aunt Cynthia arose and swirled off, leaving us staring after her, which was, I'm sure, the desired effect.

Dinner was served. The Asian-French fusion menu was elegant and delicious, the wine and champagne were superb and plentiful, and the tablemates were shrill and annoying. We were with two of David's college buddies who, Tricia whispered from behind her napkin, she had seen drunk and naked far too often while visiting David at Brown. Brent was an investment banker who kept leaving the table to scream into his cell phone, so he didn't really even count as a tablemate.

Then there was Jake Boone, a documentary filmmaker who kept trying to explain his vision of "wordless cinema *du monde,*" which sounded suspiciously like silent movies. And his Portuguese girlfriend and camera assistant, Lara Del

Guidice, who kept interrupting Jake every time he approached making a point. Usually, she wanted to expound on some obscure cinematic theory that baffled even him. I began to understand the appeal of silent movies for Jake: He clearly had a very noisy home life.

I could tell Cassady had already decided she didn't like him at all because she kept asking him questions, just as he was about to put food in his mouth. Between Lara and Cassady, the guy was going to starve to death. Unless pretension can sustain life by itself.

"Then, your 'wordless' cinema," Cassady prompted, just as Jake got a dumpling all the way to his lips, "emphasizes image over story."

The fork hovered in front of Jake's mouth for another split second, but the temptation to talk overrode his hunger. He put the fork down and began to pontificate. "The image *is* the story." He was momentarily distracted as Lara picked up the fork, ate the dumpling, then started drawing on the tablecloth with the fork. "That allows the story to transcend image and makes words irrelevant," Jake pressed on. "Words are weighed down by their emotional connotation and distort the true expression of ideas, which is found in the silent image."

Lara fed him a dumpling and took over. "Jake's vision for cinema recharges film with its mythic power by stripping away the verbal. Words, unlike images, have no existence beyond their immediate function in film. Their relationship is syntagmatic and not paradigmatic."

I've often wondered if people who are full of hot air are aware of it and just don't care. Maybe they just can't help themselves.

"Any form of communication that relies on words is inferior," Jake informed me when Tricia explained what I did for a living.

"So this conversation is useless," I said, as pleasantly as possible.

"It will suffice, but it will not transcend."

I was considering showing him how my middle finger could communicate and transcend, all without words, but I didn't want to help him make his point. "You'd prefer that I draw people a picture?" I tried to imagine the pictographs that might answer some of the letters I get, particularly the ones about love triangles gone bad. On the other hand, there'd be a great after-market in the modern art world. Hang that over your sofa, baby.

Jake shook his shaggy head with great disdain. "I want people to escape the tyranny of the word by rejecting their media-dominated lives and embracing the purity of noneditorialized experience."

"For a guy with no faith in words, you sure talk a lot," Cassady pointed out.

"Words can be a beginning. Foreplay. But for the union of thoughts and passions to truly illuminate, it has to live in a space beyond words. Not everyone's equipped to dispense with words, but we're moving there. Now, it's cell phones with cameras. Soon, it'll be motion-capture gloves and 3-D visors so we can make art on the move. In the streets. Without words." Jake leaned over, trying to get closer to Cassady, apparently operating under the delusion that he was winning her over.

His moment was derailed by the semigrand appearance of a brunette beauty with her breasts barely corralled within a neckline that made Cassady's look tame. As she leaned over to kiss Jake, all I could think was, *Avalanche!*

Lara, surprisingly, did not interrupt as the woman and Jake exchanged a disconcertingly sloppy kiss. She simply moved her hand, holding the fork, under the table.

"I didn't realize tongue was on the menu," Cassady said, not as quietly as she might have.

What tender piece of meat Lara speared with the fork I can only imagine, but Jake sat up rather abruptly, nearly knocking his new visitor over as he wrenched his mouth away from hers.

"Hello, Veronica," Tricia called with forced brightness.

"Hello, Tricia!" Veronica cooed. She leaned over again and for a terrible moment, I thought she was going to chew on Tricia for a while, but Tricia turned her cheek so all Veronica kissed was air.

Lara placed the fork back on the table and Jake wiped his mouth with his napkin while Tricia made gracious introductions. Veronica Innes was an actress who had done a short film with Jake last year—an "experimental deconstruction of the musical experience" that Jake said led him to develop his wordless cinema theory. Didn't say much for the songwriting, I thought. Or for Veronica's singing. Now, she was Lisbet's understudy off-Broadway. My concern for the quality of the play increased immensely.

"I love your work!" Veronica gushed when Tricia identified me.

I resisted sneering at Jake and thanked her. "I'm afraid I haven't seen yours."

"Sure you have." Holding her arms parallel to each other, Veronica framed her bust. "Victoria's Secret. Mainly the underwire styles."

"Wise choice," Cassady nodded.

"Play your assets where you find them, girlfriend," Veronica said. "It's a waste, otherwise."

"A very generous outlook," Cassady replied.

"Veronica's a generous girl," Jake leered.

Lara reached for something and I was ready to hand her

the fork myself, but she grabbed the digital camcorder off the table instead, aiming it at Jake and Veronica. "How interesting when ancient, dried-up paths cross again. Let me take a picture of old friends."

Veronica didn't appreciate being characterized as an "old" anything, it was clear, but she still kicked on the smile for the camera. She leaned in and I wasn't sure if she was going to kiss Jake, Lara, or the camera, but I knew I didn't want to see it.

This pivotal moment in cinematic history was interrupted by Aunt Cynthia announcing that we should adjourn to the great room for dessert and digestifs. Tricia, Cassady, and I almost scaled over the backs of our chairs in search of more entertaining company.

The great room, despite its elegant decor, could be pressed into service as a town hall in the event of a civic disaster. The outside wall was a series of floor-to-ceiling French doors that provided a heart-stopping look at the ocean without completely distracting you from the crystal chandelier that glowed overhead or the Monet above the fireplace.

The combo moved inside with us and shifted to the dance section of their playlist. A few new arrivals drifted in, mainly guys who looked to be buddies of David's who had underestimated the time it would take to drive down from the city and had missed dinner. That swelled the ranks of guests to about fifty, with even more people expected to join in over the course of the weekend.

Glasses of champagne were distributed to all in preparation for toasts by Mr. Vincent and others, but the glasses quickly were supplemented by entire bottles, all bearing the label of the upstate vineyard Aunt Cynthia had acquired as a parting gift from ex-husband number two.

"Richard and Davey must have found the cellar keys," Tricia said.

"Your aunt doesn't seem to mind," I pointed out, watching Aunt Cynthia work the room and encourage people to partake.

"She believes being sober after dinner is a breach of etiquette."

"Who are we to insult the hostess?" Cassady asked, snatching a bottle from the tray of a passing waitress.

So it was left to Lisbet to come up with the memorable breach of etiquette. While the postdinner partying had been proceeding along at a civilized pace, the champagne had pushed the fast-forward button. Lisbet had now slid a champagne flute down the front of her dress, which was quite easy to do, given that the dress didn't really have a neckline so much as it had an open pathway to her sternum. There were so many women at this party on the verge of flashing their breasts, it was like being at a David Letterman taping.

Somewhere under the few pieces of fabric that did attempt to keep Lisbet clothed, there was apparently sufficient underwiring to press her breasts together firmly enough to keep the glass in place. It was this marvel of engineering, perhaps previously modeled in an ad by Veronica, which had caught the full attention of quite a few men and several women in the center of the room. Then Lisbet started charging the glass with the bottle that dangled from her hand and challenging each to figure out the best way to drink from the glass while spilling the least champagne.

"Oh, look," Cassady hissed. "Dinner and a show."

Richard and Rebecca stood next to Tricia's parents, Rebecca with an unmistakable pucker of disapproval on her face. Could she be seriously trying to reform? Had losing Richard shaken her up sufficiently to make her want to change? Why else would she be sneering at Lisbet and cozy-ing up to her mother-in-law, whispering quietly into her ear? Six months ago, she would have been encouraging men to line up for their shot, passing out numbers and offering tips for success.

For the moment, Jake was the only one taking a shot. He and Lisbet were grinding against each other with NC-17 fervor and both had seemed to forget the objective was to empty the champagne glass. I hoped for an objection from Lara, but she was filming the whole thing, occasionally call-ing out in Portuguese either instructions or curses, I couldn't be sure which.

The group of friends standing around them laughed and clapped in encouragement, but you could feel the tension mounting in the rest of the room. Mr. Vincent took a step forward, but Mrs. Vincent put her hand on his arm and he stopped. Did Mrs. Vincent want Lisbet to embarrass herself, assuming that was possible, or was she concerned that a more painful scene would ensue if Mr. Vincent stepped in?

"Where's Davey?" Tricia asked, scanning the crowd anx-iously. "This is no way to start the weekend."

"Want me to look for him?" I volunteered. There were a number of people in the room growing increasingly un-comfortable with the floor show, but everyone was defer-ring to Mr. and Mrs. Vincent about interceding. David would be able to call a halt to the proceedings with the least amount of political repercussions.

"Davey or Aunt Cynthia," Tricia agreed. She started for the door, making urgent little circles with her hands to indi-cate that Cassady and I should walk with her.

We weren't more than a dozen steps along when Aunt Cynthia and David entered of their own accord. Well, Aunt Cynthia did, anyway. She had David by the elbow, the instinctive pincer hold women use when they're guiding a small child or an unwilling man.

"Wonder where they've been?" Tricia murmured.

"Behind the woodshed, from the looks of him," Cassady suggested.

David did have a bit of the whipped dog about him. Whatever conversation he'd been having with his aunt, it hadn't been nearly as entertaining as the one we'd had with her. And his expression just got harder and colder when he stepped into the great room and saw Lisbet and her dance team. Especially since two of Jake's compatriots were now trying to hoist Lisbet up in the air upside down, so the champagne would pour into Jake's eagerly open mouth. Lara and the camera got in so close it looked like Jake was going to swallow that, too. There was much fluttering of fabric and legs, a glimpse of panties, a lot of guffawing, and then David's voice cut through the babble with an ice-cold edge.

"Time to go, Lisbet."

The two guys holding Lisbet were still sober and sane enough to respond to David's tone and put his fiancée down right away. Jake was buzzed enough to look bummed that his fun was over, but lucid enough to shut his mouth and stay quiet. Even Lara had the presence of mind to shut off the camera. It was Lisbet who rose to the occasion in a way everyone had hoped to avoid.

"Excuse me?" She wobbled a moment before finding her center of gravity, which, in a pair of Marc Jacobs perforated suede pumps, is no mean feat even when you're perfectly sober. Once she'd stabilized, she put a hand on her hip and frowned at David. "What's your problem?"

Tricia and her brothers grew up as camp followers for more political campaigns than any one of them could count, but they all developed the gift of the glib as a fringe benefit. "There doesn't have to be a problem and I'd rather that there wasn't one," David assured his fiancée, who was beginning to sway a little. "It's just time to go."

"See, that's a problem. I donwanna leave."

David's smile was thinning rapidly. "I usually love a good debate, but not now. Let's go."

Lisbet screwed her face into her approximation of a cute pout. "I don't think so."

"Then permit me to sweep you off your feet." David scooped her up into his arms. He pivoted slightly so he could address the whole room. "Thank you all for being here tonight. We love you all, but we love each other more, so if you'll excuse us . . ." He waggled an eyebrow and most of the crowd laughed politely, if not wholeheartedly. Mrs. Vincent looked like she'd never laugh again and Mr. Vincent was staring out the French doors.

David strode toward the main doors. Lisbet squirmed a little in his arms. "How dare you?" she began.

"Shut the hell up," he growled under his breath as he carried her past us. Color rose in his cheeks and he couldn't help but glance over at his sister. Tricia gave him a small nod of encouragement and held her breath until they were gone. Jake grabbed the camera from Lara, turned it back on, and tracked David and his burden out into the hallway like some bloodhound paparazzo. Lara trailed after him. It was the first time I'd seen her smile all night.

Mr. Vincent was the one who stole the microphone from the keyboard player this time. Before the buzz of people whispering to each other could even begin, he nipped it in the bud. "We'll let the lovebirds be early birds, but we hope the rest of you will stay with us. The night is young and the bar is open."

Tricia fidgeted, watching her mother with Richard and Rebecca across the room. "Well, aren't we off to a smashing start."

"David was marvelous. Dashing and romantic," I told her.

"Davey is so in over his head." She sighed. "What *is* it with my brothers and their taste in women?"

"Guys don't want women with good taste, guys want women who taste good," Cassady suggested.

Tricia's head bobbed in something like a nod, but she really didn't seem to be listening all that closely. "I'll be back in a minute, I'm just going to talk to my parents."

But as Tricia started toward them, Mr. and Mrs. Vincent walked out of the room. They weren't snubbing Tricia, they weren't even looking in her direction, but she still froze in the middle of the floor.

I nudged Cassady and we caught up with Tricia. "I'm sure they're just checking on David and Lisbet."

Cassady slid an arm around Tricia's drooping shoulders. "Help your dad out and keep the party alive. Grab the best-looking man you can find and drag him out on the dance floor."

"Where are Richard and Rebecca?"

Cassady and I looked around, but we couldn't spot them either. "Maybe the whole lovebird/early bird thing appealed to them, too."

Tricia's shoulders slumped. "I really cannot handle any more implications about my brothers' sexual activities tonight."

I couldn't restrain my inner advice columnist any longer. "They're grown men, Tricia. You don't have to clean up after them."

Tricia cut her luminous brown eyes at me so sharply I

thought I had crossed a line. "Thank you, Dr. Freud." Okay, I hadn't crossed it, but I had walked right up to it and poked at it with my toe.

Still, I'd gotten through to some extent. Tricia took a deep breath. "Let's dance."

"With each other?"

"No, there's been enough excitement for one night."

We all spent some time dancing with David's friends and trying to keep the energy in the room up. People seemed game at first, but after a while, people began drifting out. When it got down to a handful, Tricia suggested that we head upstairs and get comfortable. "I'm going to make a nightcap tray and bring it up. Then we can really unwind."

Moments later, Cassady and I were settling into our room. It was such a treat to be in a place where the furniture was older than the plumbing. Tricia busied herself with the contents of a large silvery cocktail cart she had requisitioned from behind some swinging door deep in the center of the mansion.

Tricia clunked ice cubes so hard that I feared for the safety of the crystal. "Absolutely revolting. She's dreadful and embarrassing and Davey deserves so much better." Tricia dropped down in an armchair, glass still in her hand. She was flaring her nostrils and keeping her eyes a little too open, a sure sign that she was trying not to cry. Cassady and I swung into action. I moved over to sit next to her and Cassady took the glass from her and started mixing White Russians for all three of us.

"Your Aunt Cynthia looked like she was going to have a rather pointed conversation with both of them. She strikes me as quite able to straighten them out," I said.

Tricia raked her small hands through her hair, but the chestnut bob fell perfectly back into place. Even in great distress, Tricia is the picture of poise. "I don't want them to straighten it out," she admitted quietly. "And I feel terrible about that."

"You want what's best for your brother and you don't think she's it. There's nothing wrong with that," I assured her. "Particularly because it's a pretty widely held opinion just about now."

Cassady handed Tricia a White Russian. "As is the opinion that you have earned your nightcap. Drink up."

Tricia lifted her glass, ready to drink deep, but froze when someone knocked on the door. "I don't want to talk to my mother about this," she whispered. "I'm not ready."

I got up to answer the door while Tricia moved herself out of the line of sight. Cassady kept mixing, but with one eye on the door.

I eased the bedroom door open a crack, prepared to plead partial nudity, depending on whom the visitor was. At first, I couldn't see anyone, but then something moved against the wall to the left of the door. Before I could open the door further, David's face slid into view, our noses almost colliding as I peered out.

"David, you scared me."

David looked pretty scared himself. "I need Tricia."

I smelled alcohol on his breath, but there was something else, too. Chlorine. I inched the door open a bit more, trying to see him more fully. "Have you been swimming?"

"Where's Tricia?" There was a panicky edge to his voice, but before I could question it, Tricia came up behind me and threw open the door.

"What is it now?" Tricia asked, a tad peevish.

David closed his eyes before answering. "Help me. Someone killed Lisbet."

3

First impressions are so crucial in business, dating, and homicide investigations. The fact that I was standing poolside, not far from a dead body, barefoot, in my Nick & Nora cami and drawstring pants, was less than helpful in my effort to establish credibility with the professionals on the scene. This weekend had been intended as a getaway, not a hook-up opportunity, and I had packed accordingly. Good thing. A lacy chemise would have really sent the wrong message to Detective Myerson, who already seemed perplexed by me. At least I'd left my Washington Redskins sleep shirt at home.

As soon as what David had said sunk in, Tricia, Cassady, and I had rushed out to the pool with him. I'd grabbed my cell phone as we went, but David said he'd already called 911, after finding Lisbet in the pool, dragging her out, and trying CPR. Still, we all flew down the stairs focusing on the vain hope that he might be wrong, that Lisbet was somehow alive.

But once we saw her, there was no question. She was lying at the side of the pool, her body unnaturally neat and symmetrical as a result of David's CPR efforts. Her wet hair clumped on either side of her throat, her skin was still wet but already too pale, her dress was ripped at the shoulder, and she was barefoot. It looked like a Helmut Newton photo shoot gone irrevocably bad. Even so, I felt for a pulse because it seemed to be a place to start.

"She's dead."

Tricia shrieked in surprise and I gasped pretty hard as Aunt Cynthia walked out of the pool house. She was wearing a red silk robe and matching mules; she'd been getting ready for bed, too. Lisbet's Marc Jacobs pumps dangled from one hand and an open bottle of champagne was clutched in the other. "I've called the police," she informed us.

"I already did," David said weakly.

"David, do you know what happened here?" Aunt Cynthia asked with a cool detachment that either came from shock or an effort to keep larger emotions at bay.

Shaking his head, David started to crumble. "I was looking for her and she was in the water and I tried . . ." Tricia put a protective arm around him and he didn't finish.

Aunt Cynthia nodded slowly. "I thought I heard people in the pool, which struck me as curious at this hour." She held up the champagne bottle and the shoes. "She must have decided to go swimming and hit her head or was just too impaired."

"But she's fully dressed," Tricia pointed out.

"Alcohol encourages stupid choices," Aunt Cynthia said as though that was the end of the discussion. I couldn't believe how composed she was, standing over a dead body and talking like a public service announcement. How drunk was she?

I didn't get a chance to ask because the paramedics arrived and the noise of their arrival brought Mr. and Mrs. Vincent down. The paramedics didn't have to do much to confirm that Lisbet was dead and they tried not to move her any more than necessary to preserve what might wind up being a crime scene. Mrs. Vincent almost fainted, but Mr. Vincent, like his sister, reacted with glacial composure. But his was shot through with anger, even though he mainly seemed furious that something had happened without his permission and outside his control.

When the heavy hitters—the medical examiner, the county homicide detectives—started arriving, Mrs. Vincent tried to get David to move inside, but he refused to budge. He said he needed to keep an eye on Lisbet. So he sat hunched on a chaise lounge; his mother sat beside him, her arms wrapped around him, trying to keep him warm and calm. She seemed to be losing on both fronts.

I could understand. The night breeze off the water was starting to get to me, as was the enormity of the situation, and I was several steps removed on the emotional involvement scale. Still, I was trying desperately not to shiver. I kept my jaw clenched and hoped the detective didn't take it as a sign of obstinacy or belligerence. He had already gotten plenty of that from Mr. Vincent and Aunt Cynthia, who had talked to him with the clipped tones of regulars displeased with the service at their favorite restaurant.

Tricia and Cassady huddled together on another chaise. Cassady was watching the crime scene come together, but Tricia was watching David. There was something odd about the way she looked at him that I couldn't quite pinpoint. It wasn't pure concern, there was something darker and disquieting mixed in. She glanced up for a moment and caught me watching her. I nodded in encouragement, but she looked away. She was thinking something she didn't want anyone to know about and Tricia knows how to keep her secrets.

Richard and Rebecca sat a few chaises down, taut and silent. Rebecca had attempted to console David and Mrs.

Vincent, but both mother and son had rejected her overtures. She'd retreated to sit with Richard and quietly watch the horrible proceedings unfold.

"When's the last time you saw the deceased?" Detective Myerson asked me. He was a spindly fellow—Ichabod Crane with a buzz cut—and I distracted myself wondering how he could stay warm with absolutely no built-in insulation. He was wearing a suit coat that smelled of old cigarettes and French fries, but I would have gladly taken it had he offered. He didn't.

"David carried her out of the great room about ten."

He sniffed significantly, then squinted as though he were in pain. I couldn't tell if it was an editorial comment or a sinus condition. He'd already spoken to everyone else and we'd all talked to the uniformed officers before he arrived, so he had to see our stories were consistent. But the problem with consistent stories is, they don't give you much to go on. You need something to stand out. "And you didn't see her again?"

"No, we tried to keep the party going. It seemed like the polite thing to do."

"Were you successful?"

"Briefly."

"And then what?"

"People left, we went up to our rooms."

"Everyone?"

"Other than the . . ." I groped for the word. Household servants? Domestic employees? It wasn't a concept I dealt with on a daily basis, so I wasn't sure what the current politically correct term was. "Staff. They were still cleaning when we went upstairs."

He made a note of that, then squinted a little harder at

what he'd written. Was something already emerging and worrying him? Or did he just need glasses?

"And where we are is . . . ?" a voice behind him asked and Detective Myerson's squint deepened into a grimace of pain.

"Just getting warmed up," Myerson said with the forced cheeriness I use when telling a small child on a airplane to pretty please stop kicking the back of my seat. Did we have a homicide detective who didn't like homicides?

Or did we have a cop who didn't like his partner? The owner of the voice stepped around from behind Myerson now, a tall woman with close-cropped blond hair and icy blue eyes accentuated by high cheekbones and a sharp jaw-line. She looked like some Nordic avenging angel, ready to whip out a flaming sword and dispense justice where she saw fit. She wore a simple black suit with a skirt that was going to make it hard for her to kneel to collect evidence and a jacket so tailored that she'd never get it buttoned over her pistol. A string of onyx beads and moonstones was tucked inside her gray silk tee. She'd been called away from something fun to be here, which partially explained the tightness of her expression and skirt and Myerson's uneasiness. She put a hand on his arm in greeting and he didn't seem happy about it.

She moved the hand quickly and offered it to me. "Darcy Cook, Suffolk County Homicide."

I shook her hand, trying to analyze her demeanor and Myerson's reaction to her. "Molly Forrester, Manhattan civilian."

Her Maid of Valhalla mask didn't shift one iota. "What's your relationship to the deceased, Ms. Forrester?"

"Tenuous."

"Could you be more specific?"

"Friend of the sister of the fiancé."

"And what's your understanding of what happened here?"

"Your partner can fill you in," I said, as much in his defense as in my own. Detective Myerson was staring passively at his notes. Apparently, this was Detective Cook's standard operating procedure—start up the bulldozer and see who jumps out of the way.

"I'd like to hear it from you."

"Go ahead, Ms. Forrester," Detective Myerson said, eyes still on his notebook.

I played the highlight reel for her: engagement party; Lisbet as human champagne flute; David sweeping her out; David coming to get us. "He said he'd found her in the pool, he tried CPR, and he called 911."

"Do you know what he told 911?"

"No," I said, slowly and distinctly for emphasis and to test if it would irritate her, "I wasn't there."

"He said someone killed her. That's why we're here."

A little sigh of frustration escaped before I could stop it. It hadn't occurred to me to ask David what he'd said on the phone. We didn't need impulsive statements messing things up. Which meant I needed to be very careful about everything that came out of my own mouth. I shook my head. "Hyperbole."

"And you think so because . . . ?"

"He was upset, not thinking clearly. That plus champagne equals hyperbole."

"What did he tell you when he came upstairs?"

"That he'd called 911."

"That's it?"

Detective Myerson finally lifted his sad brown eyes from

his notebook. He'd already talked to Tricia and Cassady. They would have told him the truth. That meant I had to, as well. Playing games with the truth this early was only going to make things worse. "He said someone had killed her."

Detective Cook wrinkled her nose like an unpleasant smell had just slid by on the breeze, then waved it away. "But that's just hyperbole."

"Yes."

"Even though he said it twice."

"Yes."

"And no one asked why he was saying it?"

"It seemed more important to go see if she was even dead."

"You didn't believe him."

"Didn't want to believe him. That's different."

"You seem angry, Ms. Forrester."

"So do you, Detective Cook. And you'd probably get back to whatever oily DA or married man you left at the bar a little quicker if you'd listen to what Detective Myerson has to say and give the rest of us a minute to catch our breath. This whole thing sucks and you're making it much worse than it needs to be."

Dear Molly, When confronted by a social situation in which the most emotionally satisfying reaction would be to smack someone, do I at least get points for keeping my hands to myself and letting my words do the smacking? I could use some points right about now. Signed, Trigger Happy Tongue

When I'm stressed, I write imaginary letters to my column in my head. It helps me vent, gives me perspective. I should've written the letter before I opened my mouth. And I shouldn't have opened my mouth before I remembered she was carrying a gun. But the important thing was, I closed my mouth now.

And waited. Detective Cook struck me as the sort who was going to mess with me—and potentially, all of us—because she could. And because we were responsible for calling her away from whatever fun she'd intended to have. The only thing that made me feel slightly better about exploding forth was that Detective Myerson, who had returned his gaze to his notebook, was trying quite hard not to smile.

"Detectives?" Saved by the ME. The medical examiner was calling from across the pool and when the detectives turned to look at her, she gestured for them to come join her where she stood above Lisbet's body.

Detective Myerson turned back to me first. "We'll be back in a moment. Please don't leave the grounds."

Detective Cook didn't say anything, she just headed over to the ME. Detective Myerson walked beside her, but they didn't say anything to each other. I've seen warmer, cuddlier pairs wind up in divorce court. But, to cut them some slack, I know how hard it can be to get cozy with a homicide detective.

With no answer presenting itself, I gladly retreated to where Tricia and Cassady still sat on a chaise, arms around each other. Everyone else was gone.

"They're inside," Tricia explained as she and Cassady scooted over to make room for me. "Mother insisted and she and Aunt Cynthia dragged Davey in. Dad's calling Lisbet's parents. They can't hear it from a reporter."

I hadn't even thought about how the press was going to descend on this one, especially the tabloids. It wasn't just the death, it was the setting, the circumstances, the number and kind of people who'd been at the party, all of whom would have something to say . . . It had huge potential for being really ugly.

"There's nothing sensational here, just a tragic accident. Maybe they'll leave it alone," I said, trying to be reassuring.

"Wow, you get major points for optimism," Cassady responded. "Who's the angry blond?"

"Detective Myerson's partner. I don't think they get along very well."

"Not a job that brings out the best in people," Cassady ventured.

"Excepting Kyle," Tricia said.

"Of course."

We were too far away to eavesdrop on the detectives. Straining to hear, all I could pick up was the occasional consonant cluster from the ME floating on the night air. I noticed Myerson kept his eyes either on his notebook or on the ground, while Cook kept glancing from the ME's face to Lisbet's body.

I found myself, against my will, thinking of Jake's wordless cinema as I tried to discern what information was being communicated. The gestures were pretty vague. Until the medical examiner brought her hand to her forehead in a sharp movement that I thought for a moment was a mock salute. But then she did it again and I realized she was demonstrating a blow to the head. The phrase "blunt force trauma" leapt to mind, despite my efforts to block it with commercial jingles and other meaningless padding available in my brain.

"Aw, crap," Cassady said, realizing the same thing.

A compacted sob pushed out of Tricia. "Davey said someone killed her. I didn't want to believe it."

"The detectives already do."

Detective Myerson tapped the handrail of the pool ladder. The medical examiner shook her head, then motioned over a technician and pointed to the handrail. Detective

Cook gestured to two uniformed officers and made a large, circular motion that encompassed the whole lawn. They had to be looking for a murder weapon now.

Tricia started shivering so hard I could feel the vibration through Cassady, who sat between us. Cassady rubbed Tricia's arms and tossed her head at the house. "We should go in."

Being an unexpected adjunct to a family tragedy is a delicate situation at best. Something about the grandeur of the setting and the Vincents' impeccable manners made me want to rise to the occasion and come up with the perfect gracious thing to do or say that would get everyone to relax. But Emily Post doesn't cover the aftermath of murder in her helpful little guidebook and even my experience with Teddy's death didn't yield anything helpful to offer as we entered a drawing room filled with silent despair.

This was a room I hadn't seen yet, with wood and brass that shone from generations of careful polishing, walls painted such a deep green you expected dew to form on the baseboard, and dense Persian carpets that enforced quiet and reserve. I took my cue from the carpet and kept my mouth shut, except when taking sips of the Carlos I brandy that Nelson pressed upon everyone. There were plenty of champagne bottles still around, but it seemed inappropriate to drink something celebratory now.

Aunt Cynthia and Mr. Vincent were on separate phones, Aunt Cynthia browbeating a charter pilot she knew in Los Angeles and Mr. Vincent making arrangements with Lisbet's parents. He looked far more ashen than he'd looked outside, even in view of Lisbet. Telling her parents must have been awful. I couldn't even imagine the horror of being on the other end of the phone.

Richard and Rebecca flanked David and Mrs. Vincent on the main couch. Tricia and Cassady sat, arms interlocked, on a loveseat. I got up and wandered, not because I didn't have anyone to huddle with, but because I couldn't stop thinking about the detectives out by the pool. I had actually learned my lesson, having been down this path once before, about how dangerous it could be to get involved in a murder investigation. Still, I couldn't help but speculate about what the detectives were thinking, who they were suspecting, what was going to happen next.

Nelson offered a brandy to Richard. It seemed to trigger a thought in Richard. "We will get Grandmother's emeralds back, won't we?"

"Richard," his mother said with frigid warning.

Nelson held a brandy out to Rebecca and she bolted unsteadily to her feet. "I don't want anything to drink."

"Yes, ma'am," Nelson replied quietly and moved on.

"I don't want anything to drink ever again," Rebecca continued. "Look where drinking gets you."

Richard stood and put a consoling and/or restraining arm around her shoulders. "Take it easy," he told her, indicating his father and aunt on the phone.

"How can I, when Lisbet's dead?"

"Thanks, that helps," David moaned.

"Stop it. Both of you," Mrs. Vincent commanded in crisp, frosted tones.

Richard stood next to Rebecca. "We're all overwrought and looking for a convenient target for our anger and grief. It's not going to happen. It wouldn't be fair to Lisbet to let it happen. We have to accept this pain and still manage to be human to each other. That's a tall order, but if we all work in the same direction, it's feasible. And I don't know how else any of us are going to get through this."

The trouble with people who have a way with words is that their moments of true eloquence are hard to distinguish from their moments of crafted doublespeak and so most of what they say is suspect. But I'll give Richard credit: I knew he'd been working campaigns with his dad since high school and I still believed he meant every word he said.

Understandably, David was not so easily swayed. "Rally the troops somewhere else, you pompous bastard."

Mr. Vincent slammed the phone down. For a moment, it seemed he was upset with whomever had been on the other end of his conversation, but it quickly became apparent that he'd heard his sons beginning theirs. "Shut up."

"Hear that, Rebecca?" David said with a sneer.

Rebecca's face, already flushed with emotion, went florid with anger. "I'm sharing an epiphany. I'm evolving."

"No," David pressed, "you're assuming someone cares what you think."

Richard's civility began to shred. "No one's going to blame you for acting like a prick, David, but don't feel obligated."

David opened his mouth to respond, but Mrs. Vincent put her hand on his knee. It was a light touch, barely flattening the crease in his trousers, but the effect on David was akin to a stun gun. "Grow up or get out," she said quietly.

Get a family together, especially in times of stress, and the seams are going to show. Tricia was turning a shade of white I haven't even seen in stationery collections. Richard and David clammed up immediately. Even Rebecca dropped back down onto the sofa, eyes welling with tears. Mr. and Mrs. Vincent looked at the floor.

Only Aunt Cynthia continued on, instructing the party on the other end of the phone to do exactly as she demanded. She seemed certain she would get her way, no doubt based on years of experience. Her composure was remarkable. I wasn't sure if I was envious or repulsed.

I stole a look at Cassady, who was silent in the face of so much repressed emotion. She frowned at me, but I didn't know what to do either, except stay quiet. I drifted over to the French doors and leaned as close to the glass as I dared, not wanting it to be my lipstick Nelson had to clean off the window in the morning. But just as I got close enough for the reflection from the room to give way to the actual picture outside, something thwacked against the glass, right about even with my nose. I gasped and jerked back, splashing a goodly portion of brandy on my wrist.

As I debated in a split second whether to lick the brandy off, the door swung open and Detective Cook stepped in. She gave me a tight smirk I associate with cheerleaders who have just bedded the guy you've been pining after for an entire semester. "Excuse me."

Since pointing out that she'd known exactly what she was doing and was enjoying it a little too much wasn't going to accomplish anything, I smiled back. "No problem."

We both paused a moment to silently call each other "bitch," then moved on. I retreated in search of a napkin and a better vantage point while Detective Cook strode into the middle of the room to introduce herself to everyone. Detective Myerson entered almost unnoticed behind her and quietly closed the door.

Detective Cook recited her spiel about being sorry for our loss and didn't bother to make it sound spontaneous, much less sincere, then asked Aunt Cynthia if there was a room in which she and her partner could speak to people individually.

"There are thirty-two rooms in this house but there's no reason we can't all speak freely right here," Aunt Cynthia said.

Detective Cook shook her head. "Gracious thought, but bad procedure."

"We've already given statements," Mrs. Vincent said.

"Which have given rise to a couple of questions that I can either sort out here or we can discuss at greater length at . . . my house." Detective Cook was enjoying the escalation of tension in the room. Piece of work.

"It was an accident," Mrs. Vincent tried again. "She slipped and fell."

"And you believe that because . . . ?"

Mrs. Vincent was not accustomed to people telling her when she was wrong, but she still recognized it when it happened. And didn't like it one bit. She looked to Mr. Vincent for his reaction, but he was staring at some point past the detectives, maybe out the windows and to the pool, and didn't notice.

The Vincents had been through enough, so I decided to be a good guest and redirect the heat for a moment. "Was Lisbet dead before she went into the water?"

It was a painful thing for most of the people in the room to hear, but Detective Cook was really ticking me off with her high-handed attitude and I wanted to cut to the chase. There didn't seem to be much reason for jerking anyone around at this point.

Detective Cook turned slowly to look at me, giving me ample time to register her displeasure with my question and, given the narrowing of her eyes, my very existence. "Who are you again?"

"Molly's a journalist. Molly Forrester. She investigated a murder in the city," Richard said, offering my résumé to be helpful and being anything but.

Detective Cook's eyes narrowed so tightly that they might as well have closed. She was starting to like me just as much as I was liking her. I could tell.

"The Teddy Reynolds murder. *Manhattan* magazine," Detective Myerson said. I'd almost forgotten he was in the room.

"Yes," I said, as neutrally as possible.

"How nice for you," Detective Cook said, still not trying to sound sincere. She pointed at David. "I'd like to talk to you first."

"Excuse me. You didn't answer my question," I persisted. I wasn't sure what I was going to do with the information once I had it, but I wasn't going to ignore the fact that she was trying to ignore me.

"Won't know that until the autopsy," she said, keeping her eyes on David. She gestured for him to stand up, which he seemed reluctant or unable to do.

Detective Myerson looked right at me. "Good article."

"Thank you." I made a point of smiling at him and sounding sincere. Not so much to impress him as to get under Detective Cook's skin. I couldn't tell if it worked on Detective Cook, but Detective Myerson returned the smile. I pressed my luck. "So this is a murder investigation."

Detective Cook pivoted back, to control both me and her partner. "The medical examiner believes Ms. McCandless was struck forcibly by an object and then fell into the pool."

"Have you recovered the weapon?"

"I'm sorry, I thought they said you were a journalist. You got your law degree from . . . ?"

Cassady raised her hand. "No, I'm the lawyer."

"Do lawyers need to be called?" Mr. Vincent asked. His hand hovered near the telephone, like a Western gunfighter ready to draw.

Detective Cook took a deep breath. She wasn't having quite as much fun now. "Not at all. I simply want to make sure I fully understand the situation before anyone's memory gets fuzzy or the situation gets too public or Aspen gets too crowded, that sort of thing."

Rebecca rose before anyone could stop her. In shockingly level tones, she said, "What you don't appreciate is who this family is and what we've just been through."

Aunt Cynthia moved behind Rebecca quickly and put a hand on her shoulder. "She's quite right. Your smirking inferences are an insult to all."

Detective Cook's hands slid up to her hips and rested there, pushing her jacket open. I don't know if the gesture was meant to draw attention to her waning patience or to the gun on her hip, but it did both.

"I'd like to take just a few moments to review the time line of events David Vincent has already given," Detective Myerson said, indicating David with a gentle nod. "Our thorough understanding of that timeline now will help avoid unpleasant confusions later."

Mr. Vincent knows when he's being spun. But I could see in his eyes an acknowledgment of both the situation and the quality of Detective Myerson's spinning. He nodded and said, "David," in a quiet but forceful voice.

David rose. Aunt Cynthia made a gesture Nelson seemed to understand and he led the way out, as though simply escorting David and the two detectives to the bathroom.

I checked to see how Tricia was handling all this and saw that same odd look on her face. Part sorrow and part rage. She caught me looking at her and turned away, a sure sign something huge was happening behind her poised facade.

Mr. Vincent picked up the phone. Mrs. Vincent pulled on her pearls. "She said no lawyers needed to be called."

"Which is precisely why I'm calling."

Mrs. Vincent quickly got up and walked over to dissuade her husband. Aunt Cynthia leaned in and the three of them growled at each other like puppies over a common bowl. Rebecca buried her face in Richard's chest and Cassady slipped away from Tricia to join me on the fringes.

"Should we leave?" she said quietly. She was trying to be nonchalant, but it doesn't come easily to someone as driven as she is.

"The room or the county?"

"Both."

"Desertion?"

"Good manners."

It took a moment for Cassady's absence to register with Tricia. As soon as it did, she hurried across the room to join us. She shifted her weight uneasily and picked determinedly at her cuticles. Her thumb was already bleeding.

"What aren't you telling us?" I asked her gently.

"You're the ones whispering."

I tapped her ragged thumb. "But you're the one shredding."

She hid her hands behind her back like a small child. "How bad do you think it looks for Davey?"

"The significant other is always the first suspect," I told her. Kyle had taught me that. "But they'll move on soon enough. The important thing is, we know he didn't do it."

Tricia paused just a second too long before she nodded. That's what the dark look was all about. She didn't know he didn't do it. Based on a lifetime of stolen toys, borrowed cars, and unpaid loans, you can believe a sibling capable of just about anything. Fine. But murder?

I tried to tell myself I was overreacting, that grief had slowed Tricia's reflexes, but Cassady was more wide-eyed than I was. "Tricia," she whispered with a ragged edge of disbelief.

Tricia shook her head viciously. "I know, I know, it's crazy. I'm crazy. It just looks so bad."

"So does this." Cassady gestured to the three of us, huddled between the Bösendorfer grand piano and the French doors as if we were planning which Andrews Sisters song to open our set with. The argument by the phone was still going on and Rebecca seemed to have nodded off against Richard's chest. No one was even paying attention to what we were doing. "It looks like we're plotting."

"That's a guilty conscience talking. What would we be plotting?"

"The best way to break it to Detective Ice Queen that she's nuts to think David did this." Cassady gave Tricia a stern look, lest she weaken and give in to paranoia again. "Because he didn't."

Tricia nodded right on cue this time. "I know he didn't." She shifted her eyes to me and placed her small, cool hand on my arm. "What can we do?"

I actually thought before I spoke. It wasn't like I'd be volunteering to solve the whole mess. I could just call Kyle, ask a couple of technical questions, and try to be helpful. Participate on a consulting basis, as it were. "Let me call Kyle real quick."

Cassady glanced at her watch. "Things are back on solid footing, then."

"Meaning?"

"You're comfortable calling him at this hour of the morning when he knows you're away for the weekend."

"I didn't say I was comfortable. I said I was going to do it."

I slid my cell phone out of my pocket and eased out the French doors. The night breeze would have been more welcome if it hadn't also carried the sounds of the crime scene investigation still going on at the pool. The individual sounds of people moving, talking indistinctly, taking pictures, zipping things open and shut, were mundane enough until you let them all come together and remembered what they were down there doing. Then the sounds became as oppressive as bombs exploding.

I punched the speed dial for Kyle's apartment, then canceled it before the "connecting" message had a chance to come up. Hesitating, I polished the display screen against the side of my cami. Was it presumptuous of me to call him at this hour of the night, even though it was purely for a technical reason and not, by any stretch of the overactive imagination, to check up on him? He'd understand that this was just appealing to his area of expertise. He might even find it flattering. Right?

I punched the speed dial again. The machine picked up after only two rings. I checked my watch: 2:15 A.M. His message said, "I'm not here."

He often turned the ringer way down on the phone when he was sleeping, but left his cell phone on the nightstand in case they needed him at the station. I told the machine, "I hate to do this, but I'm going to call your cell and wake you up."

I speed-dialed his cell and prepared to be gentle and apologetic when his groggy voice said hello. But the first thing I heard when the phone picked up was voices. Lots of other voices. And when he said, "Hello," it wasn't groggy. It was energetic. He was having fun. At 2:15 A.M. Somewhere. Other than where I was.

"Hi."

"I'm sorry, I thought I was calling you at home." I couldn't identify the background voices or tell if the hint of music was from a stereo or a jukebox.

"Then why'd you call my cell?"

"Because I called your apartment and got the machine. I thought you were asleep."

"Not yet."

"Clearly."

I had a sudden dreadful thought that he was working. "I don't mean to interrupt."

"You're not interrupting."

A clear female voice cut through all the background noise to call out, "Busted." As much as I wanted to imagine the voice belonging to a female police officer about to inform a suspect of his rights, I highly doubted that even a woman who loved her job would say "Busted" to a criminal with that teasing, singsong tone.

Kyle ignored the voice and asked me, "What's up?"

Cassady stepped out through the French doors. "What'd he say?" she asked urgently.

"Nothing yet," I told her.

"So why the call?" Kyle asked.

"I was talking to someone else," I told him, wishing Cassady's voice were deep enough to pass for male over a cell phone. I didn't want to be jealous; I just wanted to know exactly who had said "Busted," what she was wearing, and where both her hands were at this exact moment.

"Everything okay?" he asked calmly.

"I'm having a great time, how 'bout you?"

Cassady rolled her eyes. "I can't believe you!" I glared at her with all the irritation I felt for the Busted Babe and she huffed, folding her arms over her chest.

"I've had better," Kyle said.

I wondered what BB thought of that evaluation. "I just have one question and then I'll let you go."

"I'm not in a rush."

"I am."

"Okay." He seemed amused. I wasn't.

"What does chlorine do to fingerprints?"

I thought I heard the chair scrape as he sat up straight. His voice got taut. "What happened?"

"Just a technical question."

"In my line of work, not yours. What happened?"

"I don't have a lot of time."

"What happened?" he repeated, more slowly and, from the sound of it, through gritted teeth.

"There's just a situation I'm trying to clarify."

"You still at Mrs. Malinkov's? I'm on my way."

"I didn't ask you to do that."

"Are you asking me not to?"

Boobytraps are effective because you don't see them, no matter how well you think you know the terrain. I scrambled to keep my footing. "No, I'm asking you about chlorine and fingerprints."

"And you want to know because . . . ?" I thought I heard Cassady ask.

I waved her off. "Tell you in a minute," I said, looking up to glare at her again. Cassady shook her head and pursed her lips to indicate that she had, in fact, said nothing. I sighed, realizing my mistake. "Thanks, talk to you later," I said to Kyle and flipped my phone shut while he was in mid-exclamation.

Detective Cook put her hand on my shoulder and said, "How about you tell me now?"

4

Dear Molly, Is turnabout really fair play? Just because I call the man in my life (notice my agile avoidance of the term "boyfriend") in the middle of the night, does that give him the right to call me back before dawn? And just because I suspected him of an encounter with a UFO (Unidentified Female Opportunity), should he be able to perform telephonic bed checks on me? Will I be less grumpy about all this sixteen ounces of coffee from now? Signed, Sleepless Beauty

I was determined to answer the phone with a sweet, pleasant voice. Even though said voice would be a complete sham because I felt miles away from both sweet and pleasant, but, as I told Cassady, staying up all night with a cop will do that to you.

"Really? I thought staying up all night with a cop made you happy," Cassady yawned as I fumbled with the phone.

"Different cop, different incentive," I growled. I had just enough time to clear my throat and answer the call before it went to voice mail. "Good morning," I said, hoping to disarm Kyle with long distance charm.

"Clearly, you need a new dictionary, because I don't understand by what definition this could possibly be a good morning. File a purchase order immediately. No, wait. You work at home enough. Buy one yourself. You can take a tax deduction. That should make you happy."

I flopped back on the bed, the gorgeous, comfortable bed I had only had an opportunity to occupy for a few hours after Detective Cook finished sharpening her teeth on me. The thought that this might be a phone call from Kyle had filled me with a mixture of excitement and dread. The thought that this might be a phone call from my editor had never crossed my fatigue-addled mind.

"Hello, Eileen," I managed, and Cassady sat bolt upright in the other bed with a whoop of surprise.

Eileen Fitzsimmons was more than my editor. She was a blight upon my life. Not that her predecessor and I had been bosom buddies, but Yvonne Hamilton and I had found a method of working together and getting along that could pass itself off, to the generous observer, as amicable. Yvonne had given me a fair amount of leeway and I'd given her a sympathetic ear, even though most of the problems on which she held forth were caused by her abrasive personality and her lack of managerial finesse. But we'd made it work.

With Eileen, it just felt like work. Chewing sandy clams kind of work. Eileen made things at the magazine far more difficult than they needed to be, mainly because she liked to see people exert themselves trying to please her. She seemed to equate it with affection.

"Were you going to inform me at some point that you were down there with your little fanny parked in the middle of the juiciest story to happen in at least two weeks? Or were you just going to keep it to yourself and screw us over again?"

Eileen always spoke smoothly, calmly, but with plenty of poison around the edges. She had cold green eyes and wore her black hair in spiky bangs that often got tangled in her eyelashes and she was always batting them away with the back of her hand like an agitated kitten grooming itself.

"No, and there's no story yet," I said, wishing desperately for caffeine in any form. I had not gotten to bed until very late—more correctly, very early—and, thanks to Detective Cook, once I was in bed, I was too agitated to sleep. I was ready to suck on coffee grounds to give me the strength for the rest of this conversation. Across the room, Cassady rolled out of bed and headed for the bathroom. Yeah, a shower was going to feel good, too.

"There's a dead body, there's a story."

"Who've you been talking to?" It was horrifying to think of the story having reached Manhattan already. I knew Mr. Vincent and Richard had been up even longer than I had, maybe all night, preparing a statement and girding the families for the onslaught, but it seemed a little early for it to have hit the news.

"I have friends."

I resisted the impulse to express surprise. "Then they probably told you everything I know. The police are playing it pretty close to the vest."

"Isn't that your specialty, getting into policemen's . . . vests?"

I would have liked very much to hang up at that point, but, in the absence of a cooler head, the balance on my MasterCard prevailed. I gritted my teeth instead. "Did you call for a specific reason, Eileen, or do you always get up at six o'clock in the morning to give people grief?"

"No. On weekends I usually don't start until seven. Stay on this story."

"Excuse me?" When I got involved with Teddy's murder, I hoped it would move me into serious journalism. It hadn't occurred to me to do anything with Lisbet's death. Yet. But Eileen asking me to follow the story didn't really qualify. It didn't even make much sense. "For which magazine?"

"Ours."

Yeah, right. Immediately following the debut of *Car and Driver*'s baking column for NASCAR moms and the dads who love them. *Zeitgeist* is a "woman's lifestyle magazine," which means we write about the Three S's: sex, style, and slimming down. Or, as Cassady insists, the Three F's: fat, fashion, and . . . yeah, well, somehow Cassady can get away with talking like that. Cassady's smoky voice and offhand delivery are like a British accent—they automatically make things sound more clever.

Besides, part of the point of writing the article about Teddy's death had been to get away from *Zeitgeist*. Just because that hadn't happened didn't mean it couldn't happen the next time. If there were a next time. As long as the next time wasn't for *Zeitgeist*. I could attempt to explain that to Eileen, but she probably wouldn't follow it and she certainly wouldn't agree.

"Did we get bought out yesterday afternoon?" I asked instead.

Sold out was more like it. Eileen had come over from *Bound*, a lad mag where she'd gotten a lot of attention giving interviews explaining, with that little cat purr of hers, how she knew exactly what men want and how to give it to them. That was information the Publisher felt women needed, so he hired her to take Yvonne's place. Since she'd come to *Zeitgeist*, Eileen had been searching for a way to get her fingerprints all over the DNA of the magazine. I guess this was a start.

"The Publisher and I have already discussed ways we might add a few teeth to *Zeitgeist*. This story will fit nicely."

"Assuming there is a story."

"You already suspect something or you wouldn't be working so hard to deny it. Keep me posted."

The line went dead before I could even remember the zip code for pithy, much less fling a zinger her way. I folded my phone back up and spiked it into the pillow beside me. This was not the way I'd planned to start my morning.

Someone knocked on the bedroom door. I considered crawling under the comforter and humming Aerosmith songs until it stopped, but then it occurred to me that the knocker might have coffee. I attempted to untangle myself from my grouchiness and the comforter, and made my way to the door. Everyone in the household, and half the local police force, had already seen me in my pajamas, so a robe seemed totally superfluous. Particularly because I wasn't sure I'd packed one.

It was Nelson, looking appallingly alert and well pressed for such an early hour. I had a quick vision of him lying in his room in a coffin, manicured hands folded on his chest, fully dressed in his knife-pleat chinos and oxford shirt, awaiting his mistress's call. "Good morning, Nelson," I said, not knowing how better to hide my disappointment that he wasn't carrying a samovar.

"Good morning, Ms. Forrester. There's a gentleman to see you."

"How can he be a gentleman if he shows up at this hour of the morning?" I asked, not so much expecting Nelson to have an answer as wanting Nelson to know I had enough couth to know this was awkward.

"He has been a model of deportment thus far and I detect signs of a rough-hewn charm," Nelson reported.

"Really? Is he cute, too?"

"That, of course, would be in the eye of the beholder,"

Nelson demurred. He held out a business card. "He says you know him."

I spotted the seal on the card and almost didn't take it. I squinted at Nelson. "Model of deportment, huh? So he's not mad?"

Nelson allowed himself a small smile. "He demonstrated no anger toward me. Not that he would have any reason to do so."

"Ah, but with me, he's got what they call 'just cause' in his line of work." I took Kyle's card from him. "You can send him up."

Nelson's brow only furrowed a millimeter, but his meaning was clear. So much for proving I had couth. Nelson ran a tight ship and I was violating crew rules. I did some fast math in my head. "Or you could tell him I'll be down in twenty—make that fifteen—minutes."

Nelson's brow relaxed and his smile crept a little farther up his face. "A gentleman never rushes a lady. Under any circumstances." There was a touch of vibrato in the way he said it and I didn't know whether to blush or to tell Tricia she was absolutely right about the range of Nelson's household duties. "I'll see to the gentleman. Take your time."

I pulled myself into quite presentable form in twenty-three minutes. It would have been twenty-one, but Cassady insisted on trying to pile my hair on top of my head. First of all, my hair isn't long enough and second of all, it wouldn't so much as curl if I were electrocuted. "What is it with you and putting hair up all of a sudden?" I asked as I tried to wriggle into my skirt without knocking her off balance and causing her to rip out handfuls of my hair on the way down.

"It's what you do when you're on vacation," Cassady insisted. "And wear Lillys with no underwear."

"This isn't Palm Beach. It's the Hamptons."

"How much closer are you gonna get this year?"

"Depends how much severance I get when Eileen fires me." I executed a little plant-and-pivot I'd learned from playing basketball with my brothers and freed myself from Cassady and her comb. My hair collapsed back into the layered bob it's been in most of my life. "See you downstairs."

Once downstairs, in the deep green drawing room we'd all huddled in the night before, I was greeted by the sight of a weary homicide detective consulting his watch. His square jaw was set, his amazing blue eyes serious. His perpetually tousled hair was worse than usual, but I couldn't tell if that was from running his hands through it or from driving out here with the windows down. He looked fantastic in jeans and a casual jacket, but there was something tense in his stance. I didn't know whether to kiss him or ask for his warrant. "Sorry to make you wait."

Kyle nodded, looking me over like he was struggling with a similar dilemma. Neither of us made the definitive move, so both of us hung back. Sexual tension is a powerful force. "So what's up?"

I resisted the impulse to make a joke about what it took to get him out of town. I didn't need to mix two volatile subjects. I slid the ball back into his court. "Shouldn't that be my question?"

The fabulous blue eyes crinkled, but I couldn't tell if he was going to laugh or swear. He ran his hand through his hair and it had absolutely no effect. "You asked me to come out."

"No, you said you were coming out and I told you, you didn't need to."

"You were being polite."

"And serious."

"So the question about chlorine and fingerprints was what—cramming for a chemistry test?"

"Research."

"Why am I here?"

"Now we're back at the beginning."

"You knew I'd come."

I hated that he was right and I hated that he looked so good and I hated Detective Cook. All excellent reasons for me to go right back upstairs, pack my bag, and leave. Go back to the city, optimally with him. But the longer I was awake, the more I was convinced that Lisbet's death was not some tragic lover's quarrel gone bad. She'd made a sufficient enough scene that David could have walked away, never spoken to her again, and most people would have applauded the choice. Why on earth would he have killed her?

"Stop," Kyle said, in a low, controlled voice.

"What?" I asked, amazed that my attention could have drifted from him for even a moment. He didn't seem all that pleased about it either.

"You're trying to solve this murder."

"So you agree it's a murder."

"I agree you think it's one. I don't know what it is. I haven't heard all the evidence."

"Neither have I."

"Which isn't slowing you down a bit."

"They suspect Tricia's brother and he didn't do it."

"You're sure."

"Yes."

"Based on your vast experience."

"I'm batting a thousand, aren't I?"

"You're one for one. Retire now and preserve your perfect record."

"Have you missed me at all?"

"Of course."

He even let himself smile. That's when I knew I was in trouble. But while that was wonderful to hear and see, it wasn't enough to drive the million questions I had about Lisbet and David out of my head. Kyle was right. I was trying to solve this murder.

Which is what Tricia had asked me to do.

The night before, after Detective Cook busted me with my cell phone out on the patio, we'd had quite a little chat. I'd done my best to be professional and respectful, but you didn't have to be an advice columnist to see this woman wore both a semiautomatic and a whole lot of issues strapped to her hip, and it was hard to tell which was deadlier.

Standing outside, she'd pushed me for details about whom I was calling and why, until Cassady had objected to both the tone and the direction of the questions. In an effort to keep things from getting any more agitated for anyone, I'd thrown myself on the grenade and suggested that if Detective Cook had specific questions, she should ask them and get it over with. I could tell by the curl of Cassady's lip that she didn't approve of my strategy in the least, but I suggested she keep an eye on Tricia and let me take care of this quickly. Cassady reluctantly withdrew and the detectives and I adjourned to the small sitting room where they had talked to David.

"So you're a friend of the sister," had been her warm and imaginative segue to the heart of the matter. We were all trying to be on our best behavior, but the strain was already showing on both sides. Part of it was the setting. It was a narrow, stuffy room with red brocade Victorian couches and dark oriental wood, the only incongruous touch being the Vaio laptop on the desk. My guess: an ex-husband's smoking room, inspired by some vague memory of a bordello in a since-forgotten emerging country that his corporation ran.

Detective Myerson sat off to one side, outside the pools of light cast by the brass lamps. It seemed instinctive for him to shun the light. He kept his notebook open and his eyes on the ground, deferring to his partner. That seemed less instinctive than beaten into him.

"Tricia and I go way back," I said, trying to be amiable. I knew I shouldn't antagonize her, but Detective Cook was just one of those people who brings out the combatant in me. Not that I ever enjoy being questioned about anything more vital than "More iced tea?" It's just with some people, it's like a chemical clash, but instead of provoking the fight-or-flight mechanism, it provokes the slap-or-snub reaction.

"You know the family, too?"

"Spent time with them over the years, yes." I tried to think of this as a job interview instead of any species of interrogation. If I put my best foot forward, perhaps I could quell my growing desire to kick her in the shins with it.

"How well do you know David?"

So he still topped the suspect list, even after they'd talked to him again. "Fairly well, socially. Well enough to know he didn't do it." I thought of David standing with us beside the pool, trying not to look at Lisbet's body. The hunch of his body, the slackness of his face—it was the picture of defeat. He was destroyed. He didn't kill her.

"So you were asking someone about fingerprints because . . ."

"David's the boyfriend and you're going to look at him first."

"So, preparing to defend him, you called . . ."

I'll admit, I thought "my boyfriend," but I knew better than to say it. It's a tricky enough word when you're my age, but it's especially tricky when it has yet to be validated by use in his presence.

"A good friend of mine."

"And this friend knows about fingerprints because . . ."

"He's a homicide detective."

It was the first thing I'd said to her all night that surprised her. Detective Myerson didn't so much as glance up from his notebook, but Detective Cook stopped playing with the brass cigarette lighter she'd picked up off the console table and looked at me with new sharpness. "Really."

"Really." I could see her trying to figure out how good a friend I might be with a homicide detective, but I wasn't about to fill in any of the gaps for her. "Did the Vincents ask you to bring this detective in as a consultant?"

"You're joking."

"She doesn't joke," Detective Myerson said quietly, a conclusion I should have reached all by myself, much earlier.

Detective Cook cut him a deadly look, but she made no effort to disagree. What she did was sit down next to me in an intensely uncomfortable caricature of friendship. "You know, my job's hard enough in a town where everyone has a lawyer on the end of a very short leash and they stonewall public servants for recreation. The last thing I need is some tanked-up party girl coming all the way out here just to go down hard on my watch. The second-to-last thing I need is some perky Nellie Bly starting her own investigation and getting in my way."

She was chafing from whatever weight Aunt Cynthia had already thrown around and was suspecting there was plenty more where that came from, rightly so. Still, that wasn't a battle I needed to get dragged into. But for Detective Cook to leave me alone, I had to promise to leave her alone.

I gave Detective Cook the most sincere smile possible under the circumstances. "You find me perky? Thank you." I stood and considered trying to shake her hand, then decided not to press my luck. "Detective Cook, I won't get in your way. I just made a phone call to calm my friend. To allay her concerns about clearing her brother of the suspicions we all know you have about him. I'm sorry if I offended you and I appreciate your taking the time to explain. Now, I assume you'd prefer that I stay far, far away from you so let me start right now."

I turned and walked toward the door, expecting to hear "Wait a minute" at best and a bullet whizzing past my ear at worst before my hand reached the doorknob. But the only sound was Detective Myerson clearing his throat—at whom, I'm not sure—so I opened the door and walked out.

I'd barely gotten five yards down the hallway when Tricia came zipping out of the drawing room with Cassady right on her heels. Tricia's perfect complexion was marred by two crimson patches on her cheekbones; she'd been crying. Cassady looked pretty composed, just anxious to know what had happened. I told them briefly and quietly.

Tricia put her hand on my arm. I thought I could feel it trembling. "So do they think it's Davey?"

"I'm not sure they have a theory yet," I answered carefully.

"Molly, I need you to figure out who killed her."

I hesitated. It wasn't that I had just given my word that I'd stay out of the way. I didn't want to promise anything before I thought it all through myself. And before I had a viable suspect to suggest in place of David. "Tricia . . ." I attempted.

"Remember what happened last time," Cassady warned,

but I wasn't completely sure to which one of us the comment was directed.

"She was right," Tricia insisted.

"In the end," Cassady said.

Tricia shook her head. "I can't just stand back and watch. Whoever did it, I need to know."

Cassady slid Tricia's hand off my arm. "Why don't we all get a good night's sleep and talk about it in the morning?"

The night's sleep had not been terribly good and here it was, morning, and to further complicate matters, here was Kyle. Who had come all the way out to the Hamptons on the basis of one impulsive phone call. Which both impressed and puzzled me.

"It's not so much about solving it," I explained to him. "I just want to give Tricia something to hold on to. She's freaked."

"Because she thinks he's guilty or because other people do?"

The Pause is no better in person than it is on the phone. Still, I had to employ it because I didn't want to lie to Kyle, but I didn't want to paint too bleak a picture either. "She's confused and upset."

Kyle nodded, adding up the nonanswer and the Pause. "Which is why you called about the fingerprints. Besides it being the simplest way to get me down here."

"Yeah. Whenever I see a dead body, it makes me think of you."

"I'm not used to such flowery compliments." He sighed and buried one hand deep in his pocket. The other hand pinched the sides of his lower lip together, which meant he was trying to make a decision. After a moment, he released the lip and nodded, having reached one. I expected him to give me a quick kiss on the cheek and say good-bye, but he said, "There don't seem to be any usable prints on the body. They haven't gotten much in the way of trace evidence off her yet, but that only makes it look worse for your boy."

It took me a moment to realize he was reporting, not speculating. "You've already talked to the police."

Kyle nodded again. "You visit somebody's backyard, you check in and say hello first."

"Doesn't sound like you stopped at hello."

He shrugged in semisurprise. "She was pretty forthcoming."

She. Of course. How could I have expected anything different? And how could I have not been there to engineer that meeting, to control the topics of conversation, to make sure they didn't take a shine to each other? "You talked to Detective Cook?"

"She's the lead, she's the one to talk to."

"Yeah, I've already had the pleasure."

Kyle tried to squash it, but his amusement danced right up to the Big Blues. "She mentioned."

"And?"

"How can I help?"

"Change the subject back to Detective Cook."

Kyle stepped closer, eyes still laughing. "C'mon. Why do you want to talk about her?"

"Why don't you?"

He stepped even closer. Was he teasing me, soothing me, or distracting me? It was sort of working on all three levels. "Because she's just trying to do her job, but she obviously ticked you off in the process. They teach us at the academy, crossfire's deadly."

"So you're keeping your head down?"

He lowered his head to demonstrate, then turned it into a masterful approach for a kiss. Just as his lips touched mine, the door boomed open and Tricia sailed into the room, full of caffeine and angst.

"You came!"

In her rush to embrace him, I doubt she even realized she'd interrupted what was promising to be a delicious, much overdue kiss. Instead, she planted a sweet peck of greeting on his cheek and squeezed his hands. "Thank you so much."

"Tricia," I warned.

She looked at me, perplexed, then looked back at Kyle, even more so. "You are here to help?"

"He came to tell me to behave," I said.

"To make sure you were all okay," Kyle said firmly, not interested in opening up a debate of his motives. "I'm sorry for your loss."

"But you can help," Tricia continued stubbornly.

"Tricia, there are rules. It's not my case. Not even my jurisdiction."

Tricia hadn't let go of his hands yet and I was trying to figure out the best way to distract her while there was still some circulation in Kyle's fingers. "Let's take it one step at a time, Tricia," I urged.

"Cook seems like a very smart detective," Kyle said.

Tricia and I both said "Oh?" at the same time. The trouble was, her "Oh?" was a pretty, round little sound, full of hope and trust. My "Oh?" was a flat, grating tone, full of envy and dread. Tricia didn't hear mine, she was so focused on Kyle. But Kyle did and tilted his head slightly as though checking the calibration of his ears to make sure he'd heard it correctly.

"He didn't do this, Kyle," Tricia said with a little more calm. "Detective Cook has to see that. She has to know how much Davey loved Lisbet, how happy they were to be getting married. It was a dream."

I knew how much Tricia had disliked Lisbet and it made me love Tricia even more to see her engineering enthusiasm for a relationship she had seen as awful, all in the hopes of helping her brother.

Kyle took a deep breath, framing a statement that I was pretty sure was going to take some of the hope out of Tricia's "Oh?" But before he could get it out, Nelson walked in from the hallway and closed the door behind him.

"Nelson?" Tricia finally let go of Kyle's hands and stepped toward Nelson, who paused by the door for a moment, framing a statement of his own. "What is it?"

Nelson walked in closer to us. His face was grim and there was a droop to his shoulders that I wouldn't have thought was physically possible, given his usual ramrod posture. "Pardon my intrusion, but something has come to my attention and I thought I should bring it to yours. I was packing Lisbet's things, preparing for her parents' arrival. I found this in the wastebasket." He held out his closed fist, fingers down. Tricia held her hand out underneath. Nelson opened his hand and a four-carat solitaire framed by terraced baguettes dropped into Tricia's palm.

"Lisbet's engagement ring?" Tricia looked like she might cry. "She wasn't wearing it?"

Over Tricia's bowed head, Kyle's eyes met mine. Why do you take off your engagement ring and throw it in the trash, especially when its fair market value could sustain the economy of a small Caribbean nation for a year? Why else? That's the problem with dreams. They end.

5

Death certainly brings out the worst in people. Not that there aren't plenty of folks who make absolute fools of themselves at weddings or sob their way through christenings or show up for their college graduations with hangovers that would cripple a lesser being and manage to sit through three hours of pomp and circumstance in the blazing sun without ralphing and still plaster on a smile and kiss Grandpa when they're done. But death brings out a raw panic in people that translates itself into such bizarre behavior that I was beginning to think it's a good thing you don't get to go to your own funeral. At least you end the day with your reputation more or less intact. As long as you didn't die under embarrassing circumstances.

Not that this was Lisbet's funeral. It was the champagne brunch that was supposed to have kicked off a day of engagement celebration and frivolity—swimming, golf, tennis, and drinking, not necessarily in that order. But given the circumstances and thanks to Aunt Cynthia's masterful working of the phones, it had morphed into a memorial gathering of people who were still trying to absorb the news that Lisbet was dead. Aunt Cynthia had been so organized in her calling, in fact, that most of the guests had heard the news from her and not from the police; they were a step behind her in contacting the guest list and making their inquiries.

"And it was too late to cancel the caterer," Cassady hypothesized as we milled on the lawn and watched other guests arrive in varying degrees of shock, grief, and disbelief. Aunt Cynthia had at least persuaded the caterer—or promised to pay him extra—to switch to more muted linens, so people were wiping their tears with dark blue napkins instead of the fuchsia and yellow Lisbet had originally requested.

Lisbet's parents were still inside with the Vincents. They'd arrived shortly after Kyle, and Aunt Cynthia had quickly cloistered the four parents to give them a chance to talk privately. Lisbet's mother, Dana Jeffries, had appeared to be deep in the grip of some major tranquilizer when Lisbet's father, Bill McCandless, had walked her into the house. Bill looked pretty haggard himself, but his gait had been stiffened by Crown Royal, not softened by Xanax.

Mr. and Mrs. Vincent had requested that Cassady and I station ourselves on the lawn to encourage the guests to congregate there. It didn't seem to matter that we hardly knew anyone. It was the principle of party physics in which guests are drawn by the gravitational pull of other guests into a central space until an overpowering force, such as the bar opening, interrupts that pull. I theorized most of our gravitational pull was due to Cassady's sheer Tadashi accordion-pleated top and mesh skirt.

While Cassady and I aerated the lawn with our high heels and tried to remember faces and names from the night before, Kyle and Tricia were touring the grounds. This had been explained to Aunt Cynthia as an introductory tour for a friend from the city. But when I volunteered to go along, its true purpose was made clear: Tricia was literally showing

Kyle the lay of the land in the hopes that he would discover something to compel him to help us figure out what had happened to Lisbet.

I wasn't sure we were going to convince him to help. One of the things I admired most about Kyle was his commitment to his job. It still bothered him that he and I hadn't started our relationship under the most pristine of circumstances and I could actually respect that in the moments that it wasn't driving me nuts. But this was a lot more complicated, especially because Detective Cook was liable to have him strung up by his badge if she caught a whiff of impropriety.

It was also more complicated because David didn't look as innocent as I wanted him to be. It was only connect-the-dots at this point, but the lines from walking out of a party where your fiancé has embarrassed your upstanding, uptight family to a row in your bedroom that ends with her throwing your expensive engagement ring in the trash to a fight poolside where you catch up with her and crack her skull open were pretty easy to draw. If I was sketching them in, Detective Cook was bound to be going over them with an indelible marker.

Cassady returned from charming one of the young men who was circulating with the cocktail tray and handed me a Bellini. "Apparently at least a few bottles of champagne escaped consumption last night."

I took the glass but paused, not sure I was ready to start quaffing quite so early. There was so much buzzing around in my head I was concerned about adding champagne to the mix.

Cassady noticed. "Why didn't we get invited on the garden tour?"

"It'll be faster for Tricia to show him around without us tagging along," I attempted.

"Did he tell you not to come?"

"Not precisely."

"What was the approximation?"

" 'You wait here. We won't be long.' "

Cassady winced and took a sip of her drink. "So what's up?"

"He doesn't want us to get involved."

"How Freudian is that?"

"I mean, he doesn't want you and Tricia and me getting involved in investigating this crime."

"Of course."

"But we already are."

"Are we back to the first 'we'?"

"I wish I knew."

"I know he drove out here in the middle of the night based on a brief-and-tearless phone call. Gotta count for something. Quite a lot, as a matter of fact."

I didn't have a good answer for that so I decided to have a sip of my drink after all. And to change the subject. "Why did Lisbet take her ring off?"

"How can you be brave enough to solve a murder and still too much of a coward to deal with your feelings about a man?"

I moved from sip to swig. "You should be proud I know my limitations. I figure out what I can."

Cassady raised her glass in momentary resignation. "Lisbet took off her ring because she was mad at David."

"He's the one who should have been upset."

"Maybe he told her to take off the ring."

"A man wants the ring back, you don't throw it away."

"True. You throw it at him."

"And he puts it in his pocket, not the trash."

"And then three months later, you see it on the pudgy

finger of some corn-fed Midwestern cow at a breast cancer benefit and you're supposed to laugh it off."

I waited the obligatory three seconds to make sure she was done. "Whatever happened to him?"

"I don't know who you're talking about."

She knew exactly whom I was talking about, his home and work addresses, current availability, and last girlfriend, as well as what she was wearing and what he was drinking the last time she'd seen him. But you gotta let a girl have her pride. "Where is David?"

"That wasn't his name."

"David Vincent."

"Of course. Because I'm so far past the other thing."

David hadn't emerged from the house yet, not that I blamed him. In his position, I would have locked myself in the attic, even if my crazy old governess was up there sucking the marrow from pigeon bones, and refused to come out. But maybe David hadn't read as many gothic novels as I had.

I was ready to venture back into the house and subtly search out David when Kyle and Tricia returned from their tour. They seemed somber, but composed. While Cassady and I were improvising wardrobe, attempting to show respect for a tragic situation while living out of suitcases filled with party frippery, Tricia had fortuitously packed her black jersey Ellen Tracy contrast trim dress and Prada black velvet bow pumps. With her hair clipped back, she looked entirely appropriate.

And Kyle looked fantastic. Maybe it was caused by the same sea breeze that was tousling his hair, but I felt a marvelous chill along my spine as he walked toward me. Was I overthinking his weekend reticence? Did I need to keep moving forward and pray for the best? If I was willing to do it for Tricia and David for the sake of an investigation, why wasn't I willing to do it for the sake of . . .

Oh yeah, there's the central problem. How do you do something for love when your mind rebels at simply thinking the word, even as a gorgeous man walks across a rolling Southampton lawn toward you with a hint of a smile playing at the corners of his fabulous blue eyes? Just because he hadn't said it, I couldn't say it or think it or act on it?

Cassady, thankfully, said something before I did. "Got it figured out, Kyle?"

Kyle slid his hands into his pockets and twitched a quick grin to acknowledge Cassady's joke. "Large open area, lots of people, minimal trace evidence. They have their work cut out for them."

"They?" Cassady asked.

"The local professionals," Kyle replied, his implication that the matter should be left to them undeniable.

"I still want Molly to talk to Davey," Tricia said quietly. "I think he'll tell her things he won't tell you because you're a cop and won't tell me because I'm his sister."

"They do call her column 'You Can Tell Me,' " Cassady pointed out.

"If you insist on doing something," Kyle said, his tone growing sterner, "you're going to give the ring to Detective Cook and explain why it wasn't on Lisbet's finger. And then leave it alone. All of you."

Tricia said, "Mother," very crisply and forcefully. I thought she was offering him an uncharacteristically profane opinion on the matter, but then I realized she was acknowledging her mother. Mrs. Vincent was walking across the lawn behind me, escorting one person I wanted to see and two I didn't—David and Lisbet's parents.

David looked like a duck being delivered to the hunter's

feet by a couple of black Labs. He'd tried to go all country gentleman with the Ralph Lauren slacks and sweater, but his appearance was still beyond bedraggled. He was ashen and morose and looked ready to cave in on himself.

And what do you say to a couple when they've just lost their child? Especially when, as she walks up to you, the mother is spewing bile into her cell phone. "I can't talk to you anymore. I have to mourn my dead daughter."

Dana Jeffries had regained some color under the pallor with which she'd arrived that morning, largely thanks to Estée Lauder. The rest of her was packed into a black Max-Mara pantsuit with her blindingly white shirt collar open far enough that you could see that the dermatologist had done his best to help her lie about her age, sandblasting the sun damage off her chest and not just off her face. Her hair had been stripped so blond that it was almost transparent and her green eyes were small and dull.

She snapped her phone shut and turned to her husband, who looked like he hadn't been sober in two marriages. Bill McCandless had a tennis player's hard-baked tan but you could still see all the broken blood vessels in his nose and cheeks. His Armani suit and perfectly groomed and dyed hair were immaculate, his gold bracelet and signet ring were incandescent, but his smile was crooked and his blue eyes were pale and rheumy.

"That bastard!" she exclaimed.

"Which one, hon?" he asked blandly.

Dana spun to include us all in her outrage. "A certain production designer, who will remain nameless until my lawyers can file the papers to sue his ass, the man I hired to design their West Coast engagement party, is not only claiming he's pay or play, he says he doesn't do funerals."

Bill held out his hand for her phone. "Let me get my

people on this right away." He punched a number into the cell phone and turned his back on us.

Mrs. Vincent, who had been visibly stiffening during this exchange until she was approaching some form of paralysis, managed to nod in our general direction. "This is David's sister Tricia and some of her friends."

Tricia held out her hand and Dana grabbed it between both of her own, like a crocodile chomping down on a dove. "Thank you for understanding the enormity of our loss and being here today to support us," Dana oozed.

As Tricia managed to come up with a warm memorial anecdote to tell Lisbet's parents, which I strongly suspected she was making up as she went along, I seized my moment. I leaned over and whispered to David, asking if I could talk to him for a moment. Out of the corner of my eye, I saw Kyle trying to get my attention without getting anyone else's.

"What about?" David whispered back.

"Guess."

David shot a look back over at Tricia, who glanced away from Dana long enough to implore him to go with me. Kyle edged away from Tricia in an effort to head me off at the pass, but Mrs. Vincent thought he was stepping in closer to her, put her arm through his, and returned her attention to Tricia's touching story. Kyle weighed the ramifications of his next move just long enough for me to put my arm through David's and hustle him away.

Conscious of all the other little knots of people populating the lawn, I propelled us on a course that snaked around them like some demented slalom, moving fast enough that no one would invite us to stop, but slow enough that no one would think we were running away.

I'd always enjoyed David. Of course, I'd never had to

clean up after him the way Tricia had. Still, I felt awkward about just diving in with all my questions. "I'm so sorry," I said genuinely, wanting to start from a solid place.

David's eyes narrowed in confusion. "Oh. Thanks. Appreciate that. It's just . . . not what I thought you were going to talk about."

"It's not," I admitted, "but I wanted to say that first."

David's eyes narrowed further, this time in pain. "Crap, Molly. Don't play with me."

"I'm not."

"I can't handle it right now. If you've got something to say, say it."

I usually saw David in a social setting where he was infallibly charming and smooth. It was a bit of a shock to be up close and too personal when the effort to be anything approaching charming was obviously beyond him. How much of the David I knew—thought I knew—was an act? The only way to find out was to keep pressing. "Okay. Why'd you break up with Lisbet?"

"What're you talking about?" David's voice leapt up in volume and shrillness, but I squeezed his arm and he cleared his throat and dropped it back down. "We didn't break up. Who's saying we did? We had a fight, that's all."

"Then where's her engagement ring?"

"Ask the police. They haven't given back any of her personal effects yet. Believe me, my father's ready to send a private guard down there to sit on the emeralds until they do."

"It wasn't on her finger."

He stopped walking, fortunately not too close to any one group. "Someone stole her ring? Someone killed her to steal her ring? That's crazy. Is that what happened?" I could see in his eyes a moment of elation when everything made sense, but they quickly clouded over again with confusion.

"But what idiot would take her diamond and leave the emeralds behind?"

"That's not what happened. Her engagement ring was in the wastebasket in your bedroom. Nelson found it this morning."

David lurched away from me, heading toward the beach. I stayed with him, though I understood his desire to walk away from everything about now. "Where'd you leave her?"

"Is this an interrogation?" The idea seemed to both amuse and infuriate him. He stopped clumsily and turned on me, his face pale except for the bags under his eyes. "You going for a scoop, Molly?"

"Not at all."

"You're not working on a story."

"No." Eileen had called, but I hadn't accepted, so I wasn't even lying, which was always nice.

David glanced back across the lawn from whence we'd come. "My sister put you up to this. The things you let her do to you." He shook his head as though I were suddenly the one under investigation.

"Excuse me?"

"C'mon. Craig Fairchild."

I flinched at the memory immediately, but it took me a moment to remember that David had also attended that horror of a cocktail party. "One blind date from hell doesn't constitute a pattern of abuse."

"He vomited on the caviar."

"Which has nothing to do with what we're talking about."

"Except Tricia's ideas aren't always the best. She can ask me her stupid questions herself. I didn't kill Lisbet."

"I know that, David," I said to placate him.

It didn't work. "Bullshit. You suspect me just like everyone else around here suspects me. My own parents can't even look me in the eye. Everybody's figuring, 'Aw, man, David went off the deep end and now Lisbet's dead.' "

I expected him to lurch away again, but he vibrated in front of me, waiting for some sort of response. "Why would people expect you to go off the deep end?" I'd seen David rowdy, but never violent.

"I've got a temper. So what. I didn't kill her."

"Make her mad enough to take her ring off?"

David took a deep breath, as though he could suck back in all the energy his anger was radiating out. "You saw the . . . performance. She was a mess. It was embarrassing and you do not do that to my parents. I had to go upstairs and tell her to get a grip. Lisbet went off on me 'commanding' her, threw me out of the bedroom. I left. Took a long walk. When I came back, she wasn't in the room. I looked all over and finally found her—" His voice cracked as he groped for the words.

I shook my head to let him know he didn't have to continue. "You left her alone in the room. Wearing the ring."

"And about to pass out, I thought. I figured I'd see her in the morning, moaning for coffee and sunglasses, not . . ." He screwed his eyes shut and shook his head vigorously, wanting to erase the image of Lisbet in the pool. I waited, trying to show respect for his pain and also trying to figure out what piece of the puzzle to pursue next. Suddenly, he grabbed my upper arm hard and pulled me tight against him. "Figure out who did this so I can get to them first."

The sudden ferocity of his tone was alarming. "Stop it."

"David, let go of her, people are watching." Tricia had glided across the grass to warn us. As I turned to look at her, I could see the mosaic of bunched people laid out across the lawn, with at least half of them turned to peer at David.

And me. But David was the one who'd gotten angry and the one who could least afford that sort of public display at the moment.

David released my arm. "You're not even sure I'm innocent."

"Don't get paranoid," I said quietly, trying to imbue the words with a moral surety I didn't feel at the moment.

He hung his head. "I'm sorry. It's all making me crazy. And this"—he gestured to the guests—"what is this supposed to be?"

"People showing their respect," his sister responded with admirable evenness. "You could stand to do the same."

Rage flashed in his eyes again, but a whole lot of upbringing kicked in and he tamped it down quickly. The concept of being buttoned down took on a whole new meaning before my very eyes. "Perhaps," David said, in overly measured tones, "you could tell me what exactly it is that's expected of me right now and I'll comply."

Tricia's lip curled in a direction I didn't know was possible. "Don't Dad me, David. It won't accomplish anything positive."

Suddenly feeling like an intruder, I eased back to let them have it out in private. I'd gotten everything I was going to get out of David at the moment anyway; I was going to have to find a hole in his story before I could challenge it.

So I headed back across the lawn to intrude on another conversation. I'd thought the most I might return to would be Cassady grilling Kyle on his plans for the rest of the weekend or, perhaps, the rest of his life, just in the interest of keeping me well informed. What I returned to was Cassady trying to communicate with only her eyebrows that I should hurry my buns across the lawn because Kyle was engrossed in intense conversation with Detective Cook.

The parents had moved on to work their way across the lawn one group at a time. Kyle and Cassady were where I'd left them, but now Detective Cook had joined them. She seemed dressed for business this time, with a gray department store pantsuit, white cotton blouse, and utterly sensible black pumps.

"Good morning, Detective Cook," I said as I walked up, thinking the sweet approach might catch her off-guard. Besides, I needed to go easy with Detective Cook if I expected to learn anything useful from her. Not catfighting in front of Kyle was worth considering, too.

But the Hand blew that nice little plan right out of the water. Rather than acknowledging me or even just ignoring me, Detective Cook reached back with her left arm and gave me the Hand. The "wait just a minute, young lady, grown-ups are talking" Hand. The "I'm on Safety Patrol and you'll stop when I tell you to stop, little dork" Hand. Detective Cook even combined the Hand with leaning in to finish what she was saying to Kyle in lower, more intimate tones. What could one little catfight hurt?

Cassady diplomatically gestured to the house. "Maybe we should go inside and see if there's anything we can do to help."

"I'm helping right here," I said, ladling on a politeness I wasn't feeling.

"And that fascinating theory is based on . . ." Detective Cook didn't even turn to look at me, she just glanced back over her shoulder. Kyle gave me another warning look, but I returned this one. Why should I let this woman snark away at me and not respond? She was an officer of the law, fine, but she was also a leggy blond who was standing a little too close to my . . . male friend of an extremely intimate nature.

Then again, did I want to give her the satisfaction of knowing how far under my skin she was getting? Maybe a sudden change in course would help keep her off-balance. While I would have found it quite pleasurable to yank her hair out by the handful at this juncture, I refrained. "Hope," I chirped. "I'm hopeful I'll find a way to help."

I couldn't get a feel for whether my change in attitude since the wee hours this morning was disarming her, but it was making Kyle very nervous. He knew I was up to something and he wasn't sure what it was. And all it was was a fairly blatant attempt to distract Detective Cook, from me and from Kyle.

However, all I succeeded in doing was eliciting a steely stare over the top of her sunglasses. She tipped her head forward and the sunglasses slid a little down the bridge of her nose, then stopped as if she had them trained. "I want your cooperation, not your help, thank you," she replied coolly.

"Then you have a suspect? And a cause of death? And a murder weapon?" I pursued.

With each question, Kyle's face got a little darker. But Detective Cook listened impassively until she was sure I was done. "This is an ongoing investigation and I'm not at liberty to share that information with you."

"So you don't have any of those."

Detective Cook looked at Cassady and Kyle in frustration. "Is she always this bad a listener?"

"She's a good listener," Cassady answered quickly.

I nodded in affirmation. "It's a big part of my job. Don't you find the same?"

"Molly," Kyle ventured, "there's probably a better time—and way—to compare notes with Detective Cook."

"No, this is actually a fine time," Detective Cook corrected him as she marched over, grabbed my arm in almost the exact spot where David had grabbed it, and marched me away from Kyle and Cassady. As I twisted in her grasp to keep my footing, I caught a glimpse of Cassady starting to follow us and Kyle stopping her. There was an explanation I was going to look forward to.

Especially since I wasn't sure I was looking forward to the one I was about to get from Detective Cook. "Since you have a 'friend' who's a homicide detective, you must not have some issue with cops in general," Detective Cook began. "So why can't you get out of my face?"

I literally dug my heels in, throwing my weight back so the four-inch heels of my Stuart Weitzman Dramahalt pumps dug into the soft lawn and yanked us both to a stop. Detective Cook fumbled for her footing while I silently hoped serving as a drag anchor wouldn't ruin the black satin on my shoes. Nevertheless, extreme situations require extreme gestures.

I decided to let the "friend" thing go for a moment—just a moment—and concentrate on the larger question. "*Me* in *your* face? I've been a heck of a lot nicer to you than you've been to me."

Detective Cook let go of my arm but looked like she was thinking about going for my throat. "'Nice' isn't in my job description. I have to be good, I don't have to be nice."

"What about being right?"

Detective Cook bared her teeth at me in a grim approximation of a smile. For a moment, she resembled a lioness ripping the flesh off an innocent zebra. I, of course, was feeling very pro-zebra. I was about to tell her so when she blindsided me. "What's the deal with your 'friend' anyway?"

"Excuse me?" I took a moment to pull my heels out of the soil and pull my thoughts together. Was she deliberately changing subjects to hide a larger intent?

"Is he single or are you two a couple?"

How dare she ask a question I didn't dare ask? I did my best to mask my surprise with a more generalized offense. "How can that possibly be relevant?"

The lioness's smile got bigger and lazier. Contented even. "Don't want to classify it or can't?"

"Don't want to get your own life or can't?"

Detective Cook's mouth contracted into a tight knot of discontent. "You've got a hell of a lot of nerve giving me attitude when you're withholding information."

"I am not," I protested sincerely. How could I withhold information when I didn't have any yet? Suspicions and feelings aplenty, but no information. "If I had information, I'd give it to you. You think David Vincent did this, but he's innocent."

"And your impassioned stance is based on . . ."

"Lisbet wasn't wearing her engagement ring when she died. She and David had a fight after the party last night, she took the ring off and threw it away. I think she went off and got into a fight with someone else, not David, because he didn't know she'd taken off her ring and he would've noticed that. Even a guy would've noticed that."

"So you're suggesting . . ."

"Someone else killed her. Someone who was irrationally upset with her behavior last night."

Detective Cook thought a moment, then picked up on my train of thought. "Someone who resented the way she'd acted and the way it reflected on David."

"Exactly."

"Someone who wasn't so much mad at her as . . ."

"Protecting David."

"Someone with an investment in David or the family."

For a shining moment, I liked Detective Cook. Liked her

a lot. Because she was thinking what I was thinking and that's always a grand place to begin a friendship. It was a little early to invite her over for a beer and a barbecue, but it was a start. "Yes."

"Maybe even a family member with a weak alibi."

"What?" So much for liking her. So much for being on the same wavelength.

Detective Cook shrugged. "Someone who was alone. Or vouched for only by friends."

I gaped at her in horror, unable to get my mouth out of neutral and say something that would stop her in her tracks the way she'd stopped me. I tried to cut her off, but she kept talking. "You can't seriously—"

"Friends who insist upon telling me who's innocent."

"Think that it's—"

"The only person who meets those criteria is . . ."

"Tricia."

Detective Cook smiled at me with tremendous satisfaction. I swore I could see shreds of zebra meat caught in the lioness's teeth.

6

"Maybe you should just stop helping."

While some may find it naive, blindly optimistic, or futile, my worldview is shaped by the notion that you're supposed to do the right thing whenever possible because if we all did that, the world would be a better place. Plus, if you do the right thing when no one else is doing it, you get a good seat on the moral high ground and there's a pretty nice view from up there.

Of course, once you're up there, it's amazingly easy to lose your balance and tumble headfirst from that good seat and watch your ethics, dignity, and ego go splat on the pavement. But with any luck, you'll survive long enough to hear someone you really care about say, "I told you so." Or, as some translate it, "Stop helping."

It had not been my intention to get David out of trouble by getting someone else in trouble, especially Tricia. And it had never been my intention to get myself in trouble with anyone in the process, especially with Kyle.

We were back in the deep green room, a place for which I was quickly losing affection. It was starting to feel a little oppressive. Though not as oppressive as the bordello room, to which Tricia and Detective Cook had retired since the detective had latched on to the ridiculous idea that I was suggesting Tricia was somehow connected to Lisbet's death. I wanted to go kick the door down and explain to Detective Cook just where in the order of evolution I placed her, but Kyle was not in favor of that plan. In fact, Kyle was not in favor of my ever talking to Detective Cook again, even to comment on the weather.

"She's talking to Tricia to tick me off," I protested.

Kyle fixed me with his amazing blue gaze. I felt both chastened and breathless, which was not a combination my already precarious emotional state could incorporate easily. "Cook's talking to her because you presented a pretty logical construct for Tricia's motive," Kyle explained with thinning patience. He wouldn't sit down and I couldn't figure out if he wanted to keep his distance from me or if he was just moving to hold his temper.

"No, I was leading her away from David," I insisted.

"Why?"

"Because he's not guilty and Tricia asked me to help prove that."

"Why?"

"Because she loves her brother."

"But she's worried enough about how it looks that she needs to bring in outside help."

"She's afraid. Wouldn't you be?"

Kyle shrugged with maddening objectivity, moving back in my direction. "I don't know everything Tricia knows. And I don't have all the evidence."

"Neither does Detective Cook," I said, thinking of the show Lisbet put on before her death. I couldn't shake the feeling that her display was linked somehow to her demise.

He slid his hand up under my hair, cupping my cheek but not pulling me to him. Yet. I didn't want him to feel me clenching my jaw, so I held my breath to help me concentrate. When you're first attracted, strongly attracted to a man, you find yourself thinking that maybe you should just kiss him so you can get past obsessing about what that first kiss is going to be like. The problem is, if the first kiss is great, you wind up obsessing about getting another one and it wreaks havoc with your powers of concentration.

He rubbed his thumb lightly along my cheekbone. I'd like to claim it's an acupressure point and that's the reason I felt light-headed, but Kyle has had this effect on me from the very beginning, despite all my best efforts to be resolute. Or at least, a little coy. I should at least get points for not melting into his arms right then and there.

"I'm not on the job and you shouldn't be either," he said quietly, but with notable authority. "I know you want to help, but sometimes, the best way to help is to stay out of it."

I was about to admit that he was right when I had a disturbing flash of Dustin Hoffman gaping at Anne Bancroft. I slid his hand away from my cheek and took a step back. "Mrs. Robinson, are you trying to seduce me?"

Kyle made a sound that was part laugh, part question mark. "Molly, I'm trying to offer a little perspective here. I think it's time to go home."

Nothing makes me want to stay in a place more than someone telling me I ought to leave. But this was more than being contrary. I still had the feeling that we were all overlooking something and I didn't want to leave until I'd found it. Or helped find it. And now that I'd created questions about Tricia, I needed to clean up my mess before I went home. "I can't."

Kyle nodded, hands sliding deep into his pockets. Apparently, this was the answer he'd expected. No way I was getting predictable this early in a noncategorized relationship.

Was I? "Most people see a dead body and they can't wait to run the other way. Why do you want to stick around?"

"Unresolved childhood traumas, no doubt," I said, sounding only slightly snippier than I felt.

"Let's work through them somewhere else," Kyle said, sounding quite a bit snippier than I felt he should feel.

"I thought you came out here to help me."

"I came because you called. Good move on my part."

"It was a good move. I appreciate it. I just don't appreciate being told it's time to go."

"Sorry. It is."

"And that's your decision to make."

"Yes."

"As the professional."

He reached for me again. "And the personal. Someone who—"

In the split second before the verb came out, all the blood in my body raced to other locations in anticipation of some monumental statement. What we got instead was the door to the room banging open and Aunt Cynthia charging in, wearing a black dress and a blacker expression.

"Where's Cassady?"

"I'm not sure," I admitted, wondering if we looked like we'd been interrupted doing something inappropriate.

Not that Aunt Cynthia was interested at all. Her focus was elsewhere. "I need a lawyer. Mine is already on his fourth cocktail and not being particularly helpful."

"What happened?" I asked.

"Policemen are going through my garbage," Aunt Cynthia said with disdain. I wasn't sure if the disdain was for the police or for their task.

Kyle was already heading for the door. "Wonder what

they're looking for." Aunt Cynthia followed him quickly, her bangles bouncing noisily.

"I thought we were leaving," I called after them, more angry that Kyle hadn't finished his sentence than at his sudden departure.

He shot a dark look back at me, but Aunt Cynthia answered. "You can't leave before the brunch. It would be unseemly. Besides, I need your young man," she said as she swept him out of the room, pulling the door closed behind her.

Yeah, well, I needed Kyle, too. I needed Kyle to finish his sentence. I also needed a chat with Tricia and Cassady. I was determined to stay put until I'd solved this thing for myself, if not for the police. Or for Eileen, of whom I had mercifully not thought for some time.

As I emerged from the house, I found Richard and Rebecca on the back patio, not so much waiting for me as lurking in my expected path. Richard was drinking a Bellini, but Rebecca was cradling a coffee cup.

"The police are back," Richard said, without benefit of preamble.

"I heard."

"What else did you hear?"

I shook my head, feeling awkward and defensive. "I don't know any more than anyone else."

Rebecca pressed her coffee cup against her chest as though it could warm her. "Then why did you tell the detective to question Tricia?"

"I didn't. I said something the detective misunderstood. It was her idea to talk to Tricia."

Rebecca's eyes misted. "And you couldn't stop her?"

I didn't know which was more troubling, Richard's anger or Rebecca's sorrow. "I don't have any influence with her."

"But you brought a cop in from Manhattan," Richard said.

I shook my head emphatically. "He's . . . here for personal reasons. And I don't have any influence with him either."

Richard didn't seem to like any of my answers, but he accepted them. For the moment, anyway. Rebecca wiped her eyes delicately with her cocktail napkin, expertly managing not to smear a bit of makeup. She put her arm through Richard's and started to walk him away. "I hate this," she offered in parting. I nodded in agreement and continued on my quest.

Cassady and Tricia were farther out on the lawn. I'd expected Tricia might be shaken by her encounter with Detective Cook, but she was infuriated. With Detective Cook and not me, much to my relief.

"That woman has no manners," Tricia said as I hurried up to them.

"She went to the police academy, not finishing school," Cassady pointed out.

"You can be flip. She didn't interrogate you," Tricia snapped.

"Not yet. But give Molly another try and I'll be in the hot seat before you know it," Cassady said with a wink.

"I never intended to say anything disparaging about you, Tricia," I assured her. "And I didn't. She just sort of backed me into a corner and then pounced before I knew what was happening."

"I saw that movie on Cinemax. Three times," Cassady said. She was doing an admirable job of trying to prop up everyone's spirits.

"Where's Detective Cook now?" I asked.

"Her partner came and got her to go look for something." So that's where the warrant came from. As I tried to figure out what particular object they could be seeking, Tricia continued. "But not before she made me give her Lisbet's ring."

"How'd she know you had it?" Cassady asked.

"I told her Lisbet wasn't wearing it," I confessed.

"I don't think either one of you should talk to policemen without me present from here on in. And," Cassady continued, eyebrow slanting, "we may have to put Kyle on that list if you're not careful."

Tricia frowned. "It's awful to have someone accuse you of doing something terrible."

I nodded sympathetically. "I remember how I felt when Kyle suspected me."

"Twice," Cassady said. "Tell me again why you two are together?"

"I've seen relationships start off on worse footing," I protested.

"Name one," Cassady challenged.

I had to scan my memory banks for a moment, but Tricia had the answer immediately. "You and Kevin McNamara," Tricia said with a tip of her glass to Cassady.

Cassady's lower lip curled in a showy mix of revulsion and petulance. "That was different."

"Because you had someone else arrest his girlfriend instead of doing it yourself."

"For the record, she was guilty."

"Of tax evasion."

"Good enough for Capone." Cassady sighed expansively. "Okay, it was a little over the top, but who among us hasn't gone a little too far to clear the path to a man?"

Of course. That made more sense than anything else so far. "Including murder?" I asked.

Cassady looked like she actually was scanning the memory banks now, but Tricia zeroed in on my meaning right away. "You think Lisbet could have been killed by someone who wants Davey?"

"Or wants David back." As the possibility took shape in my mind, I realized it was quite likely that an ex could lose control, pushed by the weight of accumulated anger and hatred. "How many of David's exes are here this weekend?"

Tricia's shoulders slumped. "Dear lord. Look at it this way. I think the only people we can safely exclude from that list are my mother and my aunts and the three of us." She hesitated. "I can exclude the three of us."

"Absolutely," I said, instinctively giving the Girl Scout salute.

No such salute from Cassady. Tricia and I both looked at her, Tricia's eyes widening in disbelief and mine narrowing in anticipation. Cassady sniffed at us both. "We're talking actual congress, right? Being wickedly drunk on New Year's Eve and pawing each other for an hour or so in a dark corner should hardly put me on a suspect list."

Tricia swallowed hard. "You and Davey?"

"Let's devote our attention to Molly's fascinating hypothesis and forget all about it, shall we?"

"You and my brother Davey?" Tricia repeated.

"*So* momentary. And this is why I never said anything. But you asked directly and I never lie to you, and now we're moving on."

Tricia wasn't moving on. She wasn't moving at all. She was standing still and staring at Cassady with a mix of awe and distaste and complete bewilderment.

"Maybe we should go sit down," I suggested, trying to guide them both toward the tent. "What time did Aunt Cynthia say brunch would be served?"

"We could ask her," Cassady said, pointing to where Aunt Cynthia and Kyle were returning to us from their garbage safari. Kyle was expressionless, which is his personal default mode, but Aunt Cynthia looked shaken, something I didn't know was possible.

"They are looking for champagne bottles," Aunt Cynthia announced.

"Not something that should be broadcast, Mrs. Malinkov," Kyle cautioned.

"You could rebuild the boathouse with the champagne bottles we've emptied in the last twenty-four hours. I don't know what they expect to find."

"Fingerprints, hair, blood," I said, not realizing I was answering before Kyle until I'd already done it. But why else would the police be going through the trash and looking for bottles? "The police must think Lisbet was struck with a champagne bottle."

The Pause reared its ugly head and then Kyle simply said, "Looks that way."

Tricia sobbed suddenly. Even though she cupped her hand over her mouth to try and hold it in, it was a sharp, startling sound. Aunt Cynthia and Cassady each took an arm and started to walk with her to the tent.

Which left me with Kyle again. "Sorry to take off like that," he said. "Just thought I might be able to help Mrs. Malinkov understand what was happening."

"Thank you."

"Ready to leave?"

Even less so than the last time he'd asked. It was good, though sad, that the police thought they had identified the murder weapon. But I'd seen a lot of champagne bottles hanging from a lot of hands the night before and I knew what an incredible task lay before them. Needle in the haystack. Then again, DNA could probably help you zero in on that needle these days.

"I'd like to stay for brunch, to be polite," I suggested. It would also give me time to come up with a compelling reason to stay beyond that. Which raised the question of why I didn't feel comfortable just saying, "You go back, I'll stay here." Mysteries abounded.

Kyle checked his watch, then turned the gesture into offering me his arm. "So let's eat."

As we joined the movement of guests toward the tent, I tried to think of the right thing to say to Kyle to steer him back to his unfinished sentence. I almost had it when my cell rang. Kyle stopped walking and released my arm, just assuming that I was going to answer it. He's a real gentleman, which is pretty amazing, given the people he deals with all day.

I checked the number and almost didn't answer it; it was the magazine. But then it occurred to me that if Eileen really wanted a story, I would have to stay and Kyle would have to understand about it all being about the job, his being a gentleman and all. So I answered.

"What *were* you wearing?"

It wasn't Eileen, it was the next best/worst thing. Caitlin, our fashion editor. She's used to summing up and dismissing fashion trends and her approach to people isn't much different.

I was sure it was going to be more efficient to skip defending my outfit and figure out why she was calling. "When?"

"Last night. You really should be wearing skirts that break right at the knee, Molly. You have nice calves but bony knees. We've had this discussion before—"

"Caitlin? How do you know what I was wearing last night?"

"I saw the video. So sorry about Tricia's sister-in-law-to-be, by the way. My point is, you go to a high-profile function like that, you're representing the magazine in some way and more precisely, it's a reflection on me if you don't look good."

Forget about the twisted logic that made any of this about her. "Go back. What video?"

"Some snot-nosed auteur has film from last night on his Web site already. Says it's an artistic statement and a tribute to the dead girl. A friend heard from a friend and called me about it. Looks like things got pretty wild. But let's get back to your dress."

"It won't happen again," I apologized quickly, hoping to get past this and move the conversation to more fertile ground. "Tell me about this film." I'd only seen one camera in plain view last night, but I wanted to be sure.

Kyle detected something in my tone and turned to look at me. I knew better than to give him the Hand, so I held up one finger—the polite finger—to ask him to wait, hoping it didn't look too imperious. He didn't seem to take offense, just fixed me with his piercing blue stare and waited to see what I'd say next.

"The lighting sucks and it's hyper-edited, but she looks great. At least people will remember her looking brilliant."

"What's the Web site?"

"Honey, you don't want to see. Give yourself some time. And get another dress."

"Caitlin, if I promise to hide my knees forever, will you tell me the Web site?"

"Deal. It's like jakesjazz.com or something."

Bingo. Jake takes tragedy and turns it into a self-serving "artistic statement." What little I knew of him thus far, it fit. "Thanks for the information, Caitlin," I said.

"Just watching out for the magazine's reputation. Are you still in the Hamptons?"

"Yes."

"What are you wearing now?"

"Nothing."

I hung up and slid my cell back into my pocket. Kyle looked at me expectantly. "Just a friend checking in from the magazine."

"What Web site?" Kyle was getting that focused look, which increases the intensity of his gaze to a practically incandescent level.

"Some goofy fashion thing, it's nothing. You want to go ahead and sit down? I just have to pop back inside and use the rest room."

"I think I should stick with you," Kyle said firmly.

"Kinky."

"If you were going to the rest room. Which you're not."

"Say I don't. Anything I see, you might feel compelled to share with your new friend Detective Cook before I have an opportunity to put it in a proper context."

" 'Cause that's my job and it's not yours."

"Which is why I'm going to the rest room. That simple."

Kyle rocked back on his heels slightly. "Nothing in your life's that simple, Molly."

"Keeps life interesting." I hurried back toward the house and resisted with every fiber of my being the impulse to turn and look to see if he was following me.

I did go to the rest room. At least, I entered and took a moment to gasp appropriately. I know people who would gladly pay two grand to rent that much space and still wouldn't expect all the marble or the raw silk window treatments. Besides, I wanted to be able to look Kyle in the eye and say I'd kept my promise.

I checked my hair and makeup and gave my knees a quick inspection. They're not bony, they're just not rounded. Thanks a lot, Caitlin. I went back out into the hallway and tried to remember which door exactly led to the bordello room.

I found it on the third try. Blissfully, it was empty and the laptop was on. Better yet, Aunt Cynthia had DSL, so I was online in what seemed like two seconds.

Caitlin's memory was better than she'd given herself credit for. At www.jakesjazz.com, I found a self-aggrandizing Web site from Jake, complete with a new notice on the home page proclaiming his great sorrow at Lisbet's passing, but touting the fact that he possessed and, of course, had posted the last footage of Lisbet ever shot. There was also some intensely creepy stuff about being able to love her on screen forever, now that we could no longer love her in the flesh. Taking a deep breath, I clicked on the link to the "memorial footage."

One of the first shots was a pan around the great room, which included Tricia, Cassady, and me. My knees looked fine. But the film quickly moved on, catching people dancing, people drinking, and finally the guys holding Lisbet upside down. Yeah, that's how she'd want to be remembered.

Feeling slightly ill, I was about to sign off, when I realized the footage continued. There was a cut, then it picked back up with David carrying Lisbet out of the room. The camera followed them out into the hallway, where Lisbet almost jumped out of David's arms. She gesticulated wildly, apparently screaming at him. There was a quick flash of someone else coming out into the hall and then the piece ended. I couldn't tell who the other person was, but Jake might remember. As for what else had been on the camera and hadn't made it onto the Web site, I was willing to bet he'd remember that, too.

I needed to make my next move carefully, so I had to get Tricia and Cassady into the loop. I dialed Cassady's cell. She answered on the second ring, which didn't bode well for the brunch conversation, and I told her that she and Tricia needed to go to the bathroom. And then to continue on down the hall to the bordello room. She made some flip comment about men who didn't like to take no for an answer to let me know that Kyle was at the table with her and hung up.

I watched the footage again while I waited, searching for clues, for some direction. Other than the fact that everyone seemed to have a champagne bottle in their hands, I wasn't able to glean much from the shaky images or identify who was out in the hall.

Cassady knocked on the door by drumming her fingernails on it, her classic knock. I ushered them in quickly. "You're probably wondering why I've called you here," I began, trying to lighten things up because I knew what came next was going to be tough on Tricia. I explained Caitlin's phone call. Cassady was intrigued but Tricia was pained, whether by this last glimpse of Lisbet or by David's obvious and potentially incriminating anger, I couldn't tell.

"So what do we do now?" Tricia asked quietly.

"We divide and conquer. You guys stay here and I'll go back and talk to Jake."

"Kyle's not going to go for that," Tricia protested.

"Were you planning on telling him?"

It's very important, whenever you have the opportunity, to give a man credit for the idea he came up with, even if your reason for finally going along with the idea diverges somewhat from his. Which is why I returned to the tent slightly ahead of my friends, sat down next to Kyle, who really had only my best interests at heart, and told him,

"You're absolutely right. I think we should go back to the city as soon as possible."

I didn't score hugely because Kyle is by nature suspicious, but I did score. And points in a relationship are like slams on his old girlfriends. You gotta take 'em where you can.

7

Returning from a weekend out of town with a man is a delicate mix of reentry, reorientation, and review. The reentry is the simple process of slipping back into the rhythm of the city, sort of like stepping onto one of those moving sidewalks at the airport; it's always going a little faster than you think it is, but once you get both feet on it, the pace is just right.

The reorientation is the slightly more complex process of checking mail, voice mail, and e-mail, educating yourself on everything you've missed, and marveling at all the contortions your friends, loved ones, and business associates can put themselves through in a weekend.

The review is the intricate and treacherous process of replaying the events of the weekend, reconstructing them to glean every possible emotional clue from each action, reconsidering their potential as anecdotes, and renewing your pledge to go out of town only with men who have demonstrated actual long-range potential because the short hops with the short bops reliably cause more problems than they solve.

Then again, I kept reminding myself on the drive back to Manhattan, this had not been intended as a weekend away with Kyle. Certainly not the weekend I'd had in mind when I'd made my big suggestion. This had mutated into a day away with him and he'd made the first move. He seemed to view it as coming to my rescue, but I couldn't quite see it that way, since I hadn't gotten into trouble.

"Yet," Kyle pointed out.

He wasn't being mean, he was being honest, and I had to acknowledge that. We'd only been on the road about twenty minutes and I didn't want to start arguing with the bulk of the drive yet ahead of us. I was still trying to reconcile the fact that he was driving an Isuzu Rodeo with everything else I knew about Kyle. I'd never driven anywhere with him before; we always met somewhere or did taxis and even the occasional subway though they make me claustrophobic and sweaty.

I picked up the CD wallet on the console between us and flipped through it, but that just added to my confusion: Good Charlotte, Fountains of Wayne, Josh Rouse, and Wilco were not the sorts of things I'd imagined Kyle listening to. Blame too many Clint Eastwood movies, but I'd expected him to be a jazz guy. If I'd had to predict a surprise, I would have gone for reformed metalhead.

Of course, what I held in my hand could very well be the musical equivalent of the fingerprints of a former girlfriend. Forensic evidence of the one who came before. Kyle had been enormously reticent about sharing any details of his romantic past, which he portrayed as being discreet and which I construed as his having a huge advantage over me since he had met—and helped to usher out—Peter Mulcahey, the guy I'd been dating when I'd met him.

Peter and I hadn't been on the best of footings. He was a fellow journalist—make that, rival journalist—and our professional vying had been a sore spot in our relationship. I was developing a knack for getting involved with men who brought out my competitive streak. Since we'd broken up, Peter had finagled his way on to the *Times*. One more reason not to think about him anymore.

"Nice CDs." Felt like a neutral-enough opener.

He shrugged. "I guess."

"What else do you listen to?"

"Whatever's on."

"On what radio station?"

"TAC one, unless we're instructed to go to TAC two."

"I meant regular radio."

"I don't usually bother."

"So what made you buy these CDs?"

"They're not mine."

I knew it. I was closing in on a subtle but telling piece of his past. "Someone left them with you?"

"She loaned them to me."

My throat tightened. Loaned? Was this the revelation of some current arrangement? "She?"

He glanced over at me, frowning at my sudden interest in his musical taste. "My niece's car. Her CDs."

"Oh." I blinked as the swirling images of another woman evaporated and a new piece of the Big Picture slid into place. He'd mentioned family in passing, but we'd never dwelt on it. Kyle as favorite uncle was a whole new concept and one that, at first blush, I found sweet and appealing. "She must like you a lot to loan you her car. On a weekend, yet."

He shook his head, grinning quickly. "She's grounded for the next fifty-four years for busting curfew, so she didn't get a vote. My sister's about the only one I can call in the middle of the night to hit up for healthy wheels." He shrugged again, but it was the first time I'd thought about all the trouble he'd taken to come to my aid.

"Have I thanked you for coming?"

"No. You've pretty much ragged on me since I arrived."

Even though he was smiling, I winced at the truth in his statement. "I just want to help protect David," I protested. "Actually, I want to help Tricia and she wants to help David."

"Detective Cook strikes me as a very competent detective."

"How else does she strike you?"

"You want to take a nap or something? I'll wake you up when we get back to the city."

"You don't want to talk to me or you don't want to talk to me about this?"

"Want me to take you back to the Hamptons?"

I took a moment to wonder how things were going back at Aunt Cynthia's. When they'd returned from their semi-covert "trip to the rest room," Tricia and Cassady had done a lovely job of expressing dismay and displeasure, respectively, that I'd decided to follow Kyle's advice and get back to Manhattan as soon as possible. Tricia had insisted that there was investigating to be done there at the house, but Kyle'd insisted more strongly that the situation was under control and that the greater the distance between me and Detective Cook, the better. I had suggested that Tricia and Cassady help me throw my things back in my suitcase while Kyle went and talked to the valets about getting his car un-blocked by all the brunch guests'.

Up in the guest room, we'd reviewed our bathroom-hatched plan. Tricia and Cassady would stay until the family headed back to Manhattan, while I tracked down Jake as quickly as possible. "Jake's gotta know more than he's post-ing and he's probably sitting on it until he figures out a way to use it to make a name for himself."

Cassady nodded. "Everyone's going to take off as soon as

brunch is over anyway. Aunt Cynthia isn't serving dinner and even this crowd will find it too morbid to hang with no buffet."

Tricia pressed her fingers into her forehead, but Cassady pulled her hands away. "You're going to work yourself into one huge zit. Pick your cuticles if you must, but don't trash the face."

Tricia waggled her fingers in the air, not sure what to do with them now. "I think Richard and Rebecca are going to take Davey back to the city as soon as Detective Cook says it's okay."

Cassady shuddered. "Whoever thought those two would be the calm, responsible ones in any equation."

Tricia sneered. "I give Rebecca eighteen hours before she's drinking again. And I give Richard a week before he dumps her again."

"Detective Cook must not have anything concrete or she would've acted on it. One more reason to join the general flow back to the city . . . Can you get a guest list, Tricia?" I asked.

She nodded emphatically. "Nelson will give it to me if I tell him I want to start writing thank-you notes. Nelson's very into protocol." She noticed Cassady looking at her oddly. "What?"

"I'm trying to imagine the note. 'Dear Friend, We deeply regret the murder of our guest of honor and want to thank you for minding your manners while being questioned by the local constabulary.'" Cassady scrunched her nose at me. "Guess you're not getting a note."

"Tricia asked me to help," I pointed out.

"I did and I appreciate it," Tricia said quickly. "And I appreciate your tackling this as a friend, and not as a journalist."

My reaction must not have been as enigmatic as I had

hoped, because Tricia's expression fell in on itself. "Please don't, Molly."

"Eileen called and asked me to follow the story, that's all. I haven't committed to anything. Except helping David."

Tricia's face contorted one more time, buffeted by all her warring fears and emotions. She leaned forward and kissed me gently on the cheek. "Travel safe," she whispered and left the room before I could think of anything to say—helpful, stupid, or otherwise.

Cassady sighed. "I'm surprised she's holding up as well as she is."

I vented some frustration on the stubborn zipper of my suitcase. "Shouldn't investigating be easier the second time around?"

"I believe that's love and I believe that's a crock. I also believe you're doing the right thing in helping and that Tricia knows that, she's just having trouble with all the other aspects of the situation. She and David have always been so close and even though she didn't like Lisbet, it's still a loss."

"Don't you ever get tired of being right?"

"I have no other experience to compare it to."

"Okay. Keep your profile low and don't tick off Detective Cook."

Cassady patted me on the head. "We'll leave that to the expert."

Kyle clearly felt I'd done enough of that already, which had been his primary motivation in getting me out of the Hamptons. Now, mulling it over as he drove, I felt all my efforts could be interpreted as helpful, even if he didn't agree. As a result, I was doing us both a favor to stay quiet about the Web site until I had a chance to talk to Jake and find out what else he might have shot. I didn't want to muddy the picture for anyone; I wanted to clarify it.

And while we were seeking clarity, this was a good time to try and get Kyle back on the train of thought Aunt Cynthia had derailed with her garbage-hunting announcement. We were alone in the car, no one's cell had rung, there was minimal traffic. Perfect talk time. But the trick was, how to dangle the hook without getting busted for fishing.

"You're right, it was time to leave."

Kyle slid me a suspicious look. "Okay."

"And I know Detective Cook's just doing her job."

He nodded vigorously. "You don't want to get in her way, Molly. She can make life miserable for all involved. You also don't want to distract her from nailing the proper party."

I hadn't intended to turn this into a cheerleading session for the devoted Detective Cook. Time to throw my weight in another direction and see if the boat turned.

"Guess I'm spoiled, having had such wonderful police cooperation the last time I was involved in something like this."

His smile slid back into place. "Cooperation. That's what that was called?"

"When it's done right."

"We were lucky."

"Lucky, not good?"

"We are good." He kept his eyes on the road, but I turned to look at him full on. It was one of those tremulous soap bubble moments when you don't want to breathe wrong, much less speak wrong, for fear of the whole thing exploding before you can absorb it.

"Yes, we are. And I can't tell you how much I appreciate your support."

"Welcome."

"Professionally and personally."

"Uh-huh."

"As someone who . . . How'd you put it?"

Kyle grinned, his suspicions confirmed to his great delight. "I didn't."

I couldn't help it. His grin was infectious and even though I should have been frustrated and thwarted, I grinned back. "But we're good."

"Yeah."

"Good enough for me to ask where you were last night when I called?"

"Out with some other detectives, having a drink. Why?"

"I just . . . heard something . . ."

He snorted. "I told Maggie she was a loudmouth. 'Busted,' right?" I nodded. "They were all complaining they had to get home and I said no one was waiting up for me and . . ."

"Sorry." The outsider had intruded on his cop world and he'd gotten grief for it.

"No." He ran the back of his hand along my arm. "It was kinda nice. We're good. Honest."

Good enough to go away for the weekend? Amazingly, I couldn't bring myself to ask. Better to enjoy this moment for itself and push my luck another time. So for the rest of the trip, I just left it alone and we enjoyed the drive and each other, talking about things that didn't matter terribly much, sampling his niece's CDs, and even being comfortably quiet a time or two. But that's hard for me under the best of circumstances and every time we grew quiet, I started trying to assemble the crime in my head, figuring out which lover of David's had come out of the shadows without realizing that Lisbet had already decided it was over, and bashed her head in with a champagne bottle. But I kept it to myself and changed the CD whenever those thoughts intruded.

The warm buzz continued as he found a great parking

spot near my building, helped me out of the car and into his arms for a kiss that was just the right length and pressure, and grabbed my bags out of the back. He greeted Danny the doorman warmly and escorted me up to my apartment without discussion. Another kiss as I unlocked the door and nothing in the world was as important as the next kiss and whether I had any decent wine.

He walked into the bedroom to put my bags down—another positive sign—so I wasn't sure what the sound was the first time. The second time, I realized it was a cell phone. Before it rang a third time, he was answering it and I was praying for a wrong number.

Instead, I heard, "Yes, Detective Cook."

It was a brief conversation and I couldn't follow it well because he was being more monosyllabic than usual. As he emerged from the bedroom, all I could say was, "You gave her your cell?"

"Professional courtesy." He slid his cell back into one pocket and dug the car keys out of the other.

I hoped my next question didn't sound as petulant as I felt. "You need your keys?"

"I have to go in for a little while."

"Out of professional courtesy."

Kyle walked toward me slowly, holding my gaze the whole time with a certainty I found exasperating at the moment. "Persons of interest live in my jurisdiction and I offered my assistance in securing information to aid a fellow officer's investigation."

"And those persons of interest are more interesting than persons currently on the scene?" I asked, trying to keep it light and probably not doing nearly as good a job as I thought I was.

"Apples and oranges, babe," he said, stopping just short of pressing his body against mine.

"Who are you checking out for her?"

"You already know way more than you should."

"Who."

"I'll call you later." He kissed me gently, lingering a moment, then walked to the door. "Stay out of trouble," he said in the doorway.

"Where's the fun in that?" I responded. Then I stood there and stared at the door for several minutes after it closed, trying to sort out the anger I felt at Detective Cook intruding on a promising evening, the frustration of Kyle knowing something I didn't, and the disappointment that yet again, just when we were finding our groove, we'd gotten jolted out of it.

And what's the best remedy for being blue about a guy walking out on you? Call another guy. Not advice I'd ever give in my column, for fear of sounding trampy, but it works.

So I called Jake, Tricia having tracked down his number before I left. The machine picked up on the second ring, probably already filled with messages as people heard about the Web site. "This is Jake. Impress me."

Interesting approach for a guy who was far more interested in doing the impressing than in being impressed. But if that was the way the game was played, "Jake, it's Molly Forrester. We sat together at David and Lisbet's party last night. What a tragedy. But I'm working to distract myself from mourning and I was really captivated by your 'wordless cinema' concept and wanted to talk to you about it. Did I mention I write for *Zeitgeist* magazine, among others?" I left my number and hoped he'd be too smitten with the idea of media coverage to check my credits and realize I never wrote about film, aside from the kind a bad cleanser leaves on your skin.

It was already after seven. Maybe Jake and Lara were out for the evening. I was in. Not because I was going to sit and wait and see if Kyle came back, but because I needed some quiet time to piece things together so I could ask Jake the right questions. And if Kyle came back, that was fine, too.

I ordered in, Pad Thai with chicken, and sat down at my computer to take another look at Jake's Web site. On my familiar screen, the images were somehow more disturbing, like porn magazines on my grandmother's coffee table. There was definitely someone else out in the hall after David put Lisbet down. As David stormed away, Lisbet turned to talk to the unseen person and the film cut. Who was it? If no one had confessed to talking to Lisbet after the big scene, did that mean the person who did, this shadow in the hallway, was the killer?

The combination of adrenaline and Thai iced tea had me up and pacing, not a place I like to be at ten o'clock at night. Jake was the next piece of the puzzle, but I was going stir crazy waiting for him to call back. And if I called Kyle, it would come off as clingy, desperate, or distrustful, none of them attractive options.

I called Cassady's cell, to see how she and Tricia were doing. Cassady answered in a hushed voice. "Tricia's already asleep."

"And you're whispering? How thin are the walls there?"

"She took your bed, didn't want to be by herself. She's a wreck, Molly."

My heart ached and that slowed my mind down a little. "Anything new from Detective Cook?"

"Detective Myerson told the Vincents they could go back to Manhattan, but nowhere else."

"That's promising for David."

"We'll head back tomorrow as soon as Lisbet's parents

finish making their arrangements. The Vincents want to help them through all that and Tricia wants to stay as long as her folks do."

I told her about leaving word for Jake and prepared to say good-bye. But Cassady wasn't done.

"Excuse me. How was the ride home?"

"Fine. Occasionally weird, but fine."

"So is he there?"

"Nope. At work. Doing some stuff for Detective Cook."

"Ouch."

"Potential ouch."

"Ouch nonetheless. Is he coming back?"

"Not my call."

"Double ouch. I think I'll call him and tell him to come back."

"I think I'll hang up now."

We said our good-byes and I paced a little more. A thought nibbled at the edge of my consciousness, but I couldn't identify it yet. The fact that it skittered away every time I tried to focus didn't help either. It was so silent in the room, I found myself thinking of the jangle of Aunt Cynthia's bangles. That's what I needed. Music. And a nightcap.

Rummaging through the CD cabinet and through the liquor cabinet are both very soothing, since both hold the promise of delicious relaxation if the proper choices are made. I decided to tackle the decision as a matched set. Years ago, Drambuie had an advertisement featuring Ella Fitzgerald, so I always think of them complementing each other. Perhaps a Rusty Nail and the *Cole Porter Songbook*? Or maybe I needed to go even more mellow: Ron Sexsmith and a Brandy Alexander? Rufus Wainwright and a White Russian? Maybe I should just go for broke: Johnny Cash and shots of Jack Black. I have more than a few friends who dabble in psychopharmacology like they're trading baseball cards: I'll give you four Ambien for two Ritalin and a Percocet. But I prefer to modify my chemical imbalances the old-fashioned way. Hey, an old-fashioned. With a little Dave Brubeck.

So I threw on my pajamas, slid in the CD, and mixed the drink. I was near the end of the CD and close to the bottom of the glass when the phone rang. Since I was finally relaxing, I decided to let the machine get it. It was almost midnight and Kyle wouldn't bother calling at this point just to tell me he wasn't coming back. And I was fine with that. Really. Duty called, he answered, and I dealt.

But when the voice on the answering machine started with a shrill, "Hey, Molly! Got your message!" I dove for the phone.

"Jake?"

"Are you screening? Am I interrupting something fun?"

"What could be more fun than talking to you, Jake?" When in doubt, go for the ego.

"Baby, not talking's what I believe in."

"I can imagine."

"Why imagine when you can see it on-screen?"

So maybe the film vaults were a little fuller than I'd suspected. I hoped I wasn't going to have to sit through anything awkward to get him to show me the party footage. "Still without words?" I asked.

"Actions speak louder, you know."

"Yeah, but I've got this silly hang-up with words and I was hoping we could trade a few."

"Anything else you want to trade?"

I could feel his leer through the phone. "Let's take our time. As a filmmaker, you should appreciate the slow build to a climax."

"You seen my tribute to Lisbet?"

"That's one of the things I wanted to talk to you about."

"What's on-screen is only half of it. I'm still building the piece."

Yes. I suddenly liked Jake a whole lot more than I'd ever thought possible. "How soon can I grab you?"

"Well, luckily for me, I'm being grabbed by someone else right now, so that's not an option."

I didn't figure it was polite to ask who might be doing the grabbing, though I suspected it might not be Lara since I didn't hear any chattering in the background. "Any chance we could talk tomorrow?"

"First thing."

"Seven?"

"You some kind of mutant?"

"I'm just so anxious to dig into this story." That was true; if he wanted to interpret that as some fan frenzy, that was his option.

"Seven isn't morning, it's the middle of the night."

"Direct me, Jake."

"Ten. You'll have to bring bagels and coffee."

I'd dress up like a bagel if it would help. "Ten it is."

"I should be upright by then. Might even be sober."

Just as long as he was able to point me to the film. I mean, if a man's going to be stupid and vain, it's a shame not to use it to your advantage.

8

"I thought I knew you."

It was not exactly the greeting I was expecting, but I was surprised that I even heard it, given that Lara had opened the apartment door wearing only jade green silk tap pants and a matching balcony bra. And Jimmy Choo Marilyn's, those amazing stiletto-heeled satin sandals with the mammoth green bows that tie around the ankle. The joint in her hand was the finishing touch on a very persuasive portrait of weekend decadence. The overall picture was stunning enough to make me give up carbs for the next three days. Or, at least, the next thirty minutes.

Before she'd opened the door, I'd been feeling pretty sleek in my Diesel black low-rise jeans, pink Juicy Couture hoody, and marvelously strappy Kate Spade santiago sandals. Of course, I'd selected the ensemble as much to make myself feel better about the fact that Kyle had never come back last night as to impress Jake and Lara. Still, confronted by Lara and her splendor with the grass, I suddenly felt Amish.

Taking great care to look her in the eyes, and only in the eyes, I apologized. "Didn't Jake tell you I was coming?"

Lara blinked so slowly I wasn't sure her eyes were going to open again. "Jake tells me a lot of things," she purred dismissively. "The doorman, he said your name and I thought of someone else."

Someone for whom it would have been appropriate to answer the door in lingerie? "Jake invited me." I raised the cardboard tray of coffee and bagels up into her line of sight. "I come bearing gifts."

Lara backed up, beckoning me to enter the apartment. It was aggressively hip, with lots of painfully austere black furniture posed on white carpet, and red accent pieces placed with great care to look as casual as possible. The living area was focused around an entertainment center designed to make mortal men weep, its centerpiece being a fifty-two-inch plasma TV. At the moment, it was tuned to a cartoon.

"Do you know Dora?" Lara asked me, pointing to the animated girl with huge eyes who was bouncing across the screen, accompanied by a purple monkey in red rain boots and a blue bull with hoop earrings and bandana.

"No," I said carefully. It had the bright colors and rounded line of kids' animation, but I was fully prepared for Lara to explain the socio-political satire at work in the piece. There had to be some symbolic significance to the bull in the earrings, didn't there?

"She's very wise. She always can find her way." Lara held her hand up to Dora's image. Was she offering the characters a toke?

"Then she's wiser than I am. Is Jake here?" I didn't want to inspire one of Lara's cultural theses, but I didn't want her to drift off and forget why I was there, either.

"He's in the shower, he'll be out in a moment, she has so much to teach us," Lara continued as though each thought flowed naturally into the next. She took a hit off the joint herself as the girl and the monkey both clutched their heads in distress. Apparently, a small star had fallen out of the sky and gotten lost. Lara nodded in sympathy. "All of us, we're lost stars."

"Swear to God, I'm gonna call DirecTV and cancel Nick right now," Jake growled as he emerged from the bedroom, buttoning his shirt slowly so I could have a glimpse of chest as he approached me. I would've restricted her smoking, not her viewing, but that was between them and I was happy to stay out of it.

Lara draped herself across the black leather couch in a languid pose. "I bought the DVD," she sniffed. "It's a powerful metaphor for the inability of the culture to embrace what is different without crushing that very individuality into nonexistence."

Jake rolled his eyes at her and opened his arms to me as he came across the room. Seeking to block his hug in the most gracious way possible, I held up my breakfast offerings. Properly derailed, he took the tray. "Thanks."

"There's a vanilla cap, a chai latte, a macchiato, and a house blend. Your choice."

"I love options," he said, plucking the macchiato from the tray. "I'm glad you called."

Let the sales pitch resume. "I was so impressed by your tribute to Lisbet and that got me thinking about your wordless cinema theory again."

"You heard any more about the investigation?" Jake glanced up from going through the bag of bagels. "Did they arrest David yet?"

"Why would they?" I asked, trying to keep my voice neutral.

"Lover's spat gone wrong, isn't that what it looks like?"

"You think David's capable of that?"

"We're all capable of anything. One of the guiding principles of my life."

"You tell the police that?"

"Course not. They'd take it the wrong way." Jake shook his head, bemused, as I tried to imagine the right way to take it. "One way or the other, sucks to be him."

Especially with such loving and supportive friends. I waited while Jake decided on the onion bagel and chomped a chunk out of it. He pointed back to the bedroom. "C'mon in here. Let me show you where I make my magic." He waggled his eyebrows to make sure I got the joke and led the way. I put the coffee and bagels on the table in front of Lara, but she didn't move as we walked by, still intent on decoding Dora and the monkey.

The bedroom was as deliberately austere as the living room. There was an unmade king-size bed in the center of the room, a massive sound system on one wall, and a dazzling rack of computer equipment on the other. Jake began reeling off the specs of all the equipment, that tech speaking-in-tongues men do. I nodded and tried not to look at the bed or wonder how well visited it was.

Jake placed me in the chair in front of the computer and thumped his fingers on some keys. The tribute sprang to life on the screen. "The core idea of wordless cinema is the primacy of the image, so it seemed so appropriate to honor Lisbet with images showing her full of life because she isn't. Anymore."

Perhaps Jake was such a fan of wordless cinema because he was so impressively clunky with words. An art form that encouraged him not to talk was making more and more sense. "You've known David since college, right? How long'd you known Lisbet?"

Jake tapped the bagel against the end of his nose and did some quick math in his head. "They started dating like four months ago, I guess."

"You didn't know her before?"

"I knew her work, but not her." He leered, leaning in much too close to me. "Interesting exception. 'Cause most of David's girls were referrals from me." He winked and I swallowed hard, trying not to grimace. "That's what friends are for."

The downside to investigating a mystery is that you wind up with a whole lot of information that you would've been happier not to know. The idea of most of David Vincent's girlfriends being scraps from Jake Boone's table was going to haunt me.

The footage had played to the final scene. I tapped the computer screen to refocus Jake's attention. "Why'd you end here? Were you trying to make a statement about the abrupt end of her life?" I vamped, trying to sound like a semiauthentic film critic.

"No, I was making a statement about Lara dropping the camera."

I chewed the inside of my lip in frustration. "So you didn't shoot anything after that?"

"Let me see." He pressed his body against mine and slid down to sit in the chair with me. I started to get up and he pressed down on my knee with his free hand. "Don't get up." Figuring he'd be more helpful if I played along, I stayed in the chair with him, edging over just enough so he could half-perch next to me. He was wearing Chanel Pour Homme, which struck me as far too classic for him. Probably a Christmas present from his mother.

He took the mouse and started clicking on icons, pulling up snippets of film. He opened and closed them efficiently, not giving me much chance to register what I was seeing before he moved on to the next one. He seemed to know what he was looking for.

"Here," he said after a moment. "This is after Lara picked the camera back up, but Lisbet's too deep in the frame for it to be an effective shot. Besides, Lady Diva marches into the shot and destroys the composition. Lara should have panned with Lisbet, but she got caught up in the emotion of the moment. She's a little high strung, but she has a lot of raw talent."

As I paused to be impressed that Jake had actually paid someone a compliment, a woman walked into the shot on the screen, just as he had said she would. I had to lean in a moment to make sure I was identifying her properly. "Veronica Innes?"

Jake stretched, yawned, and snaked his hand around the back of the chair and my shoulders like an eighth grader on his first date ever. "Wherever there's drama, Veronica can't be far away."

"I don't remember seeing her follow them out."

"I think she was already in the hallway, snitching a smoke or something. I tried to get her to leave it alone, let them work it out, but Veronica leaps to center stage every freaking chance she gets, so there was no stopping her." He tapped the screen as the footage showed Veronica following Lisbet down the hall and out of sight. David was nowhere to be seen.

I leaned against Jake, hoping it would encourage him to share more information. "Veronica and Lisbet were friends?"

"How broad's your definition?"

"They weren't close?"

"Had a lot in common. Didn't make them friends."

"Veronica was Lisbet's understudy. What else?"

"David."

In a totally involuntary rush of adrenaline, I grabbed Jake's thigh. He loved it and grabbed my thigh in return. "Veronica was with David?"

"Right after she was with me. And right before he was with Lisbet."

"Did he dump her for Lisbet?"

"Depends on your point of view. Veronica was convinced she and David were soul mates, never to be parted, all that crap, so she probably thinks so. As I recall, David burned out on the high maintenance." Jake leaned in, all but licking his lips, and I dove out of his line of fire, scooting close to the monitor again.

"Can you play the tribute for me again? Your work is so incredible."

Fortunately, the praise was sufficiently distracting and Jake turned his attention from me to the screen. As the footage played again, I pretended to study it appreciatively, nodding periodically as Jake went into another one of his declamations, and tried to absorb this new information.

Much as it prides itself on being the Big Apple, New York City can be very small. At least the circles in which you travel can be, especially when you all have the same profession or same alma mater or same bank handling your trust funds. A lot of busy people like to date what's within reach and why move on until the supply's been depleted? I know some social butterflies who've taken multiple flights around a circle before moving on to fresher flowers. So incestuous cliques are not particularly remarkable and years of round-the-clock *Friends* reruns made them palatable for the rest of the country. But I still like to take the time to be amazed by the convoluted branches of some people's dating trees.

The new pressing question seemed to be, how did Veronica feel about understudying Lisbet in more places than the theater? Hell hath no fury like a woman scorned, so God help the soul who crosses an actress. Veronica had looked pretty intent as she'd followed Lisbet out. Had she wanted to help a colleague in emotional distress or had she been closing in for the kill? Had Veronica been with her when Lisbet had thrown the ring away? Some might see that as an opportunity to get back with David, but had Veronica taken it as an insult to the man she still loved? Had Veronica and Lisbet wound up outside and come to blows?

"Can I see that last piece with Veronica again?"

"You questioning my editing choices?"

"No, no. Studying them."

Right answer. Jake nodded in appreciation and clicked. I watched anxiously as Veronica stepped into frame, then followed Lisbet down the hallway until I could see her full length, holding the glistening champagne bottle in her hand.

I sat back in the chair as much as Jake's shoulder would let me. "How does Veronica feel about being edited out of this?"

"We don't talk more than absolutely necessary."

"You seemed very close at dinner Friday night."

"That's for show. Most of what she does is for show. When she can control it. One of the big issues in our relationship. I like to call the shots, so does she. How 'bout you?"

"I'm more into give and take."

Jake pressed against me. "That's got possibilities."

"So does this article." I popped to my feet, half-hoping my sudden movement would tip the chair over. "I wanted to come by today and find out a little bit more background so I can do a righteous job of pitching this to my editor."

"Let me pitch it."

I started easing my way to the door. "I have no doubt that you'd be hugely persuasive, but that's not how it works. Not at my magazine at least. But I'm sure if I get the go-ahead on the article, she'll want to meet you. And I'll certainly be in touch if I have more questions."

"I have a lot more I could show you," Jake said, rising to follow me.

"Let's save something for next time, shall we?" I couldn't bring myself to wink at him, but I did give him my best flirtatious tone. And he was enjoying it a little too much.

I walked through the living room as quickly as I could without making it look like I was running away, but I stopped short at the sight of Lara in her lingerie dancing along with Dora and the monkey on the big screen. Her hands were in the air, eyes blissfully closed as she half-bounced, half-swayed to the song on the DVD.

I wasn't sure I should intrude on her reverie, but I felt compelled to make some sort of farewell statement. "Thank you, Lara," I attempted, not even sure she'd hear me.

Her eyes drifted open. "We got the star home. But the presentation of a happy ending is detrimental to the audience unless that happiness is possible for the masses."

"That's . . . great." This was Jake's current relationship, but he called Veronica high maintenance? What an interesting measuring scale he must have.

"I know you from the dead girl's party," she said, eyes working to focus.

"Yes."

"People get in deep water and then find out they can't swim," she said with an odd edge.

"Excuse me?" Was that a philosophical observation or a specific statement about what had happened?

Jake scooped his arm around me and, giving me little choice in the matter, walked me to the door. "She's a little . . . muddled at the moment."

I looked back at Lara, but she was already dancing again, eyes closed, lips tweaked into a little bow of satisfaction. What a trip, in more ways than one.

Jake opened the door. "Talk to you soon." He leaned in yet again and I got my cheek turned just in time.

"Thank you so much." I slid out into the hallway and closed the door behind me, feeling like I'd just dragged myself back through the looking glass. I wasn't sure whether to be concerned about them or be happy they'd found each other. Lara was in no condition for me to put much stock in what she'd said but I found her pronouncement troubling. Did she know something or was it all just jumbled up in her head?

My head was feeling pretty jumbled itself in the cab on the way back to my apartment. It was a pretty Sunday, the traffic sounds muted, and the pace on the sidewalk slightly less frantic than during the week. People looked like they were marching off to fun destinations—couples pushing kids in strollers to the park, dressed-up couples on the way to brunch, punked-out couples straggling in from last night, tourists threatening to tip over as they craned their necks back to study the tops of the skyscrapers. It was a perfect day to sit on the steps of the New York Public Library, watch the people go by, and wait for the lions to come to life as I'd always imagined they would when I was a kid.

But when I was a kid, I didn't think about people killing each other except in war or imagine that people hated each other enough to do much more than not speak to them ever again. That point of view seemed so luxurious now as I contemplated crimes of passion and the magnificently stupid and venal choices people make in the name of love.

As I got out of the cab, I was so intent on figuring out how to get to Veronica that I almost walked right by Kyle. He was waiting for me out front, perched on a planter, head bowed in thought. I walked up to him with open arms, anxious to start on a positive note this morning. "What a nice surprise."

"Really."

It might not have been the coldest greeting I'd ever gotten, but it was easily in the top ten, with lots of potential for upward movement. The Pause that followed came equipped with its own lethally sharp icicles. He only glanced up at me, then dropped his eyes back down to the sidewalk.

"You could've waited inside," I attempted.

"I'm not staying."

"Oh."

"Why didn't you tell me David Vincent has an assault history?"

The bottom of my stomach dropped, bungeed down around my sandals, then rocketed back up to the roof of my mouth. "I didn't know."

"Never charged, so nothing popped for Suffolk County, but I did some extra digging around. A girlfriend filed a complaint, then dropped it. There's also a drunk and disorderly." Kyle stood, hands diving into his pockets. "What's going on here?"

"How'd you know to dig around?" I asked gently. I knew he was angry and frustrated; I was stunned, but determined to make some sense of this.

"Because I'm a good cop, Molly. Or I thought I was, before I agreed to be part of this."

"So all of a sudden David's guilty because of dark marks in his past?"

"He's sure as hell not the poor maligned angel you were making him out to be."

The front door of my building opened and instead of any of the dozen neighbors I'd be hard-pressed to recognize in a restaurant or anywhere else out of context, it had to be

Liana Mayburn, the ancient, mountainous gadfly in 3C. You could always hear her coming, between her labored breathing and the *vipp vipp* of floral polyester rubbing against itself.

"Molly dear, good morning," she wheezed.

"Mrs. Mayburn," I answered, keeping my eyes on Kyle so he didn't take this opportunity to walk away.

"You and your young man enjoying the sunshine?"

"Yes, ma'am," Kyle answered with an old-school politeness that impressed even me.

"Young couples fill my heart. The promise of such joy. Be good to each other. Be happy." She might have suggested names for our children, but she started coughing and her momentum carried her around the corner before she could talk again.

When you have a conversation on the street in New York, it's like starting a parade. You have to be prepared for the fact that some people are going to want to jump right in and join you, while some will stand and watch, some will give you a wide berth, and some will shake their heads and critique.

Kyle took two steps backward, in the direction of the street. I circled back into his path, not ready to let him go yet. "How did you know to dig around?" I repeated, trying to trace that idea back to the source, fully suspecting it to be—

"Detective Cook."

I gave the opportunity for editorial comment a wide berth. "She had a hunch?"

"A tip."

"From someone who wanted to make sure David looked bad."

"Or to make sure he didn't get away with anything else."

"Who was it?"

"Didn't say."

"But she's immediately more credible because she's a cop and I'm a civilian with emotional biases."

Kyle grasped me by the shoulders, his contained emotion vibrating in his hands, and moved me out of his way, gently but firmly. "I'm going now." He stepped past me.

"I want to go with you."

"No."

"Please."

"No."

"You're going to see David, aren't you?"

He stopped, but didn't turn around. "Why would I?"

"Because you want to see this through, even though it's not your case. Because you want to talk to him, get your own feel before you talk to Detective Cook again and give her your take on things. Because you want to give Tricia and me the benefit of the doubt one more time. Because even though you deal with horrible things all day long, you're still an incredibly good guy."

He pivoted slowly, hands on his hips. I could see glimpses of the true blue behind the angry clouds in his eyes, but I held my breath anyway, not sure of my next step and unable to anticipate his. He pinched his lower lip, held it for a moment, then dropped his hand. "Have you ever been in a situation you couldn't talk your way out of?"

"Twice. Want my mother's phone number?"

"Maybe later." He took a deep breath. "This isn't the way things are done."

"I know."

"I want to help you, but I'm obligated to help her and you may have conflicting interests."

"I know."

"So I'm going to go see David by myself. And when you get inside and call his sister, would you please not say anything that's going to make it more difficult for me to talk to him."

I was mad at him all the way upstairs. But by the time I'd slammed a few cabinet doors, literally kicked my shoes off (for which I apologize here and now to Kate Spade; I usually treat your handiwork with the utmost respect), and inhaled three Oreos, I could see his point. That's another downside to being involved with a cop. They have might and right on their side and it makes it really tough to get indignant, or at least stay indignant, for long.

Since Kyle had already determined that I was going to call Tricia before he got to David, I felt compelled to do so. Not being sure where in her travels she might be, I tried her cell.

"Hey, honey, how are you?" she answered, sounding tired.

"I'm okay. How are you and where are you?"

"About half an hour outside the city. Cassady's driving, so we're making great time while courting grievous bodily harm. A thrilling combination. I might actually enjoy it if I'd had something stronger than grapefruit juice for breakfast."

"Where's David?"

"With Richard and Rebecca in their car. Detective Cook said he could leave Aunt Cynthia's as long as he came back to the city and stayed put for a few days."

"Kyle's waiting for him. Kyle found out about the assault complaint. And not from me because I didn't know."

I could hear Tricia's breath catch in her throat and when she spoke, she was struggling with tears. "There wasn't supposed to be any record. It was a terrible misunderstanding."

"And the drunk and disorderly?"

"What? No, that's a mistake. That never happened."

I believed her and that worried me. Because it meant Tricia didn't know everything her brother had been up to. We were working on bad assumptions. But I couldn't shake the image of David's face when he'd knocked on the bedroom door. That wasn't the face of a killer, it was the face of someone whose whole life had fragmented and vanished before his eyes.

"Well, it would be helpful if you could get the whole story from David. And tell him to cooperate with Kyle. He doesn't want to hide anything because this makes it look like we've all been hiding stuff. That's not good."

"I'll have Cassady go straight to Mother and Dad's."

"She should drop you off with them and then come meet me at the Avenue of Dreams Theater at two o'clock."

"You're going to a play?"

"Better yet. I'm going to put on a show."

9

"I should have been an actress."

"You mean you're not?"

"Professionally."

"But your acting reaps you great rewards—vacations and jewelry and lots of other pretty things."

"By that definition, all women are professional actresses."

"Yes, but most of us are the back row of the chorus in summer stock. You, Cassady, are a Broadway headliner."

Cassady and I were lurking outside the locked doors of the Avenue of Dreams Theater, the off-Broadway house that had planned to present Lisbet in her New York theater debut in two weeks. The Avenue of Dreams Company was a group of rising young Hollywood stars who had started out as starving actors in New York and had now pooled their celluloid gains to fund a theater company that made them feel less guilty about selling out and gave them a place to showcase themselves in between films and television projects. One of the founding members starred in a TV series Lisbet's mother had developed; hence, Lisbet's summer job.

Cassady hadn't quite abandoned the Hamptons aspect of the weekend yet, greatly to our benefit. Sunglasses pushed up to try and tame her hair, she was wearing Moschino jacquard floral capris and a matching halter, with gold Edmundo Castillo T-strap sandals, and she looked like the first breath of summer blowing through these spring streets.

The strapping young man who strode up to the theater door almost put his head through said door, he was so captivated by the vision. He looked vaguely familiar; I believe he'd recently played an intense young doctor on a series that had been advertised for fourteen weeks and then run for two on ABC.

He tried to turn the near-collision into a nonchalant lean. "Here for the show? We don't have a show today. The last show closed early and we don't open until the end of the month. Maybe later, because we just lost a cast member. But if you'd like to get tickets for when we do open, I could help you out with that. Or with anything else you need help with."

He did seem fully prepared to buff Cassady's T-straps with his T-shirt, if not his tongue. I felt like firing off a flare gun, just to see if he'd blink. I settled for clearing my throat. "We're actually looking for Veronica Innes."

Babbling Boy didn't seem nearly as startled by my presence as I'd expected. He nodded to me pleasantly and checked his watch. "She should be inside. She likes to come early and prepare."

I thought of Veronica framing her breasts for us at dinner Friday night and wondered if that figured into her preparation for rehearsal, too.

"We knocked and no one responded," Cassady explained.

If he'd had a tail, he would have wagged it for her. With a flourish, he pressed a buzzer next to the door, painted over the same color as the wall so you could barely see it, even if you knew it was there. "You friends?" he asked Cassady. I could see him doing the calculations of how many favors he'd have to do for Veronica to get Cassady's phone number.

"We were just with her in Southampton." I insisted on answering, really just trying to keep the poor kid's eyes moving so they didn't pulse right out of his head. "We need to talk to her for a quick second."

To his credit, he got very solemn and I could hear his libido shift down to neutral. "So you were there with Lisbet. Wow. Such a tragedy. We're really going to miss her. Veronica most of all. They got so close during this whole understudy thing."

The door creaked open and a lank-haired young woman, dressed in a formless black linen housedress and dreadfully scuffed black leather clogs, peered out. She looked like she'd last seen the sun in junior high. "You're early," she scolded Babbling Boy. She squinted at us with weak-eyed suspicion as she pushed the door open farther so he could enter. She didn't seem eager for us to follow.

"Friends of Veronica's," he told her. "This is Abby, our director," he told us.

Abby nodded, more in agreement with his introduction of her than in encouragement to us.

"We've been trying to reach Veronica." That was the truth. I'd called her once, which counts as trying, and her answering machine's obviously brand-new message had announced that she was "probably at rehearsal for my new starring role in *Sweet Twilight* at the Avenue of Dreams. Call the box office for ticket information or leave any other message after the beep." I smiled warmly at Abby, even though warmth seemed like an alien concept to her. "I don't mean to interfere with your rehearsal process, it'll only take a minute."

Abby shoved Babbling Boy into the building and stepped a little closer to Cassady and me. She gave us a frank once-over, including disdainful looks at both pairs of shoes, then stepped back again. "It'll have to be quick. I just finished re-doing the entire schedule because of—" She tapped her cheek, searching for a polite way to say it.

"Lisbet. Yes, we know. We're sorry for your loss."

Abby looked askance at Cassady. "You're not cops, are you?"

"Even undercover, they don't dress this well," Cassady assured her, vaguely insulted.

"Why would we be cops?" I asked.

Abby shrugged. "When people die, cops ask around."

She didn't seem to be speaking from any particular suspicion of Veronica, just the experiences of city life, so I let it go and trotted out the newest cover story. "We're putting together a tribute album for Lisbet's fiancé and we want Veronica to be the centerpiece."

Abby rolled her eyes. " 'Cause she's not enough of a diva yet. Fine, whatever, come in." Abby disappeared into the dark lobby, her pale hand halfheartedly trailing behind to keep the door open for us.

Empty theaters are strange places. Like empty churches. So much emotion, so many people bringing their own stories to bear, you can feel where it's soaked into the walls, sunk into the carpets so that sound and light don't bounce around the way they're supposed to, but drift from one place to another, lingering a moment longer than you'd expect.

Abby led us straight backstage to the rabbit warren of storage and dressing rooms. Walking up to a door with a piece of masking tape that said "Lisbet," she stopped, ripped the tape off the door, and knocked. "Who is it?" Veronica called from inside.

"Friends of yours," Abby replied. She reminded us sternly, "I need her in five," and walked off.

The dressing room door swung open and Veronica stood there in her best *All About Eve* pose, hair pulled back, silk dressing gown revealing a calculated amount of breast. "Hello," she said slowly. "I'm sorry, I can't quite place you."

"Molly Forrester and Cassady Lynch. We met Friday night," I said, holding my hand out.

She didn't reach out in return, still trying to remember us. Then Cassady framed her breasts with her arms and it clicked for Veronica. "Oh, Jake's table!" She grabbed my hand and shook it so enthusiastically that I declined to correct her assumption about our level of rapport with Jake at the moment. "Come in."

She pulled us into a dressing room that was a glorified utility closet with shiny black walls, a vanity table and a hat tree crammed into it. But I was happy to attempt to wedge myself in. The important thing was to get her talking and see what she might reveal about her relationship with David and her true feelings about Lisbet. That's all I was hoping for, a piece of information. Which is why it took a moment for the bottle on the vanity table to register. The champagne bottle. From Aunt Cynthia's vineyard. From Friday night.

"You brought home a souvenir," I said lightly, catching Cassady's eye in the vanity mirror. Cassady looked at the bottle, then stepped back into the hallway, looking after Abby.

Veronica seemed puzzled, so I pointed to the bottle. She flushed. "I really shouldn't have."

No way she could be confessing so easily, but my heart still skipped a beat. "Shouldn't have what?"

"Brought it home. It's tacky. Like at a really nice restaurant, when my grandmother wraps the extra rolls in a napkin and stuffs them in her purse. But in a way, I'm so glad I did. I mean, I just grabbed one on my way out because it was such good champagne, but now it's much more meaningful."

"I hate to interrupt, but where's the bathroom?" Cassady asked.

Veronica pointed. "Third door on your left."

"Right back," Cassady said, giving my arm a little squeeze, which I was supposed to be able to interpret but couldn't. My only thought was, no matter how full her bladder was, she was leaving me with a crazy actress with a murder weapon on her vanity table. Go ahead and go, but send Dick Powell in while you're gone.

"More meaningful?" I said, trying to get us both to focus.

"For the part. Lisbet's part. My part. *Our* part."

"In the play."

"Yes. *Sweet Twilight*. Have you read it?"

"Afraid not."

"My character's a young woman struggling to come to terms with her sexual addiction following the death of the music teacher who seduced her when she was a teenager and was the father of the man she's having a sadomasochistic relationship with now."

I wasn't sure if it was the explanation or the champagne bottle that made me feel slightly dizzy, but I nodded. "A drama."

"A musical. Dark, but not without its moments of humanity and humor, and ultimately, very uplifting," Veronica said. Nice she already had the review written.

"Okay, but why the champagne bottle?"

"It makes me cry. I look at it and I think of Lisbet and I cry." She gestured for me to watch. Taking a deep breath, she turned to face the bottle, reached out and barely touched it with the tip of her index finger, and started sobbing. It was a very impressive and rather alarming display, but how necessary for a musical, I couldn't be sure.

Clapping seemed like the appropriate response, so I did, gently. "Wow."

Turning off the waterworks with frightening speed, Veronica grabbed the last fistful of tissues from the dispenser next to the champagne bottle and alternated between blowing her nose and blotting her eyes. "My performance will be a lasting tribute to Lisbet. She's helped me enlarge my gift."

Now I was thinking about crying. I tried to ease ahead. "When you think of Lisbet, how do you think of her?"

"The way I last saw her."

"Dead in the pool?"

Veronica looked at me blankly for quite a long moment, then shook her head tightly. "I'd already left the party when she was found."

"So where'd you see her last?"

"In her bedroom. I tried to talk to her downstairs, but she stalked off. So I went to the kitchen to get her some coffee. I took it upstairs, we talked a little, David came in, I left. I never saw her again."

So David had been upstairs with Lisbet the last time Veronica saw her. But something, maybe the tears on demand, kept that from ringing true. "I'm really impressed by how you've been able to throw yourself right into your role. Her role. You know."

"Why are you here?" She stood and wiped her nose on the sleeve of her dressing gown, the first genuine thing she'd done since she'd opened the door.

"I wanted to talk to you about this memorial CD idea we had, but I'm not sure it'd be appropriate for you to be involved after all. Sorry to have kept you from rehearsal." I drifted toward the door.

"CD?" she asked, wiping her nose again, but taking care to use a different swath of sleeve.

"Yeah, with all her parents' clout in L.A., we figured we might be able to get it distributed, but it's really mainly for David. And if you were with Lisbet the last time he saw her, the association might be too painful. Forget it."

"No." It was sharp and tense and as she reached behind her toward the vanity table, I braced myself for her to pick up the bottle and come at me swinging. But she dug into the junk on the dressing table and came up with a limp tissue.

As she blew her nose again, I tried to steer her along the story path. "No, forget it, or no, that's not what happened?"

"Yes." She honked a few more times and sat back down. "I saw Lisbet again. Down by the pool."

"But not in it."

"Are you accusing me of something?"

Not yet. "No, I'm just trying to understand."

"You can't possibly understand because you couldn't know all the time, all the love I devoted . . ."

"To Lisbet or David?"

She flinched like I'd slapped her. "Don't drag David into this."

"But it's all about David, isn't it?"

"You think I fought with her about him?"

"Okay, what did you fight with her about?"

"I didn't, I fought with Jake."

The dizziness returned. "Jake? What's he got to do with this?"

"I left the bedroom so Lisbet and David could talk. I didn't want to go back into the party, so I went for a walk by the pool. Lisbet came wandering down, ranting and raving about having broken up with David and it all being a huge mistake and thank God she'd figured it out in time and he and his lousy family could stuff it, yadda yadda."

If she was telling the truth, that would have been after David and Lisbet had argued, and Lisbet had thrown her ring away. "So where does Jake fit in?"

"He shows up—thankfully, without that vicious little arm candy of his. But with his camera. He's got more champagne and he suggests we make a little movie. In the pool house. Lisbet and me. Or maybe the three of us."

I wasn't sure I wanted to hear the answer, but for the record, I asked anyway. "What kind of movie?"

"What do you think?" Veronica rolled her eyes in exasperation, as though men wanting to tape communal sex acts was a regular occurrence. Maybe in her social circle. No business like show business and all that.

"So is it coming out on DVD?" I said, trying to keep her from getting angry, one eye still on the champagne bottle.

"You don't think I did it."

I shrugged, not sure what answer would be more insulting to her. "Guess it was a pretty offensive request."

"To say the least. Jake has no sense of composition and his lighting always sucks."

I wanted to laugh. I wanted to be able to step outside all the questions that were running through my head and enjoy the preposterousness of this diva refusing to perform not because it was degrading but because the director couldn't guarantee decent production values. But I couldn't laugh because it was becoming clearer and clearer to me that either Jake or Veronica was a monumental liar. And whoever was lying had killed Lisbet. "So what happened next?"

"I left," Veronica said indignantly. "Jake turned on the camera and they were all over each other right away. No effort at art or eroticism, just—" She caught herself, realizing she was admitting she'd stayed a bit longer than her indignation indicated. "I left."

"With your champagne bottle."

"I wasn't about to leave it behind as a prop for Jake and Lisbet. Besides—" She turned to look at the bottle again and burst into tears. Stanislavsky—or Pavlov—himself couldn't have trained her any better.

In the mirror, I saw Abby appear in the doorway behind me. Time to throw me out, I guessed, but she didn't say anything, just stared at her weeping leading lady for a moment. "That's great, Veronica," Abby whispered after a moment. "Feel that. Remember that. We can use that."

Veronica smiled damply. "Really? You like it?"

"It's so authentic." Abby clutched the linen above her heart and scrunched it up in her hand. "Let's get that onstage and weave it into our fabric."

Veronica swept me out of the dressing room in front of her. I thought she was just going to head down the hall with Abby and leave me there, but she grabbed my hand and pulled me close to her. "I need to be part of the CD. It would mean so much to David. We have a complex history and I'm going to be an important part of his getting through this." She sealed it with a squeeze of my hand.

"I'll be in touch," I promised.

Abby looked me over again. "Are—were you a friend of Lisbet's?"

I figured the truth could be stretched a little more this afternoon. "Yes."

She pointed to a box beside the dressing room door. "Those are her things, from the dressing room. Would you like to get them to her family or should I ship them somewhere?"

"I could take them to David," Veronica chirped.

Just to prevent that collision and on the off-chance there was something telling in there, I volunteered. "No, that's okay, be glad to take care of it."

Abby thanked me and escorted Veronica toward the stage. Quickly peeking in the box, I saw clothes, a few books, makeup. Nothing with a big red neon arrow reading "Helpful" attached to it, but as the song says, "One never knows, do one?"

I picked up the box and headed for the front door, reviewing what Veronica had told me, trying to separate truth from fiction, struggling not to turn right around and grab the champagne bottle from her dressing room. During the whole Teddy thing, I'd been chastised about handling the evidence and Veronica didn't seem to feel a need to destroy it, so it was probably safe until I could inform the proper authorities. Whoever they were. But there was something else nagging at me, a sense I was forgetting something.

Oh yeah. Where was Cassady?

She was in the shadowy lobby, fixing her hair and makeup with a small compact in the available light. "Glad to see she didn't kill you with the champagne bottle," she drawled as she flipped a stubborn curl into submission.

"Me, too. Thanks for watching my back, devoted friend and comrade," I scowled, balancing the box on my hip while she finished.

"Look, she's a bitch, no question, but she's hardly an impulsive serial killer-type who's going to strike you down in a building full of witnesses who'd shoot each other to get in front of a news camera and spill their guts. I felt my time could be better spent on other avenues of investigation."

This puzzle was easily put together. "So where's Babbling Boy and how badly did you hurt him?"

"I was very gentle. I always am when they're so young."

"Have fun?"

"Even better. I have info."

"Well, well, Mata Hari. Do tell."

"Did you know Veronica had the lead in this production until Lisbet's dad pulled a few strings and suddenly, boom, Veronica's bumped to second string?"

"Fascinating."

"Wait. It gets better."

"Then it better go outside."

We exited the theater and possible eavesdroppers and headed for Ninth Avenue to get a cab. "What's in the box?" Cassady asked. "Not that I'm offering to help lug the grimy thing around."

"Personal effects from Lisbet's dressing room. I volunteered to get them to the proper party."

"After you've gone through them."

"Of course. I'm pretty sure whatever went wrong out there has its roots back here."

"You mean something like Lisbet calling Abby Friday afternoon and telling her she was leaving the play because of Veronica, then calling back Friday night and saying she'd changed her mind?"

I took a moment to absorb the news. Veronica struck me as ambitious, but ambitious enough to kill for a role? Or for a role and a soul mate? Had she thought she'd convinced Lisbet to step aside somehow and then, when Lisbet changed her mind, lashed out? "Funny how Veronica failed to mention that to me."

"Proper incentives."

"Okay, next time, I get to make out with the handsome boy and you get to take weeping lessons from the creepy actress."

"Weren't you listening? Proper incentives."

"You'd be surprised what Veronica might consider proper incentives. I've got a new fact for you. Did you know our new buddy Jake likes to film everything he does?"

"Digital or is he one of those video freaks?"

"That your only concern?"

"No, I want to know if you're going to call Kyle or go directly to Detective Cook."

I'd brought Cassady up to speed on my lovely conversation with Kyle earlier in the day. "Neither. Not yet. I want all the pieces to fit together before I say anything or I'll look like an idiot and it won't help David at all."

"Speaking of David, I wonder how his interview with Kyle went?"

"Why don't you call Tricia and check while I get a cab?" I left Cassady, her cell, and the box on the corner and stepped out into the street to flag down a cab. They would've stopped for Cassady in flocks, but she'd exercised her charms sufficiently for one afternoon. After a moment, a cab stopped and I reached back to grab Cassady and the box.

The driver leaned over and asked where we were going. I opened the back door and started to give him my address, but Cassady stopped me. She shoved me in the backseat and closed the door. "St. Vincent's Hospital and don't you tell me it's too far away."

The driver obediently threw the cab in drive and hunched his shoulders over the wheel, leaving me to gape at Cassady all by myself. "Why are we going to St. Vincent's?"

"Because David just tried to kill himself."

10

Dear Molly, I've never had a man start a fight over me. *None of my boyfriends have climbed mountains or written songs in my honor. No man I know has ever done anything more dramatic for me than pick up the check without being asked. Am I wrong to be in awe of loves that express themselves on a grander scale? Or should I consider myself lucky because those who date fire get burned? Signed, Just a Little Jealous*

"This was an accident," Tricia assured us as we walked back to the curtained area where David was being treated.

Cassady put her arm around Tricia's shoulder and gave her a heartening squeeze. I did my best to smile reassuringly, too, but I couldn't shake the thought that every time I thought I had a viable suspect in Lisbet's murder, David did something to draw the attention back to himself. Had he done this because he was sad and angry or because he was guilty? I couldn't bear the thought, so there was no way I could voice any of it to Tricia. Not until I had no other choice.

"What happened?" Cassady asked.

"No one realized he'd been drinking as much as he had and he got into Mother's medicine chest, looking for something to help him sleep. He just wasn't paying attention."

"A little or a lot?"

Tricia didn't want to answer, which meant a lot, in more ways than one. Including that she wasn't completely comfortable with the inattention scenario, which probably meant it came from her father.

David was curled up under a sheet, face pale, lips grotesquely dark from the charcoal they give you before they pump your stomach. I'd had other friends wind up in this situation, but most of them had been careless partyers, not murder suspects.

Mrs. Vincent sat beside the bed, fingers laced through David's. Mr. Vincent stood behind her, conferring quietly with Richard. Rebecca stood across from Mrs. Vincent, quiet and composed. No Aunt Cynthia. She was probably out in the hall, haranguing doctors because it made her feel better.

Everyone but David looked up as we came in and not a single one looked happy to see us. "Mr. and Mrs. Vincent," I began, not quite sure what I was going to say, much less supposed to say, in such a situation. My etiquette lessons had been sorely tested in the last few days and I was doing a lot of improvising.

"Thank you for coming by," Mr. Vincent said, smoothly cutting me off. "Tricia appreciates your support. She'll keep you apprised of her brother's condition."

I hadn't even gotten all the way to the bed and I was being dismissed. Again, I was unsure of the protocol involved, mainly because I couldn't figure out why he was blowing me off. I made an attempt: "Is there anything we can do to help?"

And then Rebecca cleared it all up for me. "Haven't you done enough? You and your stupid boyfriend," she snarled.

"Rebecca," Tricia warned.

"Tricia," her father said crisply. The effect was like a choke chain on a puppy. Her head snapped up and her eyes widened. I wanted to take her hand, but I was afraid to move for fear of setting someone else off.

Richard was the one who made the move. He walked over to Tricia, Cassady, and me and gently steered us away from everyone else. "Let's go grab a cup of coffee."

Tricia attempted to stand her ground. "I don't want coffee."

"Yeah, neither do I," he replied, half-guiding and half-pushing us back toward the lobby. He'd gotten us as far as the seating area when Tricia smacked him as hard as she could in the chest. He grabbed her hand and held it, but looked at Cassady and me instead of looking at her. "I understand what you're trying to do, but we'd really like to be left alone right now."

"Tricia asked us to come," I pointed out.

"I know, but this is family business," Richard replied. He was trying to be kind about it, but he was also hanging out the NO DISCUSSION sign.

Tricia pulled her hand out of Richard's grasp. "This is family *bullshit*," she hissed at him. I'm not sure whether he was more shocked than Cassady and I were to hear that prim little mouth utter that particular phrase, but it rocked us all for a moment. Then Tricia turned on her heel and marched for an exit and Cassady and I were the ones who hurried after her.

Even when we were all in a cab back to my place, Lisbet's box from the theater riding up front with the driver, Tricia was winding herself up to the point of explosion. Cassady and I waited, letting her find the words and the moment to uncoil. "How dare he?" she finally spat, about four blocks from my apartment.

"Which 'he' are we talking about?" Cassady asked, sharing my point of view that all the Vincent men were having a less than stellar day.

"My father. Kyle came to talk to David under some arrangement with Detective Cook and David gets all worked up, so Dad gets all worked up and David goes and does this stupid thing and somehow it's all my fault because I know Kyle."

"Which is why your dad didn't want me around either," I figured out.

"So the conversation with Kyle didn't go well?" Cassady asked delicately.

"How well can a conversation about 'When did you stop beating your girlfriends' go?" Tricia stroked my arm half-heartedly. "Kyle was a gentleman and very professional, but the men in my family didn't respond in kind."

"But what did David tell Kyle?"

"The truth. His old girlfriend filed complaints against guys as a way of breaking up with them. And he'd never raised a hand to Lisbet and absolutely didn't kill her."

What else was anyone expecting him to say? Even with the rocky history and the overdose, David looked like a mess, not a murderer. And there was no gain in this for David. Breach of decorum was a cardinal sin in the Vincent family, but it couldn't be worth killing over. The jealousy theory still fit best and it was tailor-made for Veronica; she was the one who benefited most from Lisbet's death.

Once we were up in my apartment, Tricia flung herself on the couch, Cassady got out the cocktail pitcher, and I opened the box from the theater. "I'm sorry, it didn't occur to me to leave this with your father," I told Tricia as I sat down on the floor. "He probably would've preferred to send it to Lisbet's parents himself."

Tricia rolled over enough to watch me. "I think it's fine that you have it. Who knows what Dad might have done with it."

"Meaning?"

"I'm not sure."

Cassady handed us each a whiskey sour and scooted herself under Tricia's feet on the couch. She lifted her glass in a toast. "A sour to make everything else seem sweet."

We toasted and sipped, but I wasn't ready to change the subject. "Do you think your father knows something he's not sharing?" Could Mr. Vincent be aware of something I'd missed?

"No, he just doesn't want anyone else to know things he doesn't. Which is why he was so unpleasant to you at the hospital."

"I don't expect anybody to be winning congeniality awards right now, me included." I shrugged, putting down my drink and starting to go through the contents of the box. It seemed to be mainly clothing and some odds and ends, probably the trinkets and makeup Lisbet had kept on the vanity table before Veronica banged in and swept it all away.

Tricia leaned off the couch, bitterly intent. "There's no excuse for bad manners. Ever. I believe it's the Vincent family motto. *Image vincit omnia* or *semper perfectum* or some such thing. Which is why the boys choosing Rebecca and Lisbet was so shattering for Mother and Dad."

"What about Veronica?"

"Veronica Innes?" Tricia slithered off the couch to sit on the floor next to me.

"What did your folks think of her?" I pulled a deep purple satin robe out of the box. There were heavy smudges of makeup around the collar and it smelled of Armani Mania. I tried to envision Lisbet wearing the robe as she prepared for a performance. Instead, I suddenly remembered being seven and going on my first sleepover, but taking my mother's pillow with me because it smelled of the Aquamarine body lotion she put on before bed. I really was going to have to ship all this back to her parents when I was done. It's difficult to tell what people are going to cherish as mementos when they lose someone, but I didn't want to risk keeping—or worse, tossing—something that might provide them some measure of comfort.

"I don't think they took their dating seriously because David didn't seem to," Tricia responded after a moment's thought.

"I don't think many people take Veronica seriously," Cassady offered, seizing the opportunity to stretch out on the couch now that Tricia had moved.

Folding the cool, slithery robe was trickier than I'd imagined. I laid it in my lap and smoothed it. As I ran my hand over the fabric, I felt something stiff underneath. A little poking around revealed a pocket in the seam.

Inside, there was a small envelope with a florist's name, Back to the Garden, stamped on it. The address printed underneath was just a few blocks from the theater. The envelope was hand-addressed to Lisbet at the theater, with a small notation of last Thursday's date in the lower left-hand corner. I slid out the card. The printed message on the card was: CONGRATULATIONS. The handwritten message, in big block letters, was: LEAVE AND LIVE. No signature.

I held the card up for Tricia and Cassady to look at. "I know theater people have a lingo all their own, but how does 'Leave and live' translate?"

Cassady took the card to look at it more closely. "Parse it all you want, it's a threat. Or an ultimatum."

Tricia peered over Cassady's wrist. "Veronica Innes was dating David before he met Lisbet."

"She also had the lead in that play before Lisbet came along," Cassady added.

"Your new little actor friend told you Lisbet was going to quit the play, then changed her mind?" I asked Cassady. She nodded. "Maybe Veronica was threatening her to scare her off, make her quit. Lisbet started to give in, then changed her mind."

"So Veronica killed her?" Tricia said a little too cheerily. She heard it, too, rushing her hand to her mouth as though she'd burped. "Sorry. I just . . ."

"Don't want it to be David. We know." I patted her reassuringly on the shoulder, then looked at my watch. "Now, where does a director go after rehearsal?"

Cassady raised her hand like an overachieving third grader. "I know, I know." She grabbed her purse, plunged her hand in, and pulled out a matchbook. "Where the stage manager's brother tends bar because if you're with the show, he pours with a heavy hand."

A very heavy hand, judging by Abby's demeanor. By the time we'd gotten to The Last Tankard, a dark but boisterous brass and oak tavern a few blocks north of the theater, she was already relaxed and actually seemed pleased to see us. Then again, maybe she was just a lightweight and we were catching her several drinks into the evening. Whatever the case, she seemed happy and approachable, sitting at the bar with several other pale young women. For a moment, I wasn't even sure we had the right person, her face looked so different with a smile on it.

"You tried to crash my rehearsal!" she shouted cheerily, wagging a finger at Cassady and me as we approached. Her eyes drifted over to Tricia. "Why didn't you come?"

"Sorry. I was busy," Tricia answered.

"I'm so glad I caught you. Is Veronica here?" I asked. We'd scouted as thoroughly as possible from the front door and hadn't spotted her, but I wanted to be sure before I got in too deep.

Abby's face lengthened. "You came to see her."

"No, we came to see you. We just wondered if she was here."

Abby thumped her fist on the bar. "No. I sent her home to get some sleep. She's clearly drained by the events of the weekend. How stupid was I to give them the time off for that fool party? Even though it gave me extra time with the male chorus. They just aren't coming together as a cohesive unit, which completely undercuts their dramatic weight in the swimming pool scene where—"

"Abby? I came to talk to you," I said gently, not wanting to spoil her mood, but not wanting to wait through an entire recap of rehearsal either. The two women she was sitting with leaned forward to get a better look at me, but fortunately, Cassady and Tricia flanked them and distracted them by asking for their recommendations on the house drink list.

Abby reacted with delight. "That's so nice of you."

"About Veronica and Lisbet."

Abby leaned forward conspiratorially. "I could help with the tribute CD, too."

I almost asked her what she was talking about, but thankfully remembered before I blew the cover story. "That would be so great. But before we start talking about that, I wanted to ask you about Lisbet quitting the play."

Muddy as her thinking was, that bumped Abby. "Why?"

The improvisation resumed. "If she was unhappy about the show for some reason, maybe we shouldn't pursue the idea of putting a song from the show on the CD."

Abby sat up two inches taller than I'd realized she was. "Our show? On your CD?"

"We're just talking at this point."

"It wasn't the show she was upset with, it was Veronica. She called me from Southampton Friday afternoon and said she was leaving the show because she'd walked in on Veronica and David."

"Walked in on them?"

"Red-handed. Bare-bottomed. Something. 'In the act,' she said."

"Veronica and David. Friday afternoon," I repeated back to her.

She nodded emphatically. "I offered to fire Veronica, but Lisbet said no, she couldn't be involved with anything that would keep the memory fresh in her mind. I begged her to think about it, not to decide rashly. She was sooo good."

"In the part?"

Abby now shook her head just as emphatically. "For box office."

"But not in the part?"

Abby scrunched her face up so hard that her bottom lip almost touched the tip of her reddening nose. "Hell, no. Veronica's got her limitations, but she's poetry compared to Lisbet. God rest her soul."

I nodded. "What happened?"

Abby sighed rather grandly. "Lisbet called me later that night and said she'd talked to David and he apologized and she was staying."

So not only had Veronica lost the role and the boy, she'd

done it at the same time. Despite all her best efforts. Giving the star an ultimatum and then giving the boyfriend a tumble. "Veronica must not have been very happy about losing out to someone who didn't deserve it."

Abby propped her chin up on her hand. "Veronica was making all kinds of noise about Lisbet better get the part right or she was just going to take it back. Like that was ever going to happen."

"But it has."

Abby twisted her chin on her hand to look at me more fully, eyes widening so much that mine started to water in sympathy. "Wow. Isn't that amazing. Veronica got her wish."

The question was, how much work had she done to make it come true? I thanked Abby for her help, agreed to be in touch about the CD, and persuaded Tricia and Cassady to come with me, rather than staying behind to do more tequila shots with the costume designer and the lighting designer. Amid waves and grand promises to attend opening night, we made our way back outside.

Stepping out of the bar onto the sidewalk wasn't nearly as refreshing as I'd hoped it would be. It was a muggy night, with summer trying to sneak into town ahead of schedule and spring rolling over for it. The air was damp and heavy and I felt its weight in my lungs and in my hair. Or maybe the weight came from something else.

Tricia waved for a cab. "So, what did she say?"

I let my breath out slowly, but it didn't lessen the weight in my lungs. "Your brother had sex with Veronica Innes Friday."

She brought her arm down and spun back around with such a vengeance that a couple walking past her flinched, bracing for some ninja assault. "What?!"

"You don't really want me to repeat it."

"Why on earth would she say such an ugly thing?"

"Lisbet told Abby she walked in on them. And wanted to leave the show because of it."

Tricia looked like her knees were going to give, so I grabbed her and Cassady worked her magic to get a cab. One stopped and we all slid in cozily, Tricia in the middle. I gave the driver my address. After a moment, Tricia said, "That's why he feels guilty, not because he hurt Lisbet but because he thinks he did something that caused it."

"Has he said anything to you about Veronica?"

"Not in ages. He was so completely into Lisbet, he didn't talk about any of his old girlfriends. To me, anyway."

"Sounds like Veronica was crazy enough about him that she couldn't take no for an answer. Especially after she slept with him again. And she took it out on Lisbet," Cassady suggested.

The accusation hung in the thick air of the cab like stale cigar smoke and no one knew how to wave it away. Tricia was right: Even if David was completely uninvolved in Lisbet's death, his actions had exacerbated the situation and it was easy to see the load of guilt he was going to carry for quite some time.

"Don't say anything to David yet," I suggested after several blocks.

"Until we know how bad it is, you mean," Tricia finished.

The silence returned for half a block before Cassady had had her fill. "How does Mexican sound?"

"I can't eat," Tricia replied.

"Yes, you can. I've seen you do it a number of times."

Tricia sighed warmly. "I meant, I don't feel like eating."

"That's because you haven't been properly tantalized," Cassady insisted. "We'll go to Changa and have freshly made guac, brought to the table by a magnificently swarthy young man. A little more tequila, a few more swarthy young men, and you'll be ravenous. You might even wind up wanting dinner."

The only thing more remarkable than Tricia giving in was that Cassady persuaded the cabdriver to reroute and take us the extra twenty blocks south. But she was absolutely right, as Cassady generally is: Music may soothe the savage breast, but Cuervo Reserva and guacamole can do quite nicely in a pinch.

Of course, the laughter of friends is really what makes the difference and that laughter got a little stronger with each round of Cuervo. We were laughing so hard, in fact, that we almost didn't hear the cell phone ringing.

"Oh, that's me," Tricia said, breathless from cathartic cackling over a crack Cassady had made about a couple three booths behind us. Changa is a cozy, hospitable place in the Flatiron District, filled with deeply polished woods and rich, earthy tones that give the whole place an inviting warmth. Even before shots are poured.

Cassady and I attempted to rein in our laughter, less out of respect for the couple in question than for Tricia's phone call. Which was remarkably brief. She protested to the caller that she was in the middle of dinner, listened grimly to the response, said thank you, and hung up.

"What the hell was that?" Cassady asked.

"Allow me to be twelve years old again, since that's how I'm being treated by certain people," Tricia hissed. She made a face, poking dimples into her cheeks with her fingers, and said, "My daddy says I have to come home now."

Under the table, Cassady's foot immediately found mine and pressed down hard before I could even get my mouth open to say something less than gracious about Mr. Vincent.

You know someone well when they anticipate your rotten comment before you even finish thinking it. Above the table, Cassady exclaimed, "You're joking."

I pulled my foot free, deciding that if Cassady could be inflammatory, so could I. "This is the same father who asked you to go away earlier today?"

"Mother convinced the doctors David didn't need to be kept overnight and he's being released. So the family's gathering at the apartment to welcome him home. Because despite the murder thing and the overdose thing, we're very happy to have David back home with the family that loves him." She slapped her napkin down on the table, grabbed her purse, and stood.

"You're not going?" Cassady asked.

"I have to."

"No, you don't," Cassady insisted. "You're an adult. You get to say no."

"It's not that simple," I said, reading the pained lines on Tricia's face. Cassady was right, but I could also imagine the toll Tricia would pay for taking a stand like that at a time like this. And despite everything, Tricia still wanted to help her brother. That's why we were doing all of this.

"We're gathering because it's what we're supposed to do. What's expected of us. That's what Vincents do."

"*Image vincit omnia*," I said.

"Precisely. Besides, Richard and Rebecca are going to be there and I'm not about to let them look more dutiful than me. Not when I'm the one who's talked you into solving this damn thing so we have some chance of saving Davey."

From the law or from himself was the question that went unasked, but Cassady and I could both tell it was pointless to try to change her mind. One of the toughest things in any relationship is knowing when to stop fighting and when to accept the other person's decision, however wrong it may seem to be.

But Cassady and I did insist on settling the bill, escorting Tricia to a cab, and sending her off with hugs. "I'm going straight home, so if you need to, just come. Don't have to call first," I told her.

"Yes, she does. She has to call me so I can meet her there," Cassady corrected.

"You're the best," Tricia said with deliberately false cheeriness.

"No, you are," we chorused back and blew kisses as the cab drove away.

"Oh. My. God." Cassady tapped her toe madly in exasperation. The high heel on her Castillos gave her plenty of leverage. "Bad enough that family has raised denial to an art form—they're about to start charging admission."

My heart ached for Tricia, but there are certain things— root canals, dress fittings, family cataclysms—that no one can go through for you, no matter how much they love you. "She turned out remarkably well," I said lightly.

"Because we found her young," Cassady replied. "Are you really going straight home?"

"I told her I would, so I should. Just in case."

"Okay. Me, too."

"It's just . . . ?" I prompted.

"I didn't say that."

"But there's just this thing . . ."

"Did you notice Detective Cook does that? Gives you the sentence she wants you to finish?"

I had a sudden desire to brush my teeth. "I'll never do it again. And that was mean."

"I wasn't trying."

"Just gifted, I suppose. So where do you want to go?"

"A silly little gallery thing. I'll skip."

"Go. Keep your cell on, don't go home with anyone who lives below Fifteenth and you can get to my place in no time."

"I want to be on call for Tricia, but it's that sweet young Greek thing from Allison's dinner party last week."

"The one who does installations about decomposing animals? Yeah, you don't want to miss that."

"It's a metaphor."

"So's a wheelbarrow full of manure."

"Isn't it a red wheelbarrow glazed with rain?"

"Not in this case. Have fun."

Cassady grabbed a cab and headed west to Chelsea and I headed north to my apartment, thinking about Tricia and the Vincents feeling they had to put on a show of solidarity just to bring David home from the hospital. There had to be a way to link Veronica to what had happened strongly enough that the police would want to go visit her and collect her champagne bottle. Then David could grieve, Tricia could relax, and life—for everyone but Lisbet—could go on.

I was mulling over justice and revenge, where they overlap and where they miss each other completely, as I entered my building, so it took me a minute to register that the doorman was holding up a small, clumsily wrapped package.

"Good evening, Danny," I said, not sure if I was supposed to take the package or just admire it.

"The detective was by," Danny said, pushing the package into my hands.

"It's not ticking, is it?" I shook it to support the joke and it sloshed.

Danny nodded sympathetically. "The detective said you'd had an uncomfortable conversation."

"He did?" I wasn't sure which surprised me more, the admission or the description. Danny seemed to be waiting for me to open the package, so I did, thinking only at the last moment that if it were a bottle of lubricant or even bubble bath, I was going to be staring at the floor every time I walked by Danny for a very long time.

Fortunately, it was neither. Oddly, it was a jar of green olives. Some sort of martini reference? I couldn't figure it out until Danny pointed out the note trapped under the bottle. It read: *You know how hard it is to find these things still on the branch? Call me. Kyle.*

Danny patted me on the back. "He's a good man."

I was still grinning in agreement once I got upstairs. Slipping my shoes off respectfully, I picked up the phone to call him back and realized I had three messages. The first one was from Fred Hagstrom, a former colleague at *Zeitgeist,* inviting me to a cocktail party. The second one was from my neighbor Marshall who wanted me to water his plants while he was on vacation next week. As I considered how deeply Marshall must hate his plants, the third message played. A deep, distorted voice that said, "Stop or I'll kill you next. They say it's easier the second time."

11

"Being stalked is no excuse for screwing up your priorities."

"She's not being stalked, she's getting death threats. There's a difference."

"You're going to get legal with me?"

I strive to take it as a compliment that the people in my life are willing to argue over how close they are to me, but it can also be a little frustrating, especially when one's as volatile as Cassady and one's as stubborn as Kyle.

After I heard the bizarre message on my answering machine, I did the logical thing. I listened to it three or four more times, trying to recognize the voice. It was difficult to tell if it was male or female, much less identify it. Then I played it a few more times, trying to convince myself that it was a bad joke or, even better, a wrong number. Not that I was wishing dire messages of doom onto anyone else's answering machine, just off mine. But the more I listened to it, the less I could hear any hint of humor, however misguided. And even though Probability and Statistics was the low point of my academic career, I knew chances were, the message was meant for me.

So I made the next logical choice. I called Kyle and explained the situation to him in very controlled, or at least not-nearly-as-hysterical-as-I-felt, terms. He said he'd be right over. Then I called Cassady who also said she would be right over. But when she arrived and found Kyle already there, she was somewhat miffed.

She hadn't even put her bag down before she was complaining that I'd called Kyle first. "I didn't want to interrupt your party," I explained.

"You think I'd put that before your personal safety?"

"How good was the party?"

She wasn't amused. Kyle's silence as he sat on the couch, elbows on his knees, watching her with an expression of vague disapproval, didn't tickle her either. His gaze was fixed on her feet, either to avoid looking at her or to figure out how she could walk in her shoes, I couldn't tell which. "We have a deal," she muttered to me.

We do, Tricia, Cassady, and I. Whatever happens, whenever it happens, you need me, you call me. It's that simple. And that beautiful. It has withstood time, men, jobs, and all the other complications of modern life that can muck up a friendship. But I apparently had compromised the integrity of the arrangement by calling Kyle first.

"Where's Tricia?" Cassady asked.

"Her family thing? I'm not going to call."

"Did you call anyone else?"

"Yeah, someone from the *Times* should be here any minute. C'mon, Cassady, he is a cop," I felt compelled to point out.

"Which means that he can put his little red light up and zip on over here, while I still have to flag down a cab like an ordinary mortal."

"When we found Teddy's body, you're the one who insisted we call the cops first."

"Because I was already with you."

Clearly, there was a larger issue at work here, but before I could attempt to identify it, Kyle stood. He moves with an effortless grace I'd call arresting if it didn't seem like some sort of bad cop joke. Standing got Cassady's attention, which seemed to be his point. He stepped in close enough to ask her to dance, but she held her ground.

"I'm impressed you care for each other so much. That's pretty special."

Cassady frowned. "But?"

Kyle shrugged. "Relationship that rock solid, what threat am I?"

Cassady blushed, an event I had not witnessed since our senior year of college and had not expected to see again in our lifetime. Eyes locked on his, she quietly said, "I don't want her to get hurt."

Kyle slowly shook his head. "Not gonna happen."

There was a quiet moment while they stared at each other and I tried to decide whether to run from the room or to embrace them both. The lump in my throat kept me from saying something stupid, so it was Kyle who broke the silence. "So who do we think it is?"

I wanted to explain the unwieldy path that had led me to this suspect, especially since I'd stumbled a time or two along the way in my desire to identify someone—anyone—other than David. And as much as I would have liked to lay this at Jake's insufferable feet, I had to admit that I'd moved past him and stopped at, "Veronica Innes."

"From the party?"

On the drive back from the Hamptons, I'd filled Kyle in on the interesting folks we'd met Friday night, but more from the angle of good conversation than an examination of suspects. Now, what had passed for gossip was starting to look like muddy footprints leading in a definite direction. "I can't think of anyone else. Can you, Cassady?"

Cassady shook her head. "Not that you don't have other enemies, but I think most of them have more class than this."

I nodded in agreement. "I considered Detective Cook, but I'm sure she'd be more creative. Like stake me on the beach at low tide. For that extra measure of satisfaction."

Kyle didn't say anything for a moment, demonstrating much better impulse control than I have. "This is no time for jokes."

"To cope, it's either jokes or tears and I thought this might actually be less distracting."

Kyle frowned. "Let's try the tears, just for comparison's sake."

Cassady shook her head again, this time at Kyle. "Trust me. You don't want to see that. She's a messy crier."

"Let me tell you about Veronica," I said, a little louder than necessary, just to make sure the conversation didn't drift any farther. I told Kyle about Veronica's romantic past with David, the alleged liaison Friday afternoon, Lisbet's calls to Abby, and our visit to the theater. Including the champagne bottle. As I said it out loud, it sounded coherent. Persuasive. Maybe even logical.

He listened to it all carefully, his eyes fixed on me like a camcorder lens, not missing a thing. When I stumbled to a stop, having attempted to convey the creepiness of Veronica crying over the champagne bottle, he blinked once. Slowly. That part of the Kyle Enigma Code I had deciphered. He was trying not to lose his temper.

"I was gonna tell you," I hurried to assure him.

"When?"

"As soon as I had a little more to support my theory?"

"Like another hole in your shoulder?"

"I was hoping more like a confession," I offered lamely, looking to Cassady for assistance. She was frowning in concern at Kyle's tone; if he was this upset, this threat carried more weight than we'd been giving it.

"Think carefully. What did you say to Veronica Innes to indicate that you suspected her of Lisbet's murder?"

"I didn't say anything. I wasn't even sure I suspected her until I saw the champagne bottle."

Kyle looked to Cassady, which she appreciated, but she couldn't offer anything further. "I stepped out to . . . gather some information myself," she explained.

"Lots of theory," Kyle muttered.

"How much more do they have on David?" I asked.

Instead of answering me, Kyle picked up the phone and handed it to Cassady. "Check your messages at home."

She took the phone uncertainly. "You don't think I have one of these on my machine."

"Let's see."

"You're 02 on speed dial," I offered, feeling a need to do something besides get increasingly cold.

"Who's number one?" Cassady asked as she dialed, throwing a look at Kyle.

"My parents, thank you."

Pleased, Cassady started punching buttons as her machine picked up. She rolled her eyes once or twice as she went through the messages, but she didn't seem bothered. She turned the phone off and handed it back to Kyle. "Nothing more threatening than boys who should know better asking me out again." Kyle hung up the phone and picked up her handbag, a sweet little green Dolce & Gabbana hobo, which displeased her. "I don't know whether you're looking for gum or a gun, but I'm not carrying either."

Kyle didn't open the bag, he just held it out to her. "Don't talk to anyone about this. Including Tricia. Molly will call you in the morning."

Cassady refused to take the purse from him. "What makes you think I'm leaving?"

"Experience."

I started to protest, because I didn't want either of them to leave. In fact, I was thinking about getting on the phone and inviting lots of people over for an extended party, because I wasn't planning on sleeping for quite a while. But then Cassady just nodded and took her purse. Somehow, that was even more disturbing. That meant she agreed with Kyle that we could have a serious problem.

Cassady hugged me and whispered, "Behave yourself," in my ear.

"Call me when you get home," I requested.

The eyebrow arched slyly. "But if you don't pick up, how will I know it's for a good reason?" With a wink, she swept to the door. "Keep her safe, Detective Edwards, or you'll answer to me."

It was quiet after Cassady left. Not the comfortable, cozy kind of quiet, but the thick quiet that makes it hard to breathe. "What do we need to do now?" I finally asked.

Kyle pinched his bottom lip, thinking and staring at the floor. I could feel the words building up in my throat, ready to spill forth whether or not they made sense, just to fill the silence. I swallowed hard to keep them down as Kyle walked over to me, took my face in his hands, and kissed me with such gentleness I almost wept.

"Only thing on my list," he said quietly.

"Does someone really want to kill me?"

"You evoke strong feelings in people." He traced my cheekbone with his thumb. "I'll take the machine to a buddy in the morning. But the most important thing to do right now is convince your caller that it worked and you're scared."

"Not hard," I had to admit.

"And that you are going to back off."

The Pause happened before I could come up with something to fill it with. Truth was, I couldn't answer right away. While I was genuinely disturbed by the threat on my answering machine, its existence had to mean that I'd ruffled the proper feathers and was on the right track.

"Molly." Kyle sighed my name in frustration and walked away. The benefit to having a small apartment is that he couldn't go far, as long as he didn't go out the door. Fortunately, he only went as far as the sofa. But he picked up his jacket, which he had laid there earlier, and held it in his hand. Was he leaving? "You have got to take this seriously."

"I know," I answered, tapping my bullet scar nervously.

"Because I do. And I can't be a part of this—any of this—unless you do, too."

Wait a minute. How all-encompassing was "any of this"? Were we still talking about the threat on my machine or had we changed without signaling into a much faster lane? Did this have anything to do with the weekend stalemate? Though it didn't change my answer, I realized. Whether he was asking about the investigation or our relationship, the answer was still, "I do."

He put the jacket down again. Adrenaline—or maybe sheer panic—fluttered in my throat as he turned back to me. "There are so many reasons this is a bad idea."

I walked toward him slowly, stopping a breath away. "List them."

He snaked his arm around my hips and closed the distance. "I can't concentrate when you're around."

"Is that on the list or a general complaint?"

"Both," he said, kissing me firmly. Hunger and heat had replaced the gentleness and reserve of our last few kisses and that was fine with me. I didn't want to think about Veronica or David or Lisbet anymore, I just wanted to think about Kyle and me and how we were going to make this work long term because it was delectable and right and we were going to find a way to fix everything—

Unless his phone rang.

As immensely flattering as it was that he didn't answer it right away, I felt like both a bad girlfriend and a bad citizen letting him ignore it. "Phone," I whispered.

"I know."

"Yours."

"Yeah." With a deep breath, he stepped back from me and grabbed his phone. "Yeah," he repeated into the phone. He pulled me against him with his free hand and I wrapped myself around him, imagining what piece of police business had to be dealt with quickly and efficiently so we could have the night free and clear and I could ignore everything in it except him. Instead, I felt the muscles in his arm tense. "Where? . . . Okay . . . Yeah . . ."

I kissed him on the cheek before I slid out of his embrace and picked up his jacket, determined to be good about this and not resent the intrusion of the real world on a night whose potential already had my head spinning a little. He closed his phone and sighed again. "Lipscomb says hi."

I held up his jacket and he slid into it, a comfortable gesture that I found oddly exciting. "Tell him I said hi back."

"Double homicide."

"Sorry."

"Get your stuff."

"What?" As much as I didn't want to let him out of my sight, I had no interest in accompanying him to a crime scene. I was finding enough dead bodies without him. "I'm not going with you."

"No, you're going to Cassady's. C'mon, I gotta hurry."

"Okay, but why do I?"

Kyle walked over to the console table and unplugged my answering machine with a sharp flick of his wrist. "Because I don't want you to be alone. Somewhere else you'd rather spend the night?"

"Yes, but that's clearly not an option," I answered, hoping he caught the compliment.

"Thanks. Let's go."

Fortunately, I hadn't done a very good job of unpacking from the weekend, so it didn't take me that long to toss stuff back in my overnight bag. Still, he was anxious enough to get going that he all but propelled me to the door once I was ready. "So were you going to stay with me tonight just because you think I'm in danger?" I asked as I locked up.

"What do you think?"

"That's why I asked. I'm not sure what to think."

He smacked the elevator button, then kissed me with great conviction. "Think again," he said, guiding me into the elevator.

There's something so magnificently romantic and perfectly New York about kissing in the backseat of a cab. Even a cab with duct tape holding the upholstery together, cheap incense burning up front, and a wiry young Cambodian practically giggling behind the wheel. There's the sense of catapulting forward even as you're wrapped around each other, something I'm sure was implanted in me by a film when I was young and impressionable—younger and more impressionable, anyway. Of course, I'm the one who had to buy a Danish and eat it in front of Tiffany when I first came to town, too. Still, it's fabulous.

As was the expression on Cassady's face as she opened her apartment door. It wasn't a smile of triumph, exactly, as much as an acknowledgment that she and Kyle had reached some new level of complicity, if not understanding. I felt like the MacGuffin in a Hitchcock movie, being handed off in a witty but urgent manner.

"If she's very good, can she watch television before I tuck her in?" Cassady asked, indicating that we should enter. I crossed the threshold, but Kyle stayed outside.

"That's fine. Just keep her off the phone."

"I have to go into the office in the morning," I said.

"Stay low-key and don't talk about your theories," he answered, holding up my answering machine to underline the point. He gave Cassady a look of gratitude. She nodded and he hurried back down the hallway.

Cassady's in a great building in the West Seventies. Her apartment is very inviting, lots of earth tones tying together a tailored but comfortable collection of Scandinavian Modern furniture with some strategic pillows and a wall of floor-to-ceiling bookcases that balances nice, big windows. It's the kind of place where you want to curl up in a corner of the couch to talk about current events and maybe eat fondue. I've flopped on the nut-brown leather couch and poured out my heart more times than I care to admit, but tonight, I felt uneasy about even taking off my jacket.

"This was his idea, wasn't it?" Cassady eased me out of my jacket herself. I nodded. "He must genuinely be concerned about your safety."

This time, I shook my head. "How did Veronica figure this out? I thought we were careful."

Cassady pulled my overnight bag out of my hand and set it down on the floor. "We were," she said, steering me to her kitchen. "But one of the benefits of being paranoid is that you spend a lot of time wondering who's out to get you. And I'd imagine, after you kill someone, you're bound to be paranoid."

In the kitchen, on the immaculate heather gray Corian counter, which complements all the stainless steel so nicely, there was a mad jumble of color. Cassady had pulled half a dozen liqueur bottles out of her cabinet.

"That's only just, since I haven't killed anyone and I'm getting paranoid," I acknowledged.

"But people actually are out to get you, Molly. So you're not paranoid, you're perceptive. But you're not going to get any sleep tonight if you don't think about something else for a while. So here's our arts and crafts project for the evening." She gestured to the bottles. "Pousse-cafés."

I rarely have the patience to gently pour each liqueur on top of the other so they float in scrumptious bands of color and never mix, but I could see the benefit of concentrating on such a task now. And then downing the masterpiece when it was done. Cassady poured her first shot, then pushed the shot glass, a pousse-café glass, and the bottle of grenadine down the counter to me.

"But if Veronica feels the need to threaten me, then she's basically confessing she did it."

"Stop pondering and start pouring. You're not doing anything more complicated than this tonight. Detective's orders."

"Since when are you and Kyle on the same team?"

"Since I figured out that he adores you almost as much as he should." She didn't look at me, just pushed the bottle of yellow Chartreuse to me, but I could still see her smile. And

I adored her for it. Nothing like having someone out to get you to make you appreciate who's on your side. Confident in that, I was prepared to relax and enjoy Cassady's company and my pousse-café tonight. And not think about going to question the florist until morning.

12

"I should kill you myself."

Not a phrase to be bandied about lightly, especially among friends. Particularly among friends who are trying to solve a murder. But Tricia didn't mean it lightly. She was furious. Also scared and tired and frazzled, but at the moment, she was concentrating on furious. I was concentrating on making sure our discussion didn't turn into a floor show for my colleagues at *Zeitgeist*.

Since I work at home a fair amount of time, I don't have an office at the magazine. I have a desk out in the bullpen, the large, open central area of our Lexington Avenue office space, which is inhabited by the assistants and junior staffers. While the bosses sit in their offices and look out over the city through their glittering windows, we sit in row upon row of mass-produced desks and look in on the bosses through their narrow doorways. It's how the caste system expresses itself in American business.

I actually don't mind being out in the bullpen—better access to snacks and gossip—but I'm forever finding other people's stuff in my desk and on it. Still, I understand the lure of available space in a crowded, institutional setting and I try not to complain. Unless the stuff is smelly, obscene, or otherwise repugnant. Then I demand its removal. On the other hand, if it's edible, especially if it's chocolate, it's fair game.

Cassady had insisted on escorting me to work, a noble gesture slightly undercut by the fact that she had a meeting two doors down. She'd deposited me at my desk like a mother dropping off a kindergartner, despite my protests that Veronica wasn't about to try to take me out in the vast and densely populated bullpen. Unconvinced, she'd all but lashed me to my chair before promising to call in a few hours to discuss a "secure location" for lunch and then departing with the fever of having a mission still radiating from her.

Then, seemingly only moments later, Tricia was standing before me, pale and fragile. And furious. I'd turned off my cell so I didn't have to think about it ringing with another threat. But it hadn't occurred to me, when Kyle had unceremoniously disconnected my answering machine, that a friend might call and, getting neither answer nor machine nor cell this morning, think the worst. Which Tricia had done.

Then I, because I'm so good at it, made things even worse. "I didn't think you'd worry because you didn't know about the death threat."

"Death threat?" Tricia echoed with enough volume and passion that my colleagues rose and turned as one, like meerkats catching the scent of a predator as the savanna winds shift.

I laughed as convincingly as possible, as though Tricia's exclamation was the punchline to a hilarious joke. "I hadn't heard that one," I said, a little too loudly, waving dismissively to my coworkers with one hand and yanking Tricia down into a chair with the other. Once we were seated knee-to-knee, I kept the smile, but stopped laughing. "On my answering machine. I don't want to talk about it here."

Tricia went rigid. "You think it's someone here."

I tipped my head uncertainly. "No. But no one here knows anything yet and I'd rather keep it that way."

"Then you'd best get up and come with me now, because we have talking to do." Tricia stood up again, a perfectly polite smile on exhibit for anyone who was still craning to see what we were up to.

"Let me check in real quick, then we'll go," I said, pointing in the direction of my editor's office.

"Just don't get sucked in to some lonelyhearts debate. This is more important."

"This is my job."

Tricia leaned in, her lips almost at my ear. "Are you getting death threats because you recommend honesty and good communication in a relationship?"

"No. I don't think so."

"Then this is more important."

"Point taken." I hurried past three rows of colleagues who rushed to look engrossed in their work and presented myself at the desk of Genevieve Halbert, gatekeeper to the beast. Make that, personal assistant to the editor. Genevieve is a preternaturally perky young woman who either does some fairly heavy medicating in the morning or is just wired like no one I've ever met. She's sorority-girl blond and pretty and comes off kind of buttoned-down, all Ann Taylor and Talbots, but she has a toothy, relentless smile and this eerie, irritating, monosyllabic chirp.

I made sure to speak loudly enough to please the eavesdroppers, too. "Morning, Gen. She in?"

"Yep." Genevieve lifted her hands off her keyboard and placed them on her desk, showing me I had her full attention.

"May I see her?"

"Nope." Genevieve pointed with one French-tipped nail

to the light on her phone that indicated Eileen was talking to someone.

Perfect. "Okay. Tell her I checked in, but had to go out to do some research."

" 'Kay."

My duty done, I cruised back to my desk. "Research?" Tricia whispered when I returned. "Will she buy that?" I nodded, this not being the moment to elaborate. Tricia and I picked up our handbags and I aimed us at the elevators.

A moment too late. "Molly Forrester, what's your deal?" The voice shrilled across the bullpen, but this time, the meerkats ducked. They recognized the cry of that predator and knew to stay out of its path.

Eileen strode toward me, a sheaf of paper crumpled in her hand. By "strode," I refer more to the purposefulness of her steps than their size, since Eileen is a very petite woman whose stride is roughly equal to my mince. I thought briefly about trying to outrun her, but then decided that facing the music now might make for a slightly less angry song.

Quickly reviewing my last set of letters in my head, I tried to figure out what had set Eileen off. The letter from the woman who'd given her boyfriend a threesome for his birthday and now couldn't figure out how to top that for Christmas? Or the one who wanted to throw a divorce shower for her best friend and wondered if male strippers would be inappropriate?

Eileen wore a form-hugging Lilly Pulitzer of lime green cotton sateen with pink straps and accents. Her Kate Spade patent leather pumps in matching pink had three-inch heels that boosted her clear of the five-foot mark. As she stopped before me, scowling and hands on her hips, she reminded me of Buttercup, the green Powerpuff Girl. The mean one.

"Good morning." She didn't correct me, so I plunged

ahead. "I'm sure you have notes on my column, but I'm on my way out, so could I talk to you when I get back? Thanks."

"I told you I wanted an update on your article first thing," she snarled, batting at her spiky bangs with the sheaf of pages.

"I stopped by, but you were on the phone," I explained, realizing with quick dread where this conversation was headed and wondering how on earth I was going to keep from having it in front of Tricia. "But that's why I'm going out, actually. Let me do some quick research and I'll fill you in when I get back."

Eileen shifted her scowl over to Tricia. "This is research?" she asked, as though Tricia were a stack of books.

"I won't be long," I said as evenly as I could, trying to ease Tricia and myself back toward the elevator.

Tricia, whose proper upbringing never fails her and whose reflexes are faster than mine, held out her hand in greeting before I could stop her. "Tricia Vincent. You must be Eileen."

Eileen gave Tricia's hand a perfunctory squeeze. "So it *is* research. How's your brother?"

Tricia's expression didn't change a whit, but her eyes slid over long enough to give me a glimpse of fury, then slid back to Eileen. "As well as can be expected."

"Maybe you should write your article from Tricia's point of view, Molly," Eileen suggested. "A unique perspective. We appreciate your cooperation," Eileen purred to Tricia, who was digging at her cuticles with a fervor I'd never seen before.

"Thank you, Eileen," I said with the extra lilt that makes it mean "go away."

Eileen knew exactly what I was trying to do and deliberately stood her ground. "What's wrong with your column?"

"Nothing. Why?"

"Because you thought I was going to complain about your column. Why?"

"I write a column, you were looking for me, and you sounded upset. I drew a natural conclusion."

"Hope you investigate a murder better than that." Content now that she'd been cruel, Eileen strode away.

I stood still for a moment, beaming pure loathing at her departing back and waiting for her hair to burst into flames. No such luck. When I turned back to Tricia, my own hair seemed to be in danger. "And you're getting death threats. Imagine that," Tricia hissed. "I should kill you myself."

The main difference between friends and lovers is how easily they can hurt you. You expect a lover to hurt you, at least for the first six months, so you keep your guard up. But you don't expect a friend to kick you in the gut, so not only are you unprepared, it hurts a lot more.

Tricia's anger stunned me and left me fumbling for my breath and a clear thought. I felt cornered, scrambling for a defensible position. What I wanted to do was scream, "This was all your idea!" but what I did was lean in and keep my voice down, hoping Tricia would follow my example. "I haven't agreed to write the article yet."

"Your editor doesn't seem to know that."

"She'll figure it out."

"Why can't you tell her?"

"Because if she thinks I'm doing the article, she'll back off."

"How nice for you." Tricia braced her Ferragamo silver bow clutch in her hands like a board she was going to present for my karate kick. Or maybe like a board she was going to smack me with. "I came here to talk to you about what happened last night, but since I don't want that to wind up in this or any other magazine, I'd better go." She pushed past me.

"I want to discuss this."

"I don't." Tricia headed for the elevator and I followed her with my head at the proper angle so I didn't have to catch the eye of anyone else in the bullpen, but not so low that it looked like I'd been chastised. Even though I had.

I caught up with Tricia at the elevator. "I'm just using her desire for an article as a cover for my own investigation."

Tricia's eyes slid to me again and this time, I could see tears brimming. "Who else are you using, Molly?"

It was another kick, but this one felt different. I was sort of ready for it. And instead of surprised hurt, it made me angry. I wanted to kick back. "You asked me to help. Everything I've done has been to help you and David."

"And what about your article?"

"What about it?"

"What about my family's privacy?"

"If your brother is arrested, what kind of privacy are you going to have then? I'm trying to keep that from happening."

"And if you get another career boost, that's fine, too."

"Tricia, stop it!"

The elevator doors opened and Tricia stepped on without looking at me. "Fine. I'm done. How about you?"

The doors slid closed before I could scream or kick or do any of the several highly mature things I was considering. I moved on to other options. I thought about going back to my desk. I thought about going back to my apartment. I thought about going back to school and majoring in something easy, like quantum mechanics.

I was working hard to put this encounter in perspective. Tricia was devastated, that was clear, and I reminded myself that she was lashing out at me because she knew she could. Because I was there. Because I'd forgive her. Because she thought I deserved it. It was that last one that galled me.

I'd gotten involved in this case at Tricia's request. I hadn't thought about an article until Eileen had suggested it and even then, I'd hesitated. But I couldn't stop now. Someone was threatening to kill me, so I had to be doing something right. And whether I wrote the article or not, I needed to solve this murder so I could figure out who wanted me dead next.

I got out onto the sidewalk by rote and hailed a cab. I had no idea how things had gone with her family the night before. I was so caught up in being right and being threatened that I wasn't thinking about the toll this had to be taking on her. No wonder Tricia was angry.

And no wonder my cell rang as I was getting in the cab. "I'm going to skip right over the fact that you've left your office without an escort and go straight to Tricia," Cassady said with frigid crispness.

"Is she all right?"

"In a word, absolutely not."

"I still have to do this," I responded. "If the florist can confirm that Veronica threatened Lisbet before the weekend, that'll increase the case against her. I know Tricia thinks I'm betraying her, but all I want to do is help David."

"Let's ignore the fact that you have a point," Cassady said, warming slightly. "You're still running around town without protection. Kyle will have my head if something happens to you."

"I'll be the soul of discretion. I swear."

"Do you want me to meet you at the florist?"

"No. If I go by myself, I'll be less memorable. No one ever forgets talking to you."

"Don't try to distract me with flattery. That's such a guy move."

"I'll call you the moment I'm done. Try to get Tricia to come see you."

"She's already on her way."

"I like the way you think."

"Then after the florist, you'll hand everything over to Kyle and be done with it?"

"That's what you think I should do?"

"Uh-huh. Like it?"

"Oh, look, I'm here. I'll call you back." I snapped my phone shut.

The cabdriver, a tall Ethiopian man with deep creases around his mouth that emphasized the length of his face, caught my eye in the rearview mirror.

"We're not there yet," he said with a hesitant politeness.

"I know. I was just done talking."

He frowned and the creases deepened drastically. "Don't lie to friends. They always find out."

I started to get annoyed with his pronouncement, before realizing you can only get so annoyed with the truth. And if I was on the side of truth, upsetting everyone around me in a search for it, then I supposed I should be telling it.

Unless it got in the way. Which is why I bit my lip hard enough to make my eyes tear up before I told the florist, "I worked for Lisbet McCandless, the actress."

The flower shop was a deep, narrow profusion of greenery and blossoms. Walking into it was like wedging yourself into *The Secret Garden*, with Harry Connick, Jr., on a boombox standing in for the birds. The florist was a stork among the rushes, a tall woman with impressively sharp elbows and knees that Caitlin would have banished from the planet. Her name tag read DOROTHY. She wore a smocked tie-dyed sundress that had to have been purchased out of the back of a VW van at a Grateful Dead concert, with hemp sandals flapping on her bony feet. The progression from Jerry Garcia to Harry Connick intrigued me, but I needed to stick to the subject.

"Then you're out of a job, I guess," she replied. Hardly the nurturing, earth mother response I'd been hoping for. "I'm not hiring."

"Not why I'm here," I said, trying to lean away from the razor elbows as she squeezed by me to get eucalyptus sprigs out of the refrigerated case. "I'm tidying things up, for her parents really, and have a question."

"A question for me?" She craned her long, thin neck at me, emphasizing the stork resemblance.

I held up the card, back in its envelope. "This is from here, right?"

Dorothy snatched the envelope and inspected it near-sightedly. "Yeah, it's one of mine." She pointed to the date in the corner. "We delivered them Thursday."

"Do you know who sent them to her?"

She squinted at me suspiciously. "Why?"

"Lisbet's family is a real stickler for good manners," I vamped, managing not to choke on the words. "Lisbet always wrote thank-you notes to everyone who sent her flowers. Her mother has asked me to send notes to everyone she hadn't gotten to before . . . you know. Anyway, this card was tucked in her stationery box, but doesn't match anything on the list of notes she'd written. And it's not signed, so I don't know to whom to write the note." I threw in sad eyes to seal the deal.

There was a tense moment while Dorothy weighed my story. Just when I figured she'd found it wanting, her narrow face twisted in despair. "That's beautiful. Who's got that kind of class anymore?"

"She was special," I agreed. She squeezed past me again, slipping behind the counter and fishing out an accordion file. She checked the date on the envelope again, then withdrew a day's worth of receipts from the file. As she paged through them, I wondered if Veronica had left behind any other clues to her mounting hatred of Lisbet.

Dorothy's face brightened and she held a receipt aloft. "I remember now. He was cute."

"He?" That couldn't be. "I thought the flowers were from a woman."

"Why? Was there something about the arrangement that suggested that?" Dorothy asked, her artistic instincts challenged.

"No, I thought Lisbet said something about it. Were there any other flowers delivered to her that day?"

Dorothy zipped through the other receipts, shaking her head. "Not from me. He was the only one. I remember now, because it was odd he was sending them to her when the show was still in rehearsal. It's usually an opening night thing, you know."

I nodded distractedly. Had Veronica gotten someone to place the order for her? Cassady's new actor friend? Someone else connected with the show?

"Oh, but he was the one . . ." Dorothy slapped the receipts on the counter and picked up the envelope again, sliding the card out. She beamed, turning the card so I could read LEAVE AND LIVE, as though I hadn't already. "Yes. He said he was waiting for her to make a decision and he thought flowers were a nice way to remind her."

I tried to stay calm and pleasant while my theory came crashing down around me. "Did you get his name?"

"No." Dorothy pressed the card to her chest. "It was so romantic. He said she'd know who he was, but he couldn't afford for anyone else to know."

I bet. "Did he say why? I mean, this doesn't strike me as a particularly romantic message."

"Oh, but it is. See, she was involved with someone else

and he was asking her to leave, but he didn't want it to get ugly for anyone if it didn't work out."

I wondered where along the spectrum of "working out" he would place Lisbet being murdered. Had he killed her because she hadn't made the choice he wanted her to make? Was Veronica not the killer after all? "So, no name or number."

Dorothy cocked her head at me, intrigued. "You don't know who it could have been?"

"No," I said patiently. "That's why I came to see you."

"Then they must have been really careful about their affair, if you worked for her and didn't know anything was going on."

I nodded slowly, trying to think of some shred of information I could take away from this, other than the great big question mark I now had to hang next to Veronica's name on my mental list of suspects. The problem was, David was the only man on that list. Wait. Could this have been some game of David's? "This is important. Did he say 'affair' to you?" I asked, figuring her fiancé wouldn't use the term.

Dorothy took a moment to remember, rubbing the card against her cheek gently. "Actually, he didn't."

An ice cube dropped into my chest. So it could have been David.

"He said he was asking her to leave one love and go to a new one and live more fully. Which is a lot more poetic. Romantic, even, don't you think?"

The ice cube melted. "Absolutely." So it was someone trying to get her to leave David. Veronica wanted David, but who wanted Lisbet? "Can you describe him to me?"

Dorothy scrunched her nose shyly. "He's tall and hot and has kind of wavy dark hair and nice eyes."

At least we'd gotten past "tall, dark, and handsome," but

not very far. That described half the men who'd been at Aunt Cynthia's. "Anything else?"

Dorothy thought another moment, then shook her head. I held out my hand and she reluctantly returned the card to me.

"Thank you very much for your help. I'm sure you can understand that the family would prefer that this sort of thing stay quiet. The circumstances of Lisbet's passing are tragic enough without her fiancé having to deal with a revelation like this."

Dorothy grew wide-eyed, whether at the implication of a scandal in the making or of her complicity in it, I wasn't sure. "I won't tell a soul," she assured me.

"Thank you," I told her again and tried to find the space to turn around and find my way back through the greenery to the front door.

"After all, it's like he said. Words just cause trouble."

I stopped abruptly but made a point of turning around slowly so I didn't startle Dorothy. "He said that?"

Dorothy nodded. "He said he liked flowers and film because they spoke without words."

"Any form of communication that relies on words is inferior."

"Yes!" Dorothy cried. "So you do know who he is!"

Oh yeah. "Yes, I think so."

"Did you know?"

"No. I didn't suspect him until just now."

Dorothy unfolded her arms to their full length and gestured to her shop. "People reveal things here they would never reveal anywhere else. How sad for him to have lost her before he ever really had her."

Unless it was his fault she was lost.

13

Dear Molly, Okay, if every man has his price, then I suppose it's not surprising that every woman does, too. But why do so many women have to be so blatant about their price tag? And don't the women who are willing to sell for less destroy the market for the rest of us? What happened to holding out until you get your asking price? How are those of us who are committed to delivering a quality product supposed to compete with those who are willing to flood the market with cheap product that's not going to last? Signed, Embittered Econ Major

"Where's my present?"

Lara had the apartment door open far enough for me to enter, but she hadn't invited me in yet. She looked at me expectantly, taking a hit off a new joint. Thankfully, she was clothed this time—although it was a relative state, given the shortness of her BCBG floral poplin skirt and the painted-on fit of her Generra ruffled tank. Still, even the suggestion of clothes made it easier to look her in the eye, although she was wearing Giuseppe Zanotti pink satin sandals, complete with pink crystal flowers and four-inch heels, so I had to look up to do it.

As I'd hurried out of the flower shop, I'd realized my next move had to be talking to Jake. The idea of Veronica being pushed into the understudy slot yet again and Jake assuming the role of killer was becoming more compelling by the moment. Jake had given Lisbet some sort of ultimatum. Had she ignored it and that made him mad enough to kill her? Dorothy had said leave one love and go to a new one. Was Jake's lust for Lisbet, or at least for taking away Lisbet, so strong that he'd given her an ultimatum and when she didn't make the choice he wanted—him over David—he'd killed her? Could Veronica really be blameless in all this? Well, blameless in the murder, because her seducing David couldn't have helped matters. Was it Jake's voice on my answering machine and not Veronica's? The voice had been so distorted it had been almost impossible to discern its gender, but I'd had a hunch it was female. Though with all the little electronic filmmaking gadgets he had, Jake could probably have altered his voice to sound like a twelve-year-old girl if he'd wanted to.

Did it make sense that Jake would post footage from the party if he was the one who'd killed Lisbet? The best defense is supposedly a strong offense. And given what Veronica had said about Jake liking to film everything, it made sense Jake would see the footage as a trophy, like those ghastly serial killers who keep body parts. I wondered if Jake had filmed Lisbet's death, but the idea was too sickening and I pushed it out of my mind. Besides, how could he have swung the champagne bottle and held the camera at the same time?

If Jake was the one who'd threatened me, how could I approach him and not bare my neck to the executioner? But I had to talk to him. Maybe there was a way to play this with innocence, an approach Jake was probably completely unfamiliar with. Besides, there was a chance that if I went to see him, he'd think I'd taken him off my list of suspects. Because who would be bold/foolish enough to go grill someone who had threatened to kill her unless she stopped asking questions? That would be me.

So I'd called him, planning to give him some song-and-dance about the article. The maddening article. Even if I did come out of this with a byline, I was going to wind up with enemies, too. One story wasn't going to please all masters. Unless I wrote about everyone's investment in the piece and how a subject's expectations conflict with the writer's goal. Hey. That had potential. But I still needed to talk to Jake.

Lara answered the phone, her voice distant and chirpy. I'd caught her smoking and better yet, she didn't seem to recognize my name when I offered it. So maybe Jake hadn't let her in on his campaign against me, which was greatly to my advantage. When I asked to speak to him, she coolly informed me that Jake wasn't home. And when I asked when she expected him, she said, "I never expect Jake. I experience Jake on his own terms."

Some people stay in film school so long they forget how to interact with the real world. "When do you suppose Jake's terms might bring him home next?" I attempted. I stopped where I was on the sidewalk, trying to beam all my energy through the cell phone and into Lara's fuzzy brain to get her to focus.

"Why do you want to see Jake?" she asked petulantly.

"To accuse him of murder" was what I thought, but what I said was, "To talk to him about his filmmaking some more. I'm the magazine writer," I added, in case the vague promise of publicity might work on her as well as it had on Jake.

"He could not make these films without me," she replied, a touch of haughtiness replacing the petulance.

Right. She'd shot the footage of David and Lisbet and Veronica in the hallway. She'd been messing with the camera when Veronica and Jake were flirting at dinner. What else had Lara shot and/or seen that I didn't know about yet?

"Then you should definitely be in the article." The ever-expanding article. The Article that Ate New York City. Or at least my career. "Can I come talk to you, even if Jake isn't home?"

"I don't know," Lara responded with the automatic coyness of a woman who's accustomed to trading on her looks and charm.

A store across the street caught my eye. "I'll bring you a present."

So now, like some perverse dealer, I was standing in the stuffy hallway with a Blockbuster bag in my hand, trying to bribe my way into the apartment. And for the promise of getting her name in a magazine and a new DVD, she was going to let me in.

Lara squealed with excitement when she took the *Dora the Explorer* DVD out of the bag, then gave me an enthusiastic hug that semidragged me across the threshold. "You are so kind!"

"I hope you don't have this one," I said, trying hard not to feel ridiculous.

"No, I didn't even know about 'The Pirate Adventure,'" Lara assured me. She grabbed my hand and led me into the living room. Pushing me down onto the couch, she ran over to the DVD player. She wasn't really expecting me to watch it with her, was she?

I tried to strike a nonchalant pose on the couch, but the couch's angle and my mood were all wrong. "Lara, I'm sure it's a great piece of cinema, but I need to talk to you. About the films you and Jake make, remember?"

Lara paused, weighing the pleasure of talking to me about herself with that of watching her new DVD. For a moment, I thought I was going to lose, but then she put down the DVD. "What would you like to know?"

"Do you do all of Jake's camera work?"

"Not all," she said. "Most. The good stuff."

"You must've shot more than was on the Web site."

Lara's face darkened suddenly. "You're talking of David's party."

"Yes."

"Why? What do you know?" Lara's long legs carried her to the couch in the blink of an eye and she leaned over me, preventing me from getting up. How had I upset her?

"What should I know?"

Lara bent down to get in my face. Her pupils looked pretty normal, so maybe she wasn't all that buzzed, but that didn't make her any less unpredictable. "You're trying to trick me."

I wanted to laugh this off, but her intensity was disturbing. Was Lara the one who was trying to trick me? Did she know more than she was letting on? Had she done more than I could imagine? Was she also involved in Lisbet's death? Her leaning over me was suddenly making me very claustrophobic. I pushed against her legs, trying to get her to move so I could get up. She recoiled from my touch, jumping back. It was startling, but at least I could stand.

"It's you," she gasped in horror. "You did it."

"Did what?" I asked indignantly. It was one thing for me to show up at her apartment thinking her boyfriend was a killer, but it was another thing entirely for her to suspect me. Of anything. I'd given my theory a lot of thought and she was just accusing me in the heat of the moment.

"You made Jake go away."

"I did not. I haven't talked to Jake since I was here yesterday. If I'd made him go away, why would I come here looking for him? Where did he go?"

"You have to leave. I can't talk to you anymore." Lara shoved me in the direction of the front door with surprising strength.

"Why did he go, Lara? Did he say where he was going?"

"I thought you were my friend."

"Yeah, there's a lot of that going around. I need to talk to Jake, Lara. It's important. Really, really important. A matter of life and death."

"Out! Get out now!"

The Zanottis gave her impressive leverage and with another sharp shove, I was out in the hallway, minus my dignity and the information I'd come looking for. And the cash for the DVD. But I'd gained a huge new question. What did Lara imagine I'd done that made Jake go wherever he'd gone? It made sense Jake would want to hide if he'd killed Lisbet, but why had he waited until now to go? Had I tipped my hand and spooked him? What sort of story had Jake fed Lara to make her so protective? Or had he just blown her off and she was eager to lay some blame?

More important, how was I going to find Jake now? Lara was stonewalling me and the only other person I knew who knew Jake was David Vincent. I was willing to bet Lara's ability to toss me out on my ear didn't hold a candle to Tricia's ability to keep me away from David while she was still angry. But Jake and David were the two people I needed to talk to the most. I had to get David's story on what had happened with Veronica and his insight on where to look for Jake. But I also had to be careful or Tricia was going to blast me yet again for impure motives and other assorted character flaws.

So I called Cassady. I felt positively old-fashioned holding my cell phone to my ear, but I've never found a comfortable enough earpiece that didn't make me feel like I was practicing to be on tour with Janet Jackson. Earpieces have become so prevalent in New York that it's hard to tell the bankers from the crazy people as both storm down the avenues, railing at unseen tormentors. "I know you have other things to do today," I began as I walked back to Sixth to get a cab.

"Nothing more important than this."

"You're such a good friend."

"Cherish me. What's up?"

"I need to talk to David."

"What're you going to talk to him about?"

"Are you asking as a lawyer or a friend?"

"As an interested party. Specifically, a party interested in minimizing the damage on all sides."

"I want to hear his side of the story about sleeping with Veronica."

"That would be interesting."

"So you haven't talked to him about it either?"

"I haven't seen him. I've only talked to Tricia. Apparently, her parents are confining David 'on doctor's orders,' which is Park Avenue-ese for locking your child in his room, no matter his age."

"I need you to get me in there."

"Into David's room?"

"I'll settle for just inside the front door, as long as David's within hollering distance."

"So what you're suggesting is that I come up with some sort of plan that gets you into the Vincents' apartment under false pretenses and gives you the opportunity to grill their son about illicit sex he may or may not have had prior to the commission of a murder of which he may or may not be guilty."

"Pretty much."

"The disgusting thing is, I can do that."

"I know. That's why I called."

"But it can't be until this evening. Before dinner. Anything sooner's going to look transparent and needy."

"Heaven forbid."

"All I'm saying is, that never wins over anyone."

True. Still, this was a lip-chewer. I didn't want to wait that long. On the other hand, I couldn't imagine any other way I was going to be able to get the information. I stopped chewing and admitted, "You're right."

"Of course. Tricia's spending the afternoon with her family, poor thing. I'll tell her we'll meet her there. At six-thirty. You show up, on your best behavior, and ask your questions quickly and quietly. Then we'll go out and mend fences between you and Tricia."

"Sounds planlike. Thanks."

"You're being careful, right?"

"Absolutely."

I hung up and hailed a cab. As I was getting in, my phone rang again. I almost answered without looking at the number, assuming Cassady had thought of something else, but I glanced down at the last minute. It was the office, so I let it go to voice mail. Let Eileen grouse into a digital chip for a while.

I did keep my phone out and call Kyle. I wasn't sure if he hadn't gotten back to me because his new case was overwhelming or because he hadn't found out anything helpful about the threat on my answering machine. Of course, there was always the possibility that he was done with helping me. Or done with me. There are so many options to consider when you're a wary, weary, worried single woman in Manhattan. The city's full of men who want to finish you off, one way or the other.

He answered quickly, which was a good sign, and sounded concerned, which I also found hopeful. "Hey. You okay?"

"Fine. You?"

"More or less. What's new?"

"You got a minute?"

"Maybe even two."

"Okay. Forget what I said about Veronica."

The Pause was excruciating. I could hear the effort he was exerting to breathe evenly. My jaw started to tingle and I realized I was gritting my teeth, bracing for the response. When it came, it was way too controlled and way too quiet. "Why?"

"I've come across information that suggests a new direction," I said, trying to sound as clinical as possible.

It didn't help. "Stop."

"Stop what?"

"Everything. Just stop."

"What did you find?"

"I can't talk to you about this right now. It'll have to wait."

"Can I afford to wait? Do you know whose voice is on my answering machine?"

"Not yet. Just stay at work and I'll call you as soon as I can."

I didn't bother pointing out that I wasn't at work, since he already sounded pretty upset. That was just great. Kyle thought I was a flake, Tricia thought I was a traitor, Lara thought I was stalking Jake. I was building up quite a fan base. And it wasn't even lunchtime.

Though I dreaded returning to the hollow halls of *Zeitgeist* with more questions than I'd left with, I had no choice.

I needed to check back in, lest I raise Eileen's curiosity and ire. Plus, the computer on my desk was thirty blocks closer than the computer in my apartment. If I wasn't going to be able to talk to David until later, maybe I could spend some-time trying to find Jake. And if Jake had vanished, maybe his Web site would give me a clue as to where he'd go to hide.

I did my best to hide as I slunk back into the office. Eileen was going to want more than I had and my colleagues were going to be smirking about the little sideshow Tricia and I had put on for their entertainment. But I hadn't even gotten half the distance from the elevator to my desk before Genevieve appeared in my pathway, like the Grim Reaper in a mint green sweater set.

"Hey," she chirped.

"Genevieve," I replied neutrally.

"Busy?"

"Very."

"Visitor." She pointed to Eileen's office.

If it wasn't Jake or David, I wasn't interested. "Who is it?" Genevieve shrugged. "A happy visitor?"

Genevieve scrunched her nose in thought. "Furious."

Great. Not that I could think of anyone who would come see me at work without calling first whom I hadn't spoken to in the last twenty minutes (Kyle and Cassady), who wasn't currently not speaking to me (Tricia), who could possibly have anything happy to say to me (Santa Claus), but who else was mad at me? I actually had half a moment to wonder if it was Lara, though I wasn't sure she understood where I worked, before Eileen's office door opened and Eileen her-self ushered out my visitor. My newest fan. Veronica Innes.

They were saying their farewells, but both saw me at the same time and fell silent. Genevieve helpfully filled in the si-lence. "Here!"

The meerkats all took that as permission to stop what they were doing and observe what was about to happen. Eileen frowned at Genevieve. "Thank you, Genevieve. We can see that."

They were quite a pair, framed in the doorway, Eileen in her Lilly and Veronica in her Diane von Furstenberg multicolor wrap dress, which wasn't wrapped quite tightly enough. Unlike Veronica. I hoped they'd been chatting about the play or fashion or world peace. Then Eileen beckoned imperiously for me to join them. I hesitated, inciting Veronica to scream, "You bitch!" across the bullpen at me. She yelled it at just the right frequency to change my reluctance to talk to her at all into a burning desire to make her apologize and then shut up.

"I beg your pardon?" I asked, trying to strike the proper tone of outraged innocence as I walked up to them. Genevieve tagged along at my heels like a miniature terrier who'd retrieved a bone twice her size.

The actress in Veronica took over and she centered herself, fixing me with a frosty glare as I approached. Her voice was well modulated and complete ice. "What are you trying to do to me?"

"Nothing."

"The police came to the theater and destroyed me."

As hard as I was trying to look like the injured party here, I faltered a step. The police had done what? And how had she connected it to me? Was this why Kyle had been unhappy when I told him I wasn't sure it was Veronica anymore? "I don't understand," I told her, possibly the first wholly sincere thing I'd said to her.

Eileen gestured again, a little more impatiently. "Why don't we step back into my office?"

I still flinched every time I walked into Eileen's office,

having been so accustomed to it being Yvonne's office. Yvonne's space had been aggressively homey, with lots of dark wood. Eileen's was like something a set designer in the sixties might have designed for an office in the new millennium. Lots of twisted, lacquered acrylic in primary colors, abstract art on the blindingly white walls, and a floor painted Chinese red and buffed to such a high gloss that you wanted to take your shoes off and slide across it, just once. It was also the only intimation of fun in the entire place, Eileen included.

She leaned against the edge of her desk since she wasn't quite tall enough to sit on it, while Veronica perched on the lip of a shiny red chair in the shape of a question mark. I stood.

"Ms. Innes is quite upset," Eileen recapped.

"I can see that and I'm sorry, but I don't understand what it has to do with me."

"They took my champagne bottle," Veronica explained.

I was pretty sure my face stayed composed, but my stomach flipped twice. "Champagne?"

"I showed it to you. Remember? The bottle from the party."

I don't like to play dumb, but sometimes it's the simplest approach. "I think I recall talking about that."

"You're the only one who knew I had it and suddenly the police come and take it. What did you tell them?"

I didn't have a story ready. I'd been concentrating on Jake and was no longer prepared for Veronica. She'd caught me by surprise, which was disconcerting. "I'm sorry. I didn't send the police to you." I'd told Kyle I'd suspected her, but he hadn't seemed especially convinced. How could he have thought that was worth acting on officially without more information? Unless he had other information he wasn't sharing with me. He'd told me to stop and he was cutting me out of the loop to make sure I did. I inched toward that subject. "What did the police officer say when he took the bottle?"

Veronica sniffed. "She had plenty to say. And plenty to ask."

She? Kyle had sent someone else? Or . . . No. Couldn't be. I heard myself asking, "And her name was . . . ?"

Veronica slid a business card out of her pocket and flicked it at me like a miniature Frisbee. "Darcy Cook. Detective and first-class bitch."

I refrained from agreeing as I caught Detective Cook's business card. How had Detective Cook wound up at the theater questioning Veronica? Had it been an independent course of investigation? Or had Kyle said something to her about my suspicions and she'd leapt upon the lead and come charging into the city to track it down in person? If she was in town, had she checked in with Kyle, the way he'd checked in with her? And was that why he hadn't wanted to talk to me when I'd called?

"Do you know her, Molly?" Eileen seemed amused.

"We've met," I admitted, but I wasn't eager to admit more.

"This is devastating," Veronica said, glaring at me.

"Did Detective Cook accuse you of something?"

"Of course not. She asked plenty of questions about the party and Lisbet. All the same sorts of questions you asked, which is how I figured out you were in on this."

"A coincidence," I said, ignoring Eileen's smirk.

"But she didn't accuse me of anything. She just took the champagne bottle."

"Lisbet was killed with a champagne bottle, you realize that, dear," Eileen said.

"Do you have any idea how many bottles of champagne

there were at that party?" Veronica countered. "I didn't kill her."

"Then you have nothing to worry about," I assured her, trying to assimilate all this on the fly.

"I explained to you how important that bottle was to my performance. They took it, can't say when I'll get it back, and we open in a week and a half." Veronica stood for dramatic effect. "I'm ruined. And it's all your fault!"

Eileen gave a few silent claps in my direction, congratulating me on my handling of the situation. I restrained myself from responding and focused on Veronica. "Veronica, I have a thought."

Eileen crossed her arms over her chest. "Let us hope."

"You told me the champagne bottle represented the sadness of crushed dreams. So if the loss of the bottle is going to impact your performance . . ." I held Detective Cook's business card back out to her.

"Then I'm screwed," she insisted angrily.

"Work with me. Don't come from a place of rage. Come from a place of sadness. Remember what she's done to your career and then think of that career—"

Veronica snatched the card, eyes widening. "A beautiful flower trampled in its prime." I started to ask if that referred to the career or Detective Cook, but I didn't want to take a chance of derailing Veronica. Her nostrils flared, but no tears came. "Wait, wait." She took a deep breath, then stared at the card like a superhero burning holes in it with eye lasers. She took a shuddering breath and started sobbing.

Eileen winced. "Dear God, that's unattractive."

Veronica stopped on a dime and ripped a fistful of tissues out of the box on the coffee table. "You're good."

"As a writer, I appreciate the creative process in any discipline," I said, offering her a level on which we could pretend to bond.

"I'm still pretty pissed at you, but this helps." She waved the business card at me, then slid it back into her pocket. "At least I don't feel like suing you anymore. Right now."

"Thank you." I could have left well enough alone, but it's just not in my nature. "But I want you to know, I never spoke to Detective Cook about you and your bottle. I didn't even know she was in town." Though it was something I was going to look into at the first available opportunity.

"Well, you better be careful who you are talking to, because they're talking to her and who knows who else. And if it gets back to whomever did this, you could be next."

Even Eileen reacted to her matter-of-fact delivery of that gem. And I got goose bumps like I haven't had since the first time I saw *Poltergeist*. I resisted the impulse to rub my arms. Was it back to Veronica after all and not Jake? "That's not a threat, is it?" I asked as lightly as possible.

"Honey, when I threaten someone, they know it. It's just a word to the wise, that's all." Veronica gave me a chilling wink and moved for the door.

Eileen scampered to catch up with her and walk her properly out of the office. "If you have any further concerns, please don't hesitate to call me," Eileen purred, stroking Veronica's arm like they were old, dear friends who'd just been through a terrible trial together.

"Thank you, I will," Veronica replied. Eileen delivered her to Genevieve to be escorted to the elevator, then spun back into the room, easing the door closed behind her.

"Exactly what the hell are you doing?" Eileen demanded silkily.

"You asked me to find the story. I'm looking."

"Will there be other murder suspects arriving in tears?"

"Maybe you'd rather I didn't do the article."

"Maybe you'd rather not work here."

I'll give Eileen this. She draws her battle lines clearly. A little misdirection seemed in order. "I'm still seeking to impose a coherent narrative on disparate events which crystallize the societal and sociological pressures which drive people to extreme behavior in the pursuit of pleasure and love." The scary thing was, that approach could actually work. But all I wanted it to do at the moment was excite the editor in Eileen enough for her to let me out of the office.

She thought about it for a moment, which I found promising. Then she walked over and took my hand, patting it with just the proper amount of condescension to remind me why I disliked her so much. "Molly. This isn't the damn New York Review of Books. Tell me a story about sex and violence among the beautiful people. It's that simple."

"I aim to please. Guess I just wasn't aiming low enough." I pulled my hand free and walked past her, deciding to save the battle over actually writing the thing for another time.

"Where are you going?"

"To find you your story." And to find myself a cop.

14

"You need a healthier hobby. Something that involves fresh air. Or the production of something positive."

"Pottery, maybe? Baking?"

"Just saying maybe hanging with dead bodies isn't the best thing to do with your time."

Detective Ben Lipscomb is Kyle's partner. He's a tall, imposing African-American man in his late thirties who can be quite intimidating without intending it and can be downright frightening when he needs to be. He has the detective's gift for staying quiet and letting you talk yourself right into the corner where he wants you, so if he does talk, it's worth listening to.

When I'd left the magazine office, I'd considered eating my way to Kyle's office. Part of it was that it was lunchtime and I hadn't really eaten much breakfast because I'd been too stressed. Besides, to Cassady, breakfast is a cup of coffee in a travel mug. I'm still a cereal girl when I have the time and a bagel eater when I'm on the run. The closest I'd come to protein today was the hangnail I was about to pull off with my teeth.

Manhattan possesses its own special energy. Maybe it's the by-product of millions of people's individual electromagnetic fields mingling with each other day and night. Perhaps there's some glowing gem out in the harbor that keeps us all racing around on a divine jag. But part of it's gotta be the coffee. There's a Starbucks on every block—I think that's a zoning regulation now—and the streets are lined with food carts which sell every kind of portable nosh imaginable, as well as more coffee, so it's entirely possible to go from one end of the island to the other and never go more than a hundred yards without the opportunity to have something to eat and grab a cup of coffee. The city that never sleeps just can't.

Post-Eileen and Veronica, I'd adapted to today's stress level and I was starving. I thought about grabbing a hot dog, purely for comfort food purposes, but I wasn't sure whether that would go with a caramel macchiato, which was my other craving. A falafel with a chai tea latte seemed a little more harmonious. A hot pretzel and a cappuccino? Let's face it—what I needed was a cheesesteak and a Vanilla Coke, but I didn't have time to go in and sit down somewhere. I had to find out what Kyle and Detective Cook were up to.

When I got to the precinct, I asked the desk sergeant if Detective Edwards was available for a brief conversation with Molly Forrester. He called upstairs, talked to someone, then hung up. I was debating between being further frustrated or outright hurt when he told me that Detective Edwards was unavailable, but Detective Lipscomb would be down for me in just a moment.

I hadn't spent that much time with Detective Lipscomb, but he'd always been cordial to me and right now, he looked like a long-lost friend as he came down the stairs to greet me.

"Unexpected pleasure," he said graciously. He shook my hand warmly, but didn't move to lead me back upstairs.

"I'm sorry, I should've called. I'm a little scattered today."

"I hear someone's trying to kill you."

"Yeah, but the person I thought was threatening me just showed up at my office and didn't do anything but spit venom and cry on command."

"That why you're here?"

I frowned. "Guess it should be." He shrugged. I didn't know how else to phrase my question and Detective Lipscomb had always seemed to be the straight-shooting type, so I just went for it. "Is Detective Cook here?"

Detective Lipscomb frowned. "I thought you wanted to see Kyle."

"I do," I said, suddenly feeling like a teenager who's been caught with one leg out the bedroom window as her parents come in to tell her good night.

"What's Detective Cook got to do with it?"

"That's kind of part of what I want to see Kyle about. What *does* she have to do with it?"

"Well, to him, she's investigating a homicide. But to you, she's what? Spending time with your man?"

"You're good. You should be a detective."

He laughed once, then let a silence develop that he was far more comfortable with than I was.

"So can I see him?" I asked when I had to say something.

Detective Lipscomb frowned again. "He's pretty tied up."

I'd prefer not to describe the image of erotic bondage that spontaneously leapt to my mind, lest that increase the number of therapy sessions it was going to take to erase it. Or at least erase Detective Cook's prominent role in it. Suffice it to say, I muttered, "That's what I was afraid of."

Detective Lipscomb thought a moment, weighing variables he wasn't going to share with me, before he put his huge hand gently on my shoulder. "Want to come upstairs and wait for him?"

I said a quick silent prayer of thankfulness for there still being good people in the world and told him, "Yes, please."

Detective Lipscomb slid his hand off my shoulder and on to my back to guide me to the staircase. As we climbed the stairs to the detective division, he offered his observations on my needing a new hobby, concluding with, "It's never easy."

"Solving a murder?"

"Being involved with a cop." He swung his left hand up for me so I could see the bare fourth finger. "Used to have a ring."

I wasn't sure whether to offer condolences or to panic. Especially when he continued, "Good to see you and Kyle doing so well. He hasn't made it past six months in I don't know how many."

Six months. Was that some sort of watershed for Kyle? The point when he decided if he wanted to renew or cancel his subscription? Brilliantly, it was the point when I'd asked if he wanted to go away for the weekend. I retained my crown as Queen of Great Timing.

Detective Lipscomb led me over to his desk. I found our bullpen at the magazine dreary and institutional, but at least it had a little style to it. Their bullpen looked like someone had gone to a clearance sale when the War Department closed in the 1940s and bought only the most worn and battered desks and chairs and no one had gone shopping since. There were piles of paperwork on every available surface and the detectives who were at their desks looked weary but resolute. I vowed to remember that the next time I was tempted to complain about my taxes.

He pulled a spare chair up to the side of his desk. "Shouldn't tell you this, but your incident this weekend, it's gotten very political. People throwing their weight around. We caught a double last night, but the bosses still pulled him to help Suffolk County."

"I didn't mean to get him in another mess," I said quietly.

"Just wanted you to know the lay of the land. I'll tell him you're here. Or not," he corrected himself.

I thought he was toying with me, then realized he'd spotted Kyle coming across the room toward us, shirtsleeves rolled, an anguished look on his face. "What now?"

How stupid did that make me feel? Let me count the ways. I felt catapulted back past the War Department, a full century at least, a stupid hysterical female who was impeding the serious work of men.

To his credit, Kyle realized how it sounded, probably more because of Detective Lipscomb's glare than my stricken look, because he quickly amended, "Sorry. What I meant was, has something else happened?"

"Any results from the answering machine?"

He checked his watch. "Soon. Why aren't you at work?"

"Veronica Innes came to see me. At work."

Kyle's look of concern deepened. Despite what I'd told him, he still hadn't dismissed her as a suspect. I wondered what Detective Cook might have told him that I didn't know. "And?" he prompted.

"Do you have time to talk?" I asked, trying to sound polite and concerned rather than suspicious and possessive.

Kyle hesitated, glancing over at Detective Lipscomb, who grabbed his coffee mug off his desk. "Coffee, Molly?" he asked. I nodded and he walked off, stifling a smile and not looking at Kyle once.

Kyle pinched his bottom lip. "Veronica told you about Detective Cook."

"Bingo," I snarked.

Kyle stepped in close, keeping his voice down with a visible effort. Unlike the meerkats in my office, his colleagues kept right on working, though they'd probably all been trained so they could listen to our conversation and do their own work simultaneously without missing a beat of either. "Don't give me attitude. I'm in the middle of this because of you. Try to help me once or twice without adding to the problem."

"Which problem is that? Lisbet or you and me?"

"This isn't about us unless you want to make it about us."

The position I'd put him in was uncomfortably close to the situation I felt Tricia had put me in, but my mind grasped that after my mouth had already said, "I'm just trying to help. Which is why I came to tell you about Veronica. But you already know. How is Darcy?"

"Detective Cook's getting her ass kicked by the people she works for."

"I'm familiar with the feeling."

"She asked me to pass along anything I heard that might help her out."

"Really. She asked me if you were single."

Kyle pinched his lip so hard I thought he was going to rip it off. "Tell me that's not why you're here."

"That's not why I'm here."

"Damn it, Molly." He caught me by the shoulders and eased me down into the chair Detective Lipscomb had found for me. "Sit here. Give me a minute, then we'll talk."

He was being nice, doing his best to be nice, but it hit me

like the wave you don't see when you're body surfing that slams you into the sand. I'd made a mistake. A magnificently big mistake. I thought quickly—something I should do way more often than I do—and realized that I needed to reposition myself fast or I was going to destroy more than my credibility.

"Actually, I don't think that's a good idea," I began, though I could tell from his expression I could have begun better. "I should leave, give you the time you need to do what you have to do, then I'll meet you a little later and we can talk then."

He waited a moment for the other shoe to drop. When it didn't, his grip on my shoulders eased. "What're you doing?"

"I'd suggest you come to my place, but I'd like to include Detective Cook in the invitation and she might be uncomfortable there."

Now he let go of me completely. He didn't know what to make of my change of heart. Which was actually a shift in tactics.

"So how 'bout we meet at the lounge at the Algonquin Hotel at say, five?" I was really pleased with how sweet and reasonable all this sounded, since I was madly tap-dancing in my head.

Kyle straightened up. "Five-thirty."

I stood. I was about to object, knowing that I had to get up to the Vincents' by six-thirty, but I could figure that out along the way. "Fine."

Detective Lipscomb returned with his mug filled and a paper cup of coffee for me. "I forgot to ask how you take it."

"To go, thank you." He handed me the cup without further comment, scanning my face and Kyle's and picking up all the info he needed. "I'm really sorry to have barged in on you like this. Thank you for coming downstairs," I said

to him, "and thank you for talking to me," I said to Kyle.
"I'll see you later." I gathered up what was left of my dignity and went home to contemplate my next move. And my
wardrobe.

My mistake had been to keep thinking I was a partner in
this endeavor and, therefore, entitled to Kyle's information
and time. But he didn't see me that way. He saw me as an innocent to be protected. So my impulsive appearance came
off as the attack of the high-maintenance girlfriend. The
shrew who kicks at the door and demands entrance she
hasn't earned. Worst of all, I looked like I was trying to compete with Detective Cook. And maybe I was, but it wasn't
supposed to be so apparent. I was going to have to play this
differently. And get to the answer before Detective Cook did.

On the way home, I called Genevieve and instructed her
to tell Eileen I was on to something for the story, so I was
going to be out of pocket for the rest of the day. I also had
the cabbie drop me off three blocks shy of my apartment so
I could stop in at Stavros's Grill, a terrific Greek deli, and get
that cheesesteak to go. With fries, damn it. And a Vanilla
Coke big enough to bathe in.

I got home and instinctively checked the empty space on
the console table where my answering machine belonged. It
disturbed me for it to be gone, but this way, I could tell myself my threatener hadn't called again or, even better, made
any other advances into my life. It couldn't be Veronica. It
had to have been Jake, didn't it? Veronica had been scary
but, in retrospect, too involved in her own drama to be plotting against me. She was an actress, but she wasn't that good.
Was she?

Light-headed from hunger, stress, and too much caffeine,
I put on Joni Mitchell's *Miles of Aisles*, one of my favorite
pondering CDs, unwrapped my sandwich, and took stock.

Detective Lipscomb was emerging as the only positive encounter of my day. Someone wanted to kill me. My editor
wanted to fire me. A crazy actress was ready to sue me. One
of my best friends wasn't speaking to me, the other was
pretty unhappy, the man I cared about wasn't exactly
thrilled, and my prime suspect had vanished, leaving behind
nothing more helpful than his girlfriend, Our Lady of Du-
bious Lucidity.

And then there was Detective Cook.

But she could wait. What was weighing most heavily on
my heart at the moment—aside from the cheesesteak—was
the fact that I couldn't call Tricia and Cassady and talk this
through with them. Cassady would probably make time to
talk to me if I called, but it'd be putting her in the middle
until Tricia and I worked things out and that wasn't fair.
Nothing that was happening to Tricia and her family was
fair. Certainly, what had happened to Lisbet wasn't fair. I got
all that. But it was going to be hard for Tricia to see past it
for a while. I worried Tricia and I weren't going to be able
to work things out until I found Jake and uncovered why
he'd killed Lisbet.

And how was I going to find Jake? I moved my portable
feast over to the computer and logged on to take a look at
Jake's Web site again. Not that I was expecting a pulldown
of "Places I Go When I'm Hiding from My Girlfriend and
the Law," but maybe there'd be some clue there about
where I could find him. Or a way to e-mail him that cir-
cumvented Lara and her protective instincts.

Unfortunately, all there was on his Web site was a big
screen that announced "This Web site is undergoing drastic
renovation. We apologize for any inconvenience this may
cause or any offense it did cause." Everything was gone, most
particularly the "memorial" footage of Lisbet. Was it the

shameless use of the footage that had forced Jake to scrub the Web site? Or had he realized he was leaving a trail of bread crumbs that led to his own front door and the quieter he stayed, the better? But he'd shown it to me. Of course, I hadn't suspected him then. Maybe that's why he'd been so touchy-feely. Maybe he'd gotten off on showing it to me while he knew the truth and I didn't. Who had frightened, threatened, or otherwise cajoled him into taking it down now?

No matter where I looked, all roads led back to Jake. If he was, in fact, the ghost in my machine, I had to be careful about my approach. Should I play the article card again? Or did I dare approach him directly with my suspicions? That was the more dangerous choice, but it was probably also the more effective. He could ignore the chance for an article, even though that would take considerable ego-wrestling on his part, but how could he pass up the opportunity to confront a person accusing him of murder? The trick was not getting myself killed in the process.

With that in mind, maybe I should play it more subtly. Appeal to his sense of self-importance and let him fill in whatever was necessary between the lines.

Picking up the phone, I hoped I'd get the machine, because I worried about Lara's ability to deliver a message verbatim, depending on her state of mind. Of course, there was always the chance she was going to get the message off the machine and pass it along, losing it in translation, but I'd take that chance. I'd glimpsed enough of the control freak in Jake to believe that wherever he was, he was monitoring his messages.

I paced around the apartment with the phone in my hand, drafting a message in my head so I didn't have to stumble and stammer when I got through. I've botched plenty of attempts to attract men with awkward phone messages. At least that's what I like to blame it on. With this much at stake, I wanted to be careful.

"Hi, it's Molly Forrester," I thought initially. "Jake, Lara told me you're going through some stuff. I think I can help. Call me." But when I thought about that a little longer, it sounded like I was a therapist drumming up business, not a spider enticing a fly.

Try again. "Jake and Lara, it's Molly Forrester. Jake, I know you're busy but there's something I have to ask you. It's life or death. Please call me." Nah. Nice sense of urgency, but it was a tad adolescent.

Maybe something more spare. Less Danielle Steele and more Raymond Chandler. "Jake, it's Molly. I have to talk to you. You know why."

Yeah. That had real potential. Best of all, Lara would think it was about the article, but Jake would know better. And even if someone had put a scare into him, his ego wouldn't let him stay in the shadows for long. He'd want to come out and toy with a person who knew his secret and had the ability to spread it all over town. As I left the message on their machine, asking him to call my cell because my answering machine was "broken," I was confident he'd respond. I just had to pray I'd hear him coming.

15

The Algonquin Hotel is a shrine to me. The Algonquin Round Table, those bright, bitter, witty folks who hung out in the Oak Room there in the 1930s, are some of my favorite writers. Especially Dorothy Parker, a woman who knew how to balance comedy, pain, and a cocktail and never waste a drop of any of them. By asking Kyle and Detective Cook to meet me there, I felt I was creating a home-court advantage, or at least giving the spirits of Parker, Benchley, and the rest an opportunity to watch over me.

I'd taken my frustration out on my closet, ransacking it for the right outfit to set the proper tone for meeting Kyle and Detective Cook. Nothing I owned fit the bill. The Algonquin seemed to require black Hollywood trousers and a slouchy white silk blouse and unexpectedly delicate black slingbacks, perhaps with a little rosette. I tend toward the Katharine Hepburn because my shoulders are too wide to try Audrey Hepburn. Besides, there wasn't anything Golightly about my mood. It was darkening by the moment.

I kept expecting the phone to ring, hoping it would be Jake and wondering if it would be Kyle with some reason to cancel. Instead, I called Cassady and warned her that I might

be cutting my appearance at the Vincents' a little close because of my date with the detectives.

"You're not worried he's interested in her, are you?" Cassady asked disdainfully.

"I need to talk to them about the message on my answering machine."

"How do you expect to get people to answer your questions when you won't answer theirs?"

"I don't know."

"Which question does that answer?"

"All of the above."

"Don't be too late. It's not polite. And frankly, I don't
relish the thought of spending any more time there than
necessary."

"Did you really sleep with David?"

"I'm already on record, it was just holiday party pawing.
Nothing consummated."

"Who started it?"

"Excuse me?"

"I'm trying to figure out this alleged liaison with Veronica. How easily do you suppose David strays?"

"He's a man, isn't he? That's why the penis is shaped like
a handle, so they can be led around by it. Put them on
wheels and they'd make delightful pull toys."

It was difficult to keep that image out of my head as I
watched the men entering and leaving the Algonquin,
thinking of all the grand art and sex and drinking that had
taken place in this magnificent setting. The lobby is dark,
the colors and textures rich, the light suspending everything
in amber.

Not owning my dream Kate Hepburn outfit, I'd decided
on my Ralph Lauren taupe linen duster and matching pants
with a white silk blouse underneath. With Jimmy Choo

pumps, Melody in burnt orange leather, I felt I fit in quite nicely. I'd snagged a seat on one of the velvet sofas facing the front door so I'd be able to see my guests enter and told the cocktail waiter I was waiting for someone. He still came back with a drink on his tray, a deep red drink in a martini glass, and put it down in front of me.

"I'm sorry, but I didn't order yet."

He nodded knowingly. "A gift from a friend. It's the Parker, a house specialty. Named for Mrs. Dorothy Parker. Your friend said it was a toast to a long life."

I'm sure he was expecting me to be pleased, but I was alarmed. Invoking the Queen of Sarcasm in a toast for long life sounded like a threat to me, especially in my current mood. "What friend?" I asked, looking around nervously. Was Jake here, hidden in a dark corner somewhere, watching me and waiting for his moment?

"A lady. She came in right after you." He looked around, too, puzzled. "Now I don't see her." He looked back at me. "You're upset, I'm sorry. I'll take it away."

He reached for the glass, but I put my hand on his. "Did she pay for the drink in cash?" He nodded. Okay, no paper trail to help there. "Was she blond or dark?"

"A little dark."

"Pretty?"

He shrugged. "All women are pretty."

I smiled, even though I was freaking out. "Thank you. Leave the drink. I'll figure it out."

Dark, maybe pretty. Someone who had followed me to the Algonquin. Somebody who, therefore, had been watching my apartment, because no one else knew I was going to be here except Kyle, Detective Cook, and Cassady. Somebody who'd been right behind me and I hadn't even noticed. People get shot this way. I got shot this way.

I wanted to chug the drink for courage, but then again, I didn't even want to touch the glass. I'd been worrying about Jake all day and now there was a woman after me? Who was she? What did she want? Was she going to—

The hand on my arm was gentle, but I still cried out and leapt to my feet. I'd been so busy staring at the drink and trying to figure it out that I hadn't seen Kyle and Detective Cook come in. They were both in their work clothes, suits of an almost identical slate gray, though she was wearing a cream silk tee and he had on a blue oxford. There was a matched-set quality to them I found disturbing, especially because I wasn't sure if I was overdressed or just emphasizing, for good or ill, that I wasn't a member of their club.

I attempted to sound witty and light while I explained the untouched drink on the table, but I wasn't terribly convincing. Kyle scanned the room carefully before indicating the armchair next to me for Detective Cook. He sat beside me on the couch.

"I guess I've ruffled some feathers," I said with a stab at nonchalance.

"Go with your strengths," Detective Cook replied.

Now, Kyle was studying the glass as though he could make it slosh up some forensic clue. "You didn't notice anyone?" he asked.

"No one. Besides, when I look over my shoulder, I'm looking for the guy on my answering machine."

"It's a woman," Detective Cook told me.

I was equally startled, but I didn't cry out this time. "A what?" I asked stupidly.

"A woman. Kyle's tech rat couldn't tell much else about the tape, but he's willing to testify that it's a woman."

Several things stood out in that sentence. "Woman," which blew my Jake theory to shreds. "Testify," which awakened the concept of all this going to trial at some point, preferably with David not in the lineup. And "Kyle," which meant the dear detectives had progressed to calling each other by their first names.

Focusing on "woman" seemed to be the wisest course at the moment. If a woman had called me and a woman had followed me here tonight, either Jake was using Lara as his all-purpose messenger of doom or I'd underestimated Veronica Innes's acting ability and dismissed her too quickly. "Where do you stand with Veronica Innes?" I asked Detective Cook.

She looked at Kyle before answering. "And the ground rules for this conversation are . . ."

Kyle shook his head. I elaborated. "Here's one. We put our cards on the table because none of us are in a position to waste time."

Detective Cook reached into her jacket, but she brought out a notebook, not a gun, so I hadn't stepped too far over the line. "Ms. Forrester, I'm not here to make you happy."

"Congratulations on your success."

"Molly . . ." Kyle sighed.

"What? She already told me she doesn't have to be nice, so why do I? Because my mother raised me right? That's why the wolves always win. Because the rest of us mind our manners and get devoured for our efforts."

Detective Cook looked at Kyle again. "She always like this?"

"No, you bring out the best in me and I'd really prefer that you insult me directly, rather than making snide comments to him like I'm not old enough to understand."

Kyle caught the eye of the cocktail waiter and his pleading look brought the man in a hurry. Kyle slid the suspect drink away from me, possibly to keep me from throwing it on Detective Cook, and asked me what I wanted. I ordered a fresh Parker because I was feeling stubborn. Detective Cook ordered a Diet Coke and Kyle went with club soda; they were on the clock. I was on a different one. I checked my watch. I wanted to allow myself twenty-five minutes to get up to the Vincents', but I didn't want to leave until I'd gotten everything out of Detective Cook I could.

Detective Cook resumed smoothly. "I'm not trying to offend you, Ms. Forrester," she said, with the clear implication that she wouldn't lose any sleep if she did, "but I don't want you to screw up my investigation either."

"Then tell me what you have on Veronica Innes so I can figure out if she wants to kill me or just likes taking it out on me after you've gotten her all worked up. And please answer me without looking at him."

Detective Cook started to put her notebook back in her jacket. "Forget it."

"No," Kyle said quietly. "Someone's threatening her. She's part of this."

"And no one else could be threatening her because . . ."

My desire to kiss him outweighed my desire to punch her, but not by much. "Veronica Innes," I repeated.

She glared at me so determinedly, I could tell she was straining not to look at Kyle first. "The champagne bottle's clean. There were traces of the label in Lisbet's scalp. The label on Veronica's bottle was intact. Not the murder weapon."

"Which doesn't mean she didn't kill her."

"And her motive would be . . ."

"To win back the guy and the part. She had sex with David Vincent Friday afternoon."

They both reacted to that, Kyle in surprise, Detective

Cook in delight. "Which doesn't make it look very good for David Vincent."

How did she keep pinning it on a Vincent and making it look like my idea? "C'mon, Detective Cook, a guy wants to get rid of you for better sex, he dumps you, he doesn't kill you."

"I wouldn't know."

"Well, after you've had sex, you'll understand."

"Okay!" Kyle exclaimed, more for the benefit of the arriving waiter than for either of us.

The waiter astutely passed out the drinks and left quickly. My new Parker looked beautiful, somehow brighter and crisper than the other one, and I took a nice, long sip. Vodka Chambord, and a hint of lemon-lime—tart but smooth, just like Parker, and a noble goal for me. I was taking a second sip when my cell rang. I mumbled an apology and fished the phone out of my purse, sure I'd lost track of time and Cassady was calling to yell at me.

"Molly."

It was Jake. It had worked. But I wasn't sure, in the moment, whether that was a good thing or not. "Hey."

"Leave me the hell alone."

"Excuse me?"

Kyle put his hand on my knee in a very comfortable, very wonderful manner. He was watching my face carefully, trying to figure out whom I was talking to. I didn't know what to tell him and Detective Cook, because I wasn't sure how to keep her from turning Jake into a black mark against David. Especially because this conversation wasn't going in the direction I'd expected it to. Not surprising, given my track record for the day.

"Stop threatening me, Molly."

"I didn't. I asked to see you."

"The first message. The 'shut down the site or die' one."

Someone had threatened Jake, too? Or was this a ploy? "Wasn't me."

"Liar!"

"I swear."

"I closed it down."

"I know, but—"

"Satisfied now? The most beautiful thing I've done in my career and I took it down. What more do you want from me?"

"We need to talk. About leaving and living."

This Pause was choked with anguish. I could feel Jake's struggle to figure out how I knew and what else I might know. "Too late now."

"Why?"

"Go to hell."

He hung up. I kept the phone to my ear for another moment because I knew Kyle and Detective Cook would have questions for me the moment I hung up and I wasn't sure which ones I could answer.

When I finally closed the phone, Kyle asked, "You okay?"

His hand was still on my knee and I squeezed it appreciatively, then took a greedy sip of my drink before answering. "Yeah."

"And that was . . ."

I didn't want to tell her because I couldn't lay it all out neatly and win her over to a theory I hadn't fully formed yet, but I felt obligated to her since she'd told me about Veronica's bottle. And because Kyle wanted me to play nice. "Jake Boone. He was at the party Friday night."

"Why do you need to talk to him?"

I took another sip, still debating, then did the right thing because I was raised that way. "He had sex with Lisbet after the party. Right before she died."

Kyle and Detective Cook exchanged a look before Detective Cook said, "The ME told us she'd had intercourse just before death. But you learned this from . . ."

"Veronica Innes. Didn't she tell you?" Detective Cook shook her head and I shrugged and said, "She told me, so I just assumed she told you."

"And you're meeting him . . ."

"I'm not. He's gotten threatening messages on his answering machine and he thinks they're from me."

"Are they?" my dear friend Detective Cook asked.

"No, I'm a flies-with-honey kind of girl."

"I hadn't noticed."

"Where is he?" Kyle intervened quickly.

"He wouldn't tell me and neither would his girlfriend."

"Well, if David Vincent caught this guy and Lisbet Mc-Candless together, that certainly clears things up for us," Detective Cook proclaimed.

She did it again! "I have to go," I said, standing.

"That's your answer?" she asked.

"Was there a question? What I heard was you back on your wretched theory about David Vincent which must still be full of holes or you would've done something about it by now."

She stood to be able to look me in the eye. Kyle stood, prepared to keep the peace if necessary. "The wall's got a couple of cracks, but you keep handing me plaster. I do appreciate that."

I wanted to take the rest of my bright red drink and pour it down the front of her pretty cream tee and see if she appreciated that. But I also wanted to show Kyle I could keep my cool. "I'm very sorry you and I got off on the wrong foot, because I really do want the same thing you do." I exercised great self-control and didn't look at Kyle because I was trying not to muddy the waters. "I want justice. But I want it for David as well as for Lisbet."

She looked at me oddly, perhaps assessing my sincerity, perhaps holding back choice invective. I couldn't tell. Kyle slid his hand along the small of my back. "Sit down and finish your drink."

"I can't. I really have to go. I have an appointment."

"I'll go with you."

"You can't," I said, gesturing to Detective Cook. "You have important business to take care of." She sat back down and picked up her glass, looking expectantly at Kyle. That made me want to sit right back down myself, but I suspected that was why she was doing it. And I had to go talk to David. Besides, I realized with a little shiver, if I couldn't trust Kyle with Detective Cook, what was the point in standing up Tricia and Cassady to baby-sit?

Kyle was on a completely different track. "You have people following you."

"I'm going to meet Cassady at Tricia's and I'll make her come home with me."

Kyle reached into my bag before I knew what he was doing and pulled out my cell. "She number two on this, too?" He speed-dialed Cassady without waiting for my answer. I reached for the phone, but he stepped back just far enough to make it awkward.

"Cassady? Kyle Edwards. . . . No, she's fine. She's here with me, but she says she's on her way to you . . . Can I trust you to see her home? . . . Okay, I'm bringing her in a cab now. Thank you." He snapped the phone shut and handed it back to me.

I'm not sure which of us looked more stunned, me or

Detective Cook. She was looking at Kyle like one of the amber lights hanging from the ceiling had turned into a spotlight illuminating him in a blazing white glow. I was pretty impressed myself. A rare specimen of an endangered species—the classy guy.

"You want to finish your drink and meet me back at the precinct or go for a drive?" he asked Detective Cook, further endearing himself.

This time, she looked at me before replying. I did not gloat, I swear. "I'll see you back there."

"Thank you for the information, Detective Cook. I'm sure we'll be talking again."

"Count on it," she replied. I laid bills on the table to settle the bar tab and she reached out to stop me. "I got this."

"No, please. It was my invitation. It's the least I can do." And then, because the desire to pour my drink down the front of her shirt still hadn't left me, I quickly put my arm through Kyle's and walked out with him.

The doorman practically had a cab waiting. Once we'd slid in, Kyle put his arm around me like we rode around the city together all the time. I didn't object. In fact, I had the good sense to stay quiet while he relaxed and enjoyed my putting my head on his shoulder. Then it turned out that he'd just been thinking. "I don't like that someone followed you in there."

"Yeah, but here's what I'm telling myself. Whoever it was could've tried to hurt me, but she didn't. So she's probably content to just scare me." I said it with a lot of enthusiasm, hoping to win him over to that point of view, even though I was having trouble staying there myself.

"She's building up to her move. Finding her nerve." He shook his head. "Whatever your appointment is, skip."

"I can't," I protested, knowing that not only would it be hard to get another chance to talk to David, but I'd go crazy not being able to try and smooth things out with Tricia. Not to mention the cabin fever aspect of having to stay home until this was all over. And as much as I adored him, especially in the midst of his chivalrous gesture, I didn't want Kyle to stay with me. I'd never get to talk to David that way.

Kyle was quiet and again, I followed suit. I sensed he was trying to come up with an alternative plan, but by the time we got to Park Avenue, he'd shaken his head a few times, but hadn't come up with anything that passed enough muster to share with me.

He told the cabbie to wait and walked me to the door. I greeted the doorman who opened the door graciously. Kyle stepped through with me, scanned the lobby, then took my face in his hands. "Don't be brave. Or stupid."

"You be careful, too."

"No one's out to get me."

"I don't know about that."

"You're all I want." He kissed me lightly, but my knees still trembled. Words to savor. He slipped back out the front door and I got on the elevator with a big grin.

With the Vincents' apartment, "palatial" is the word that comes to mind, especially as you step in and your eye is caught by the sweeping staircase and the glittering chandelier. The floor is a pastoral mosaic I swear I saw in my college art history book and there's a table at the center of it that King Arthur must have used when the knights got together on the weekends, resting on an exquisite fringed oriental rug. And that's just the foyer.

Cassady opened the door for me, but Tricia was standing with her. Cassady obviously had high hopes for the evening, since she was wearing a Sue Wong spaghetti-strap cocktail dress, with fringe along its asymmetrical hem. Tricia had gone elegant in a Betsey Johnson turquoise Battenberg lace slip dress and Hollywould black linen ankle-strap sandals decorated with turquoise and other colored beads and stones. She was paler than usual, but I wasn't sure if that was the strain of events or of seeing me.

"Goodness, isn't Kyle racking up the sweetie points," Cassady said as she shut the door behind me.

Tricia didn't say anything.

I wanted to make a joke, but I couldn't think of anything but how sorry I was that I was there under such excruciating circumstances—needing to work things out with Tricia, needing to talk to David, trying to do both without upsetting the family any further.

"Hey, Tricia," I said.

"Molly," was all I got in reply.

Richard chose that moment to descend the staircase, brandy snifter in his hand, playing lord of the manor to the hilt. "Hello, Molly, I didn't know you were coming by."

At least he hadn't expressed revulsion at my presence, which meant there was an excellent chance that Tricia's extreme displeasure with me hadn't been shared with the rest of her family. Richard wouldn't be inclined to skip an opportunity for a barb, even a veiled one. "Hello, Richard. Just came by to tempt your sister into stepping out for cocktails."

"Why not stay here and get drunk? It's much more efficient and we're very good at it." He kissed me on top of the head as he walked by and headed down the hallway. It was so long, I wasn't sure how much time to wait before judging him to be out of earshot. Plus, I'm not used to vaulted ceilings and how they affect acoustics. Most important, I didn't know how I was going to ask where David was.

Cassady came to my rescue, though I didn't realize it at first. "So, shall we?"

"Go?" I asked, a little concerned.

"Stay here and get drunk," she replied. "Or at least, begin here while we decide where to go."

Tricia turned without a word and walked in the opposite direction from Richard, assuming Cassady and I would follow, which we did. It was somewhere between a museum tour and the walk to the principal's office, given the formal set of Tricia's shoulders and her refusal to look back at us. I found myself taking great care not to scuff my feet as I walked, out of respect for the glistening floors and not my shoes.

Tricia led us into a cool, spacious room dominated by a Steinway concert grand and glass-fronted bookcases. A mahogany bar with matching stools swept in front of one wall and David was behind it. I was sure Frank Sinatra would appear momentarily and start singing "Well, Did You Evah?," but for now, David was the only occupant of the room.

Tricia seemed startled, but Cassady was pleased. I couldn't tell whether she'd scouted his location or taken a lucky guess, but the important thing was that I was in the same room with him at last. Now, the trick was to get him to talk.

"Hello," David said without much enthusiasm. "It's not much of a party, but you're welcome to join me," he continued, gesturing to the bar stools.

"You don't mind?" Tricia asked.

"I don't seem capable of minding anything anymore," he said with some frustration. I wasn't sure if he was referring to his sorrow over Lisbet's death or if his parents' doctor had him on something. I hoped it wasn't the latter, since he had a full highball glass in his hand.

"Good to see you, David," I said, sliding onto the end

stool, rather than placing myself directly in front of him and looking too eager.

"Especially good to see me neither in the hospital nor in jail," David agreed.

"Molly's been working very hard on keeping you out of the latter," Cassady pointed out, taking the stool right in front of him. Tricia sat between Cassady and me, but turned herself toward him and away from me.

"By way of thanks." He pulled a bottle out of the minifridge behind him.

"Davey, no," Tricia admonished, but he didn't listen. He expertly pulled the cork from a bottle of Veuve Cliquot and poured four glasses.

"As Tom Waits says, 'Champagne for my real friends, and real pain for my sham friends.'" He put one glass in front of each of us with a flourish, then picked up the last one himself.

I was relieved to see I wasn't the only one hesitating to pick up mine. Tricia gave him a withering look, but it didn't hit David until he'd taken a deep swig from his glass. He sighed. "I'm sorry. This is pretty inappropriate, isn't it."

"You never listen," Tricia said, her voice suddenly thick with repressed tears. "Why don't you ever listen?"

"Ease up, Tricia," he said through gritted teeth.

"I'm sorry you're in pain, but that's no excuse for being an idiot. People are only going to feel sorry for you for so long before they start getting annoyed with your stupidity."

I instinctively put my hand on her arm, not to stop her but to encourage her to go slow. I thought she was going to push my hand away, but she put her hand on mine and squeezed it. "I really don't know why, but people want to help you. And if Molly's going to help you, she needs to know the truth about you and Veronica on Friday afternoon."

I didn't trust myself to look at David or Tricia, so I looked at Cassady, whose surprised eyes met mine over Tricia's head. I could only imagine the pressures that had been building up in the family for the past few days and Tricia had clearly reached the breaking point.

"What're you talking about?"

"Did you have sex with Veronica Innes on Friday afternoon? And don't you pull any Clintonesque semantics with me. Yes or no."

David defiantly took another swig of champagne before saying, "Yes."

Tricia turned to me, inviting me to ask the next question. Startled, it took me a moment to jump in with, "Why?"

"Veronica and I were together a while back. She hunted me down Friday afternoon and told me this whole story about Lisbet leaving me, leaving the play, that she wasn't taking the engagement seriously. She was pretty damn persuasive."

"To the point that you slept with her?" I asked, trying not to sound too incredulous.

"I know I screwed up, if you'll pardon the expression."

"Because Lisbet caught you," I said.

"Yes. And because it wasn't as good as I remembered it, so it wasn't worth it." He slouched forward, elbows on the bar, rubbing his forehead with one hand. He made it all sound like a simple misunderstanding, but these relationships had to all be a heck of a lot deeper than he was letting on for passions to have gotten to the point where Lisbet wound up dead.

"What happened when Lisbet caught you?"

"She threw some stuff at Veronica and screamed at me."

"What did you do?" Tricia asked sternly.

"Begged her forgiveness, blamed it all on Veronica being a scheming tramp. Spin control, sister dear. Spin control." He tried to smile, but he couldn't muster it. "She went with it. After all, the two of them had been having trouble at the theater."

"Did you know Lisbet was thinking of leaving the play before Veronica told you?"

He shook his head. "I asked Lisbet about it. Once she'd stopped screaming. She said she'd had an interesting offer, but now she knew we needed to stay together, work things out."

I wanted to phrase my next question very carefully, lest I be accused of leading the witness. "You think that offer might have come from Jake Boone?"

"Jerk-off Jake? Lisbet wouldn't give him the time of day," David scoffed.

"She slept with him right before she was killed." I said it neutrally, not wanting to shape his reaction at all.

He shook his head. "No way."

"You embarrassed her by sleeping with Veronica, then embarrassed her again by carrying her out of the party. Then you fought with her and she took off her engagement ring. And you still don't think she could've been mad enough to want to get back at you by sleeping with Jake?"

This time, he just sneered. "No."

But, I thought as the goose bumps came back, he would've been mad enough to lash out. To lose control. To kill her. The Detective Cook boomerang effect was taking over and she wasn't even here. Why was it that the harder I tried to prove David innocent, the guiltier he looked? Because it was true?

"This is a surprise." Mrs. Vincent stepped in from the hallway, Teri Jon pink tweed suit impeccable, Judith Leiber satin clutch in hand, face impassive. "Good evening, ladies. Time to go, David."

Tricia spun on her stool to face her mother. "Where are you going?"

"Out for a little dinner, dear. I'm sure Ingrid will cook for you and your friends if you're hungry."

David came out from behind the bar, eyes down, avoiding his sister's questioning glance.

"You're going out?" Tricia asked, puzzled.

"Just a working meal. We're planning a little get-together, an opportunity for people to show David some support during this difficult time."

"Really." Tricia tried, but she couldn't suppress all the doubt in her voice.

"It was Rebecca's idea. I thought it was quite nice."

"Really," Tricia repeated. This time, there was no doubt, only ice. "I didn't realize. I would have made different plans," she continued, gesturing to us as she stood up.

Mrs. Vincent waved vaguely for Tricia to sit back down. "It's fine, dear. We can handle it."

Rebecca and Richard appeared in the doorway behind Mrs. Vincent. Richard had pulled himself together enough to get a jacket on. Rebecca looked like she was planning on auditioning for Junior League later that evening, in a positively sedate DKNY pink linen suit with a notched collar and tailored waist and Dolce & Gabbana eel-skin pumps.

"Are we ready? Dad's waiting," Rebecca said sweetly.

"Mother, I'd like to be included," Tricia said.

"Oh, dear, no need. I'm sure we'll get it all figured out." Mrs. Vincent smiled regally, turning back enough to take Rebecca's hand. "Rebecca's been such an unexpected comfort in all this. You girls have fun tonight." Rebecca and Mrs. Vincent walked away.

If Mrs. Vincent had realized where she'd be standing in thirty-six hours, I bet she would've been a lot nicer to her daughter. But the really big lessons are the ones you learn too late.

16

Some roar in pain and make their anguish known to the world. Some fall silent as they attempt to reconstruct the tortured path that brought them to this sorry moment. But when I'm hung-over, I curl up in a ball and pray for my brain to stop rubbing against the inside of my skull, especially that jagged spot right above my left eye. I want to shave that puppy off, even if it means not being able to do long division or waltz anymore. After all, how often do I use those skills these days?

We hadn't started out drinking with the goal of overdoing it. Well, I hadn't. Looking back, difficult as it was to do that with anything approaching clarity, Tricia probably had that in mind all along. Cassady and I went along for the ride.

The ride crash-landed in my apartment in the wee hours of the morning. Tricia had been all for painting the town red, but Cassady had gotten almost strident about her sworn duty to deliver me safely home and what Kyle was going to do to her if I got popped on her watch. Besides, the cocktails at my apartment were less expensive. So we finished off the Veuve Clicquot because it seemed a sin to waste it, piled into a cab, and went to my place.

Once we were inside, Tricia announced that she was sick of hypocrisy and wanted to drink to the truth. My response was to make a pitcher of martinis. A martini pitcher is the best lie detector there is; you see if the story you get when the pitcher's full matches the story you get once it's empty.

So the first pitcher we dedicated to truth. Tricia was bold enough to tell me, "Truth is, I'm still mad at you, but I'm madder at my mother, so you get a free pass for the evening."

"I can handle that," I promised.

The second pitcher was dedicated to our families and the insidious ways in which they mold us. The third pitcher went to the many ways love goes bad. I think. And the fourth pitcher went to . . . some worthy cause, I'm sure. It got pretty hazy by then.

In fact, my next semicoherent thought was, "Someone's stealing my shoes." It didn't matter that I vaguely knew I was in my own apartment, my shoes—my beautiful Jimmy Choo shoes—were in danger and I had to act. But acting required sitting up and sitting up caused all sorts of unpleasant sensations like my stomach pitching and the room yawing and a hallucination of Kyle. Except it wasn't a hallucination. Kyle was real. Beautiful, slightly out of focus, and real.

He shook my foot once more for emphasis and I realized I was stretched out on my couch, fully dressed, a half-filled martini glass still in my hand. "Neat trick," he observed. He took the glass from me and set it on the coffee table. "C'mon. You'll feel better after you have some breakfast."

"What time is it?" I asked as he helped me to my feet. My mouth tasted like thawing Alaskan tundra and I could only imagine how bad my hair and face looked. I felt like I hadn't moved in days. It had to be almost noon.

"Seven. Danny let me in."

"Sadist!" I croaked.

"You gotta go to work."

"I'm calling in sick."

"Wimp."

He walked over to the kitchen and my stuffy nose belatedly picked up on the smell of broiling meat. My stomach shuddered. "What's that?"

Kyle checked the broiler. "Steak. How do you like your eggs? My dad always used to do a raw egg with a little hair of the dog, but that'd probably kill you." He grinned, enjoying the image, and put a frying pan on the stove.

"I am not eating eggs."

"You'll feel better. Speak now or take 'em sunny side up." He cracked two eggs into the pan without waiting for an answer.

"Have you come to torment me?" I tried to sound gruff, but I was actually delighted at this glimpse of him. The few nights he'd stayed over, we'd gone out to breakfast. When he hadn't had to leave before breakfast for a call. But he seemed quite comfortable in the kitchen. My kitchen. I found that thrilling. It almost gave me my appetite back.

"I actually came to tell you that Jake Boone called the precinct to file a complaint against you."

"What?"

"I took care of it, but it was all about you calling and threatening him."

"I told you—I told him it wasn't me. He's cooking up some stupid story to make himself sound innocent while *he's* threatening *me*."

"But it's a woman on your answering machine."

"He has a girlfriend who would happily harass me for him. She knows I'm on to him, even though I told her she was wrong. I'll bet you she was also the woman at the Algonquin last night."

He poked at the egg. "How about Cassady and Tricia?"

"I'm sure they agree with me."

"How do they like their eggs?" My confusion showed on my face because his grin got wider. "They're in your room. If you can walk that far, go tell them breakfast is ready."

There's great comfort in knowing that while you look like hell, your friends look worse. By the time Cassady and Tricia had dragged themselves off my bed, where they had collapsed fully dressed but without martini glasses, I had managed a glass of cranberry juice and was beginning to think I'd live. Kyle had made steak and eggs for all of us and was having trouble chewing his, his grin kept getting so broad.

"Good thinking to stay here last night," he commended Cassady and Tricia.

Tricia was holding her head up with both hands, acclimating to the aroma of her breakfast before daring to taste it. "It wasn't a conscious decision. More like an unconscious decision."

Cassady was tearing into her steak with relish. "This is delicious, Kyle. I may throw it all up in twenty minutes, but I'm enjoying it now."

Tricia moaned, Kyle laughed, and I got the coffeepot. I had that awful nagging feeling that something had happened last night that shouldn't have, but I couldn't put my finger on it. And we were all fully clothed with no drug paraphernalia, sex toys, or Krispy Kreme boxes in evidence, so how sinful could it have been?

Tricia saw the look. "What is it?"

"Blank spot."

"Only one? I have several and none of them in the right

place. I still have to go home and have words with my mother."

"Can I come watch?" Cassady asked.

"There's no point, because I'll lose my nerve by the time I get there."

"Eat your steak and you'll have the strength to whup her good," Kyle suggested. He got up from the table and rinsed his plate in the sink.

Tricia looked at him, inspired, then picked up her knife and fork and started eating. The image of her in her deeply wrinkled Betsey Johnson and bedhead, munching happily on the steak while dreaming of confronting her mother, was heartening to us all.

Kyle had to leave, so he dispensed instructions for us to stay sober and for me to stay away from Jake Boone. I couldn't believe that idiot had called the cops on me. I couldn't wait to return the favor, but I didn't have enough proof. Yet.

"I vaguely remember discussing Jake Boone last night," Cassady said, holding her coffee mug to her forehead like a compress. "But other than agreeing that he was a murdering bastard, I can't recall deciding on a course of action."

"You really think Jake did it?" Tricia asked, actually picking up her steak and gnawing on the bone.

"He gave Lisbet an ultimatum about leaving your brother, which, despite the fact that he slept with Veronica—" An idea hit me and I had to pause a moment to marvel at its beauty. "I bet he sent Veronica to seduce David and then made sure Lisbet walked in on them."

"Veronica would have done that for him?" Cassady asked.

"She wanted David. It served her agenda as well." I drummed on the edge of the table as I saw the pieces coming together. "And even then, Lisbet wouldn't leave David, which infuriated Jake, so they're both mad at the party, which explains the floor show. And afterward, Lisbet does fight with David, Jake thinks he's home free, Lisbet even sleeps with him, but then she tells him she's going back to David. So he freaks and kills her."

Tricia and Cassady were engrossed, nodding supportively. I tried to imagine Detective Cook and Kyle sitting in their places, nodding just as supportively, and I couldn't quite get there. But I was close.

"So where does Lara fit in all this?" Tricia asked.

"That's it! Lara," I said, drumming a little faster. "She thinks she's helping Jake but he's using her. And if she finds that out, she becomes the weak link."

"So Lara's the woman shadowing you." Cassady leaned over and pressed her hand over mine to stop my drumming. Abashed, I slid my hands into my lap. It was true; the drumming wasn't helping anyone's headache. "Who's the woman threatening Jake?"

"He's probably making it up. Or maybe Veronica's figured out he used her and she's ready for her pound of flesh. She's a wrathful sort of gal."

"So what happens next?" Tricia asked, licking her fingers.

"I have to talk to Lara without Jake, see if I can shake her loose."

"I really appreciate what you're doing, Molly, the article aside. My family doesn't deserve it, but . . ." A wave of pain that had nothing to do with our night's debauchery swept over her and a memory unexpectedly swam to the surface. Tricia sitting on my couch, her martini glass balanced on her knees, proclaiming that Einstein had proved it was impossible to be truly happy.

Cassady was lying on the floor at that point, her ankles

crossed and propped up on the edge of the coffee table, try-ing to balance her glass on her forehead. "Missed that sci-ence class."

"Einstein said we could never travel at the speed of light because as a body approaches the speed of light, its mass in-creases to the point that it slows down and can't achieve the necessary speed."

"If you say so," I encouraged from the armchair in which I sat sideways, my legs over one arm and my head on the other. Very comfortable, though it would make a chiroprac-tor flee in horror.

"Same way with happiness. The closer you get to achiev-ing that moment of transcendence, the greater mass you take on because you start thinking of all the things that can go wrong and whether you deserve happiness and other people pull back on you and you slow down and never get there." She'd lifted her glass, "To Albert."

Now, Cassady put her arm around Tricia's shoulders and I took her hand in mine. I wanted to say something profound and comforting about how it was going to be all right, that we'd get through this, her family would recover. But I won-dered if the Vincents didn't have their own physics prob-lems, with the force of the impact of Lisbet's death having revealed stress fractures that undermined the stability of the whole structure. But we could help her through that, too. As long as the three of us stayed on the same side, we could work these things through.

The one thing we couldn't get around in our friendship was that we're not all the same size. Not being able to freely trade clothes cuts down on squabbling to a certain extent, but it also forced my cohorts to face the long trip home in yesterday's clothes. As parting gifts, I gave them both Advil and hugs. The two of them left arm in bedraggled arm, a sight Mrs. Mayburn and my other neighbors were bound to whisper about for at least a month.

I went to stand in the shower until the hot water was gone. Even after two scrubbings with my vanilla aromatherapy bar, my body still shrank from anything but a sweater and jeans, but I forced it into my trusty Banana Republic brown flute skirt and white ballet neck sweater, subscribing to the theory that if you look good, you feel better. I'm not sure if Einstein came up with that one. Might've been Newton. Or Mizrahi.

Deciding that a massive infusion of espresso would put the finishing touch on my reconstruction, I slipped on my Kate Spade chocolate and lavender spectator pumps and headed out to Starbucks. The Starbucks across the street from Jake's apartment building.

My first New York boss, Rob, taught me to always be friendly to doormen and assistants because they have more control and more information than anyone ever gives them credit for. On my previous forays to Jake's, I'd been pleasant to the doorman and I hoped it was about to pay off.

I waited until I could feel my espresso double shot pulsing in my temples, then darted across the street. It was a decent May day, bright and warm. Under all the diesel fumes, the air still smelled lightly of the night's dampness burning off. Steve, the doorman, looked quite comfortable in his epauleted overcoat, but he was a gaunt greyhound of a guy who seemed like he never broke a sweat, whatever the weather or situation.

This was crossing the line from flirting with danger to making a blatant pass at it, if my theory about Jake and Lara was right. Further, if Jake had been serious about trying to get me in trouble with the police, I wasn't going to get very far with Steve. But since Kyle and Detective Cook hadn't bought into the Jake theory yet, I had to see what I could do to make it more attractive for everyone.

Steve raised a gloved hand to the brim of his cap as I approached. Good start. "Good morning, ma'am."

"Good morning, Steve. Is Mr. Boone home?" I asked cheerfully.

"Mr. Boone left two days ago," he replied without hesitation. Another good sign.

"I didn't realize." I played along. "No wonder he's been hard to get a hold of."

"Ms. Del Guidice left last night."

"Oh," I said again, with genuine surprise this time. "Gone to meet him for a little lover's getaway. How nice for them."

Steve shook his head. "It was less a getaway than a 'get away from me,' best I could tell," he said, his voice dropping to a confidential volume. "She walked him out when he left and all but gave him the bum's rush."

"Wow. I saw them together Sunday morning and they seemed their usual happy selves," I replied, leaving out a few small details like his pass at me, her stoned dancing in the living room, and then Lara giving me the bum's rush while the other doorman was on duty.

"You're a new friend, right? 'Cause I haven't seen you around here before this weekend."

"We met in Southampton Friday," I admitted. "But I thought they were charming."

"They have their moments. You must've caught 'em in a good one."

"When do you think they'll be back?"

"He'll come back eventually. We might've seen the last of her." My expression must have been more alarmed than I'd intended, because he hurried to clarify. "She just had that look of a woman who was done, you know? And I've seen it a lot. On his women especially."

So he was referring to Jake's romantic track record, not any homicidal leanings. "Do you have any idea where they are? I need to talk to her. About a project I'm doing."

"I'd say he's crashing with a friend and she's somewhere expensive with his credit card. But that's just a guess," Steve shrugged.

"Thank you."

Steve touched his brim again. "I'll tell him you came by whenever I see him. May I get you a cab?"

"No, thanks. I'm going to walk a little."

I was only about ten blocks from the office and I thought the walk might help my hangover as well as my thought process. Besides, I love walking in the city, throwing myself into the river of people moving up and down the island all day and most of the night, and letting the current carry me along. It's not good for the shoes, but it's good for the soul. The pace and the size of the city make it easy to feel disconnected, but when you walk down the sidewalk and just spend a few minutes watching the huge spectrum of people rushing along right beside you, worrying about being disconnected, too, sometimes that's a connection in itself and you feel part of something larger and more important than your own panics and problems. Maybe you're just a fish swimming along with a school, maybe you're a star in a constellation, maybe you're part of the human race. Whichever, you're not alone.

I found myself humming "Takin' It to the Streets" as I walked, watched faces, and thought. I'd come over to Jake and Lara's on Sunday, he'd left Sunday night. Then I'd gone back yesterday and she'd gotten all freaked out about it "being me." I'd thought she'd meant the one threatening Jake, but could she have meant the woman she thought Jake was cheating with? The idea was preposterous to me, but—not to pat myself on the back—I could see how Lara might construe events that way. Maybe she knew he'd been up to something when he was courting Lisbet and then I popped up. I almost felt bad for her. But then I thought of her stalking me to the Algonquin and I felt less bad.

But I felt worse again when I got to the office and saw Genevieve swooping to intercept me before I'd reached my desk. I had an absurd impulse to run to the desk, slap it, and yell "Safe!" but I was certain no one would find that nearly as amusing as I would. Eileen might have goosed the subscription numbers since she'd come, but she'd killed office morale. Everyone worked with the fear of the pink slip foremost in their minds. Being fearful for my mortality and my basic hatred of the woman pushed that one down a few notches for me.

"Late!" Genevieve proclaimed, tapping her watch.

"I'm been working," I answered with a patience she didn't deserve. "On the story. Not much I can do sitting here in the office," I explained. "But you can tell Eileen that I think I'm very close."

"Really," she said doubtfully.

"Really," I said cheerfully. Then Genevieve handed me a message slip. On it, Genevieve had taken a message for Eileen. *From Veronica Innes. Re: The Article. Message: Why hasn't anyone called me yet?* Across the message slip, Eileen had scrawled, probably in Genevieve's blood, *Molly, Call her now!*

I released the slip, letting it drift down on to my desk. The person I was least interested in talking to was the one most interested in talking to me. I was beginning to think I could divide the world into those who wanted to be in the article and those who didn't. "I'm not sure she's even part of the story. Why should I call her?"

"Orders," Genevieve replied.

"Okay," I said, looking for the magic word to make Genevieve go away. That apparently wasn't it. "What?" I asked, trying not to be shrill. I was beginning to wonder if part of Eileen's shrillness came from having Genevieve in her face all day.

"Call," Genevieve chirped.

"No."

Genevieve put her hands on her hips. I decided in that split second that if she wagged her finger in my face, I was going to bite it off. But all she said was, "Molly," in what was probably her version of low and menacing. It was only slightly less chirpy than usual.

I wanted to tell her she wasn't the boss of me. I wanted to tell her that her prep-school sense of entitlement was the most irritating of many irritating traits. I wanted to feed her the message slip in individual strips, like high-carb pasta. But all of that required more energy than I wanted to devote to her at the moment, so I switched gears. I leaned across the desk and said, "Let me tell you a j-school secret."

Her eyes went wide and she leaned in eagerly. "'Kay."

"Never go into an interview unprepared. Because the question you forget to ask will turn out to be the most important question for your entire piece."

She nodded slowly. "Right."

"So I'm going to take some time to prepare my list of questions. Then I will call Ms. Innes. I'm sure we'll all find the experience worth waiting for."

"Absolutely." Genevieve flounced back to her desk, leaving a cloud of Kenneth Cole's Black over mine.

I sank into my chair. Dale Bennett, the rotund editorial

assistant who sat the next desk over, so fresh out of school he still had blue books to use as scrap paper, threw me a sidelong glance. "I don't remember learning that in j-school. Where'd you go?"

"I didn't. But I will go to hell for lying, if that makes you feel better."

Dale quickly went back to his work and I attempted to go back to mine. I did some research on Lisbet's family, just in case there really was an article in all this, but the more I worked, the more frustrated I got. I channeled that into making phone calls to the most expensive hotels in the city, looking for Lara Del Guidice, but I couldn't find her. Finally, I switched over to reading letters for my next column and that made me feel much better. Isn't that the whole attraction of advice columns, not so much "Hey, I was wondering that myself!" as "Hey, I'm not as messed up as these people!"?

I was engrossed in sorting out a letter that was filled with so many exes on all sides that I thought I was going to have to draw a family tree like in *One Hundred Years of Solitude* when the phone rang. I grabbed it halfheartedly; statistically, it was someone I was going to hang up on anyway.

"Guess where you're having dinner tonight," Cassady demanded.

"The McDonald's in Times Square."

"Why there?"

"It's the most depressing thing I could think of."

"No depression. Only joy. Acappella in TriBeCa. You and Tricia. Eight-thirty."

"Any particular reason?"

"So you can ever so casually run into me and my dinner date. He and I arrive at eight."

"And who is this yummy man we have to come inspect so early in the game?"

"Jake Boone."

"What?" It was so loud that not only did the meerkats rise up, several of them considered bolting from the bullpen. I actually felt compelled to cover the phone and yell, "Sorry, guys," before returning to the conversation. Which I did by repeating "What?" at an only slightly lower volume. "How did this happen?"

"Remember those blank spots we were discussing this morning?"

"I remember having them, but obviously, I don't remember what they are or they wouldn't be blank spots."

"Think about this. Think of me with the phone in my hand, proclaiming that I want to finance a film."

In a queasy swirl of recollection, it came back. Somewhere between pitcher number three and pitcher number four, it had occurred to us that the one foolproof way to entice Jake was to give him what he wanted most in the world. Not sex or fame but money to produce his next movie, which would then bring him all the sex and fame he wanted. So Cassady had gotten on the phone and left Jake a message, proclaiming that, while she'd given him a hard time about his cinematic theories, she hadn't been able to stop thinking about him since meeting him and she wanted to discuss being one of his backers. She'd left her cell phone number, which Jake had called this morning and, after questioning her sincerity only once, he'd asked her to meet him for dinner.

"Cassady Lynch, you magnificent vixen. We'll be there. With bells on." Or whatever it is you wear to crash dinner with a murderer.

17

It's funny how you use a phrase for most of your life without really thinking about how it came into the language or how its meaning might have been diluted by time. And then, something happens that changes the import of that phrase for you forever. Don't expect to hear me talk about "deer in the headlights" again.

I had some trepidation about calling Tricia to arrange the dinner. What if by the time her hangover lifted, she decided she was more upset with me than with her mother after all? But I had to call her. She was invested in this, too, and I couldn't exactly go into Acappella by myself without arousing suspicion.

"I'd be delighted," she replied when I laid out the plan.

"And yet, you sound quite grim," I pointed out.

"They planned their little party, their marvelous show of support for David. And didn't include me in it one bit. You know, I'm not the one who's been accused of murder here, but I'm the one being shunned. I swear to God, Molly, I wish Rebecca would go back to drinking and messing up."

"Why?" I couldn't quite see the connection.

"Because sober, she's a little too perfect to bear. I'll pick you up at eight and I might have calmed down by then. But no guarantees."

When I met her at the cab in front of my building, she was smoldering. She looked fantastic in her flutter-sleeved Matthew Williamson red jersey dress, a keyhole cut in front and back, but she was still upset, too. She'd contained it, but she hadn't gotten over it.

"So when is this big event?" I asked as we got into the cab, aware I was stepping onto thin ice.

She slammed the cab door for emphasis and/or catharsis. "Tomorrow afternoon. A luncheon."

"You're kidding."

"If I were kidding, it would mean I saw some humor in the situation, which I don't."

"But that's no notice at all."

"The funeral's on Friday and it has to be before that. Mother and Rebecca are sure that our true friends will drop whatever they're doing and rush over to show their love. It's a test. Everything with my mother is a test."

I wasn't sure whether that was a conversation it was wise to have just now, when we should be psyching ourselves up to deceive and snare Jake. Then again, I didn't want to ignore her pain. I aimed down the middle. "Are you going?"

"I haven't decided yet. If you can put Jake behind bars tonight, I might go. If Jake pins it on Davey tonight, I might still go." She smiled weakly and patted me on the knee. "No pressure."

As we lurched down the West Side Highway, our cabbie driving like he was immersed in some marvelous video game that required he never come to a complete stop, I tried to anticipate how we were going to maneuver Jake into confessing. At the moment, it seemed simpler to walk across the Hudson River, which taunted me outside the cab window. It might have been nice to have Lara in the equation, but I still hadn't been able to find her. As my dad always says, "Do what you can where you are with what you have."

Where we were now was on Hudson Street in TriBeCa. Acappella is a marvelous Northern Italian restaurant with fantastic food and exquisite service, big on charm and low on lights. We stepped into the muted glow of the interior and Tricia gave her name to the maître d'. He asked us with a lovely, rolling Italian accent to have a seat in the cluster of burgundy leather settees behind him while he checked on our table. A compact and beautifully supplied bar was just across from us, its stools occupied by snugly dressed young women being doted on by well-dressed young men. I studied the bottles behind the bar because I didn't dare peer into the dining room for Cassady and Jake.

Tricia perched nervously beside me. "You think they're here?"

"I hope so. Otherwise, I don't have enough appetite to do this place justice." Then again, maybe it wasn't lack of hunger. Maybe it was nerves.

"This morning, I swore I'd never drink again. But right now, a shot might stop my heart palpitations."

"*Bellas?*" The maître d' reappeared and gave us a little bow, indicating we should follow him.

The seating area, dominated by an immense painting of an intense Italian nobleman, was even dimmer than the bar and it took my eyes a moment to adjust. I was still blinking when, to my great relief, I heard Cassady exclaim, "What are you doing here?"

She stood up at her table, radiant even in the dimness in a David Meister psychedelic silk halter, her hair caught loosely at the crown of her head. She looked fully prepared to seduce Jake into a confession, should that prove necessary.

The maître d' stopped politely. "Am I surprised the most beautiful women in my restaurant know each other?" He folded his hands in front of him and waited while Tricia and I put on a show of hugging Cassady in greeting.

Only after I'd hugged her did I look down at her dinner companion. The pained look on his face helped me react with surprise. "Jake. Hi," I said flatly. I'd figured he wouldn't be happy to see me, but he looked disgusted. "I'm sorry," I backpedaled, like I thought I'd stumbled on to some lover's tryst. "I had no idea . . ."

"Hello, Jake," Tricia said with extreme politeness.

The maître d' pointed out the empty chairs at their table. "What a lucky man, *signore*, you could dine with all these pretty ladies."

Jake cocked his head at me. "Your boyfriend know you're here? 'Cause he told me to stay away from you."

"I tried to tell you last night, Jake, it wasn't me."

The maître d' cleared his throat. "Or, you could have your table right over here, *bellas*."

Jake stood up and dropped his napkin on the table. "No, really," he said a little too firmly. "I insist. Join us."

Wary glances were exchanged all around, including with the maître d', before Tricia and I moved to sit down. Acappella is one of those places that seems to have slightly more than one impeccably trained waiter per table, so there's always some gentle soul appearing out of nowhere, tending to your need, and disappearing back into the darkness. The moment we reached for the chairs, two waiters materialized to seat us properly, hand us our napkins, and assure that we were properly situated.

"We're not intruding?" I asked, needing some sort of explosive to break the ice that was spreading from Jake's side of the table.

"Jake and I are discussing his next film. I'm going to invest," Cassady said sunnily.

"A short or a feature, Jake?" Tricia inquired.

"A feature," he replied, but not as sullenly as he might have.

"Self-financed? That's ambitious. My hat's off to you," I said.

"I'd rather have your checkbook," he replied, warming to the topic. He'd recognized the ambush for what it was, but he'd expected us to launch in on him immediately. Now he was starting to relax a little, thinking he'd been wrong. Silly boy.

"Would this be part of your wordless cinema?" I asked. "We didn't get that far in our talk about the article."

"You were telling us about that at David's party," Tricia added.

"Yes. Sorry about your loss, by the way," Jake said with unexpected grace.

"Thanks. It's so insane. She didn't have an enemy in the world, we just don't understand . . ." Tricia grabbed her napkin and dabbed at her eyes. Either she could cry on cue as well as Veronica or those were real tears for her almost-sister-in-law, or for her brother, or for the whole mess.

Jake sat quietly a moment, struggling with something. I managed to keep my mouth closed and let him work it out without any reinforcing stiletto through the toe from Cassady. "I don't mean to throw mud, but she did have enemies," he said quietly. "If they still haven't figured out who did this, it's important you know that."

I stared at Jake, not because of what he was saying, but the way he was saying it. I'd seen nothing but braggart and blowhard from him. This was a gentleness that was shocking. Maybe it was something he turned on when he wanted to charm people; even with that in mind, it worked.

He stared back at me. "I told you about Veronica. They weren't cool with each other at all."

"But it wasn't bad enough for Veronica to kill her, was it?" I asked, scoffing at a theory I'd held dearly for a while.

He shrugged. "People do stupid things."

"Like sleep with the guest of honor at her own engagement party?" I asked.

Jake groaned and turned to try to explain to Tricia, but then he could see she already knew. His look hardened as it slid back to me. "Who told you?"

"Veronica."

He twisted his napkin angrily. "She's just trying to make me look bad. Who else have you told?"

"Doesn't matter. What does is, why wasn't that enough? Why didn't that fulfill your ultimatum?"

Jake looked at Cassady, hurt. "You set me up."

"That doesn't mean I won't invest in your film," she assured him. "Unless you're going to jail."

"Why would I go to jail?" he asked, his voice getting a little too loud for such an intimate restaurant.

"Why did she have to leave, Jake?" I persisted.

"What're you talking about?"

"The card in the flowers. 'Leave and live.' "

"I'm the one who's leaving." Jake stood and threw his napkin on the table.

Two waiters and the maître d' teleported into position around the table, the maître d' in emergency mode. "*Signori, signore,* some wine, perhaps? A drink from the bar? Tony, where's their antipasti?"

Jake pushed past them and headed for the front door. I jumped up and followed him, trusting my far more diplomatic friends to be able to smooth things over with the restaurant staff. Jake blew through the doors and out onto the sidewalk, oblivious to other patrons and pedestrians. He started to walk out into traffic to make sure a cab stopped for him, but I grabbed him by the back of the jacket and yanked him onto the sidewalk.

"Jake, listen to me for just a minute."

"Why, you gonna read me my rights?"

"I'm trying to make sense of what's going on here. You're getting threatened, so am I. I want to know why."

"I bet you're getting threatened for asking people nosy questions."

"And you're getting threatened for being classless enough to post footage of a dead girl on your Web site."

Something, perhaps some whiff of his own culpability, caught him. His breathing slowed and his jaw relaxed slightly. "I made mistakes. But I don't deserve any of this."

"What mistakes?"

"The flowers. I shouldn't have forced her to make a decision right then. She was crazy—the party, the play opening—I shouldn't have pushed her to choose."

"Between you and David."

Jake's jaw actually dropped. "Is that what you think this was? Some warring lovers' trope?" He laughed bitterly.

"Forgive my confusion, but you did sleep with her after she broke up with David."

"Because she invited me to. C'mon. I'd have to be embalmed to pass up a shot at that. You saw her, right? Well, you shoulda seen her naked."

A wave of vertigo ran through me. Was I really that far off or was he playing me? "The decision didn't have anything to do with David?"

"Only in terms of her talking to him about it. And she kept dragging her feet about it, which is why I pushed her."

"Then what did she have to decide, Jake?"

"To leave the play to be in my movie. And live more fully as an artist."

I wanted to laugh, but I didn't, thankfully. "Your movie?"

"I wanted Lisbet to star in my movie. And I had a shot at this great DP coming off another friend's film so I had to move fast. She had to drop out of the play to make the schedule work."

"So when she called Abby and said she was leaving the play, it was because of your movie."

"Until that stupid cow Veronica seduced David and Lisbet realized she couldn't leave him alone for two minutes, much less go shoot with me in the Berkshires for two weeks, so she caved on me and told Abby never mind."

"This is all about your stupid movie?"

Jake leaned into me. I think the only reason he didn't hit me was my gender and even then, he was struggling. "It's not stupid."

"It can't be worth killing over."

"I didn't kill her!"

"Of course you did. You banged her in the pool house, made your little sex film, and figured you were golden. But then she said no, she was just having a little fun and she didn't care about you or your stupid feature. So you picked up the champagne bottle and bashed her brains in."

"The technical term is 'blunt force trauma,'" the voice behind me said. I didn't have to turn around to identify it and I didn't want to turn around because I didn't trust myself.

"Who the hell are you?" Jake demanded over my shoulder.

"Detective Cook, Suffolk County Homicide." She stepped up even with me, but I moved away. I didn't want Jake to think I was working for her.

"You met this weekend," I prompted.

"I met a lot of people this weekend and I'm trying to forget you all." Jake sneered at me.

"Are you following him or me?" I asked Detective Cook.

"I'm pursuing an investigation," she said, eyes on Jake.

"Well, investigate this," Jake suggested with a grab at his crotch, " 'cause I'm outta here."

He took a step closer to the curb, arm up for a cab. There was one on the other side of the street and I was worried it was going to swing around and pick him up before I could convince him not to go, so I stepped up with him. Detective Cook closed in on his other side. We were standing three abreast on the corner as the SUV at the curb on West Broadway peeled away and came right at us. The headlights were so bright I couldn't see the driver. Even so, I couldn't believe the SUV wasn't even trying to make the turn until it was almost too late, until people were screaming and Detective Cook was shoving us as hard as she could and I could feel the heat of the engine under the hood as the SUV clipped us, sending us to the pavement in a tangle of flailing limbs.

Somehow, we rolled out of its path as it roared up onto the sidewalk, scraping against several planters, then back down onto Chambers. It roared off as I tried to stand up. People were rushing from everywhere to help us. "Get the license!" I yelled as someone grabbed me and told me not to try to stand. Arms eased me back down to the pavement where Jake was sitting, stunned, his nose bleeding. On the other side of him, eyes closed, her left leg bent at an unnatural angle, Detective Cook lay silent.

18

"You think they were after you? You conceited twit."

"How many death threats have you gotten in the past three days, big guy? Huh? Bet I got you beat by a mile."

"Shut up, both of you, or I'll have you arrested for disturbing the peace."

"Look, just because we thought you were dead, don't expect us to go all soft and respectful now," I snapped at Detective Cook. Even before the paramedics had arrived, she'd come around, roaring in pain and anger, shouting directions, and still trying to grill Jake. Loath as I am to admit it, I had to sit back in admiration. Then again, I was probably in shock.

Now we were gathered around Detective Cook's bed in the ER at NYU Downtown Hospital, while Kyle ran interference with the responding officers from the First Precinct. Tricia and Cassady were doing their best to move the medical process along and get us all released. In the eye of this storm, Jake was still protesting that he had left Lisbet completely sexually satisfied and very much alive and, other than Veronica, he had no idea who could have killed her and why. Detective Cook continued to lay out the outstanding quality of Jake's motive and opportunity. And I tried to figure out which one of us the SUV had been aiming at, which had turned into an absurd roundelay of bragging about how many people hated us and why each of us was a prime candidate for hit-and-run target of the year.

When Kyle came in, Tricia and Cassady on his heels, we managed to settle down for a moment or two, but the combination of painkillers and adrenaline the three of us were wrestling with was pretty unwieldy. Especially Detective Cook, who had a fractured leg and a suspected concussion. Jake and I had lots of bruises and cuts, but we were going home. Kyle informed Detective Cook she had to stay in the hospital, at least for the night.

"I have a case to run!" she protested.

"We've got a partial plate and I'll let you know as soon as we get a meaningful hit. I'll call Myerson and see if he wants to come up. There'll be a uniform outside your room tonight, as a precaution."

"You think she's the target?" Jake complained. "Why don't you people understand? She wanted to kill me!"

"Why're you so sure the driver was a woman?" Kyle asked.

"Because a man would've gotten the job done right."

Tricia made a high, strangled sound of disgust and Cassady wagged a finger at Jake. "You say that with four women in striking distance? Not as smart as I'd hoped you were, Booney."

"Hard to imagine someone wants to kill him, isn't it?" I asked.

A large, unhappy nurse who walked like her feet had been sore since the Nixon Administration pulled back the curtain to join our party. She had an intimidating syringe in her free hand. "Ten seconds to clear out. Otherwise, you each get one of these and spend the night with the detective."

"Charming as that offer is," I said, backing out immediately. I gave Detective Cook a little wave she didn't bother returning. Jake, Tricia, and Cassady followed me, but Kyle lingered for a moment. I hoped it was official business and just kept walking.

"If this keeps up," Tricia pointed out, "we'll have visited every ER in Manhattan in another two years. We could have T-shirts. 'The Molly Forrester ER Tour.'"

"To her credit," Cassady countered, "I have many more doctors in my Rolodex than I used to, which I deeply appreciate." To illustrate her point, she flashed us a newly won business card before sliding it into her purse.

"Somebody's trying to kill me!" Jake whined, loudly enough that a doctor detached himself from the admissions desk and started over to us. Cassady shook her head at the doctor and Tricia and I put our arms around Jake, ushering him quickly down the hallway and pinning him against a vending machine.

"Jake, I want you to tell me who you think it was. Because I'm going to find her and help her get it right," I threatened.

"I don't know. I'd been thinking it was you threatening me this whole time and Lara thought so, too. But unless you're really twisted and set this whole thing up, it's gotta be someone else."

"I'm plenty twisted, but it wasn't me. Where's Lara?" We needed to find her and see if her story overlapped properly with his.

"Home, I guess."

"No, she's not. Doorman Steve said she left."

"Left you in your hour of need. That's cold," Cassady observed.

"He left first," I pointed out.

"Left her behind," Tricia said.

"No one was threatening *her*!" Jake would have happily squeezed himself up into the vending machine and spent the rest of the night between the stale Kit Kat bars and petrified Juicy Fruit if it meant getting away from us.

Getting away. What if that's what Lara was doing? "Did Lara know you slept with Lisbet before she was killed?"

"I didn't tell her, did you?" he snarled at me.

"No, but what if someone else did? Who else knows?"

Jake shook his head emphatically. "Just Veronica. And Lara won't speak to her. Won't speak to any of my exes."

"Poor girl travels in a pretty small circle," Cassady said.

Jake was too beaten-up to respond. "There was nobody else."

"Nobody but the person who saw you walk out of the pool house. The person who went in to see what you'd been doing and found Lisbet, figured it all out, and was mad enough to kill her for it."

Jake slumped as he envisioned Lara committing the murder. Tricia mumbled, "Dear God," and turned away. For her that path led back to David again. But I was headed in a third direction. The woman who'd been calling and threatening Jake. Could she have been the one? And she was worried that there was something in Jake's footage that could incriminate her. That's why she'd demanded that Jake shut the site down, not out of respect for Lisbet but to keep anyone from going over it too carefully.

"You still have all your footage?" I asked Jake.

"Of course. I archive everything," he said in a tone that implied of all I'd accused him of since we'd met, that was the worst.

"I want to see it. Everything." I turned to Tricia and

Cassady. "You guys can head home and I'll call you as soon as I can."

I half-expected lip from Cassady, but it was Tricia who dished up the attitude with an extra-large scoop. "You must have hit your head harder than they realized if you think we're going to sit out this round. In fact, I think we should have the doctors keep you overnight and we'll take it from here. Cassady?"

Cassady slid the business card back out of her purse. "I have a new friend who's very eager to do me a favor."

"All right," I acquiesced, "just let me find Kyle and tell him we're leaving. Stay right here."

I found Kyle coming out of the ER, looking for us. I started to explain what we were going to do and he held up a hand, cutting me off. "Go home and stay there."

"I can't," I protested, "I have to see this through."

"No, you don't. That's my job. Cook's job. Other people's jobs, not yours."

There was a lot I still didn't know about Kyle, but I knew when not to argue with him. His brilliant blue eyes go hard and dark and God Himself would have trouble swaying him. Arguing with him was just going to upset us both more and waste valuable time, so I said, "Fine. Can Jake go, too?"

"You've all given statements, you can all go."

"Great. Thanks." I turned and went back to retrieve the others.

"Molly," he said behind me.

"I know," I said, stopping but not turning around. "The job's hard enough without my getting in the way."

He caught my arm and spun me around. "The job's hard enough without the next place I pick you up being the morgue. I'm trying to protect you, don't you get that?"

I was grateful, but I was angry, too. I was trying to protect myself and people I loved and even some people I didn't particularly care for who needed protecting, just because it was the right thing to do. But I wasn't a member of the Protector's Club, so I was supposed to sit quietly in the dungeon and wait to be saved. The hell with that. I had a more complete picture of what had been happening than anyone else did and I was going to finish what I'd started because I'd promised one of my two best friends I would.

What I told Kyle was, "Yes." What I did was walk away slowly and then cram Tricia, Cassady, Jake, and myself into a cab and go straight to Jake's. I figured we had a little time before Kyle called to check up on me and I needed to use it wisely. I wanted to see Jake's extra footage, discover what secrets it held, and pinpoint our hit-and-runner accordingly.

The flaw with that plan was that, when we got to Jake's apartment, the footage was gone. It had been wiped off his computer, and his camera, with the original memory cards, was gone. Jake called Lara names I had never heard before as he ransacked the place, looking for where she might have hidden any of it. But it was just gone.

Remembering what Doorman Steve had said about Lara being out on the town on Jake's dime, I asked, "You have a credit card with just a first initial, something Lara could use?"

Jake stopped his ransacking and grabbed his wallet out of his pants pocket. "Damn her!" He showed us an empty slot in the wallet. "The production company."

Cassady arched an eyebrow at him. "You're incorporated?"

"I'm a professional."

"Professional what?"

"Focus, please." I handed Jake the phone. "Call your credit card company. Ask them the last charge on your card so you can figure out where you might have left it."

While Jake pounded through the automated menu in search of the information, I huddled with Tricia and Cassady. "If you ripped off your boyfriend, would you keep the stuff on you or ditch it somewhere?"

"Keep it," Tricia voted. "Putting it somewhere just increases the odds that you won't be able to get back to it when you need it."

"Not that I base this at all on personal experience," Cassady added, "but the whole point in taking something is leverage. You want it on hand when they come looking for you."

"Son of a bitch!" Jake screamed, throwing the phone across the room.

"Good news, Jake?" I asked.

"You know the last two places my credit card was used? The Peninsula Hotel."

I'd missed that one. Tricia shook her head. "That'll set you back six hundred a night. Unless she's in a suite."

"Where else, Jake?"

It took him a minute to be able to say it. "Hertz. Hertz Rent-a-Frigging-Car."

How about that. She moves out, then decides she's still mad, and rents a car. Maybe a nice big SUV, even. And goes for a moonlight drive in TriBeCa.

"You think she might have decided to leave town?" Tricia asked sweetly.

"She rented a car to run me down. She hates me! She wants to kill me!"

"Can't imagine why," Cassady said.

If Lara'd been following him, she could've been following me, been the woman at the Algonquin, just not for the reasons I'd thought. She could've seen him leave Lisbet, and killed her in a jealous rage. Then when I came around, she had to figure out if I was into Jake or on to her. It made sense. As much as murder could. "There are several lovely bars at the Peninsula. Anyone for cocktails?"

Cassady wound up in charge of keeping Jake in the apartment and off the phone while Tricia and I went to the hotel. Jake looked on the brink of a meltdown, but in case he got feisty, Cassady was bigger than Tricia and had a couple of self-defense classes under her belt to help her control him. Tricia brought the sympathy card to play with Lara if we had trouble getting her to confess.

"We're not calling Kyle?" Tricia asked in the cab. "I'm clarifying, not critiquing."

"No. He has other things on his mind."

Tricia, someone with plenty on her mind herself, nodded. After a moment, she said, "I know you're doing this for Davey, Molly, and I appreciate it, but I don't want you to lose Kyle over it."

I started to tell her I didn't want to lose her friendship either, but we seemed to be okay at the moment and I wasn't going to pick at wounds that might be healing. I didn't want to lose Kyle, but I also didn't want to be in a relationship where my sense of right and wrong didn't matter because I wasn't professionally charged with upholding it. "Thank you," I said.

The Peninsula Hotel is on Fifth Avenue, a gorgeous Beaux Arts building, gilded and burnished to gleaming beauty. You walk through the revolving door and an overwhelming double staircase under a massive chandelier makes you want to stop and wait for the Busby Berkeley chorus girls to descend.

Tricia picked up the house phone and asked for Lara's room. When Lara answered, Tricia asked, in flawless French, if her *grand-mère* was ready for dinner yet or if she needed more time. Lara told her she had the wrong room and hung up. Now that we knew she was up there, we sat down on a loveseat near the elevator banks and I called Lara's cell on my cell. There's more than one way to flush the partridge.

"Hello?" she answered with some irritation, probably because she didn't recognize the incoming number.

"Lara, it's Molly Forrester. Don't hang up."

"Give me a good reason."

"Jake's in trouble."

"Good." She hung up.

Damn, she was straight. Still, I dialed back, praying she would be intrigued enough about Jake's condition that she would answer again. She did. "What?"

"He's in the hospital, Lara."

"He deserves it."

"Deserves what?"

The Pause was brief, but telling. "Whatever happened."

"Where are you, Lara? Can you come see him?"

"I don't think so."

"He's asking for you. And his camera bag."

This Pause was unexpected. Was she considering it? "Too bad." Guess not.

"You really need to come, Lara. The police are here, Jake's so upset . . ."

"So am I. He's a lying bastard and a cheat and . . ." She trailed off and I thought she was searching for the word, but then I heard a sob and realized she was crying. For Jake or for what he'd driven her to?

"NYU Downtown ER," I said gently.

"Okay," she said and hung up.

"Are lies in the pursuit of truth still lies?" Tricia asked as I hung up and we moved over to stand outside the elevators.

"I'm not sure. Are ugly shoes worn by a beautiful woman still ugly?"

"Do you not like these?" she worried, looking down at her Narciso Rodriguez black leather ankle-strap sandals.

"I was staying theoretical."

"I rarely do."

"Part of your charm."

I almost didn't see Lara get off the elevator because two couples stepped off in front of her, then stopped mere inches in front of the elevator to have an animated debate about whether to have drinks at the hotel before going to dinner or to go straight to the restaurant. Lara had a Hermès scarf over her hair and Chanel sunglasses on, very Jackie O, but I spotted her when she put the camera bag down to adjust her Burberry denim jacket.

I skittered across the highly polished floor and grabbed the camera bag before she could pick it back up. "Let me help you with that, Lara," I offered.

"Put that down! It's not yours!" she protested.

"It's not yours either, but if you'd like to make a scene, I'm game." I wasn't sure where Tricia had gone, but I didn't dare take my eyes off Lara. "Then you can explain to the police why you have Jake's camera bag. And his credit card. And what you were doing earlier this evening."

She yanked her sunglasses off and I was startled to see how puffy her eyes were. She'd been crying mightily to look that bad under that much foundation. "Go away," she demanded.

I put the camera bag on my own shoulder. "Is everything you shot at the party in here, Lara? The less you hide now, the better it will be for you in the long run."

"I don't know what you're talking about."

"I find that when people say that to me, they know exactly what I'm talking about."

She shoved her sunglasses back on her face, stiff-armed

me out of the way, and bolted for the front door. I went after her, but Tricia had already circled around and positioned herself so that all she had to do was step into Lara's path and Lara went sprawling, actually sliding some distance across the highly polished floor. Several bellboys came running, but Tricia and I helped Lara to her feet and assured the staff that everything was quite all right. Each of us grasping an arm, we walked Lara to the door.

"I hate you both! Leave me alone!" Lara protested.

"It was supposed to be the best rehab program on the East Coast," Tricia said to me, just a little louder than conversationally. "I'm very disappointed."

"Can we get a refund or should we just try to send her back for another couple of weeks?" I asked. The handful of guests who'd bothered to look up shook their heads in sadness or sympathy and returned to their own affairs.

The hotel doorman opened the cab door so that we never had to let go of Lara and we slid into the backseat like one thrashing, six-legged creature. "You'll be part of the kidnapping charge!" Lara hissed at the driver.

The driver, a pockmarked Slav with big, sad eyes and a huge belly, popped open his glove compartment, consulted a small spiral notebook, and checked his watch. "There's a meeting at St. Aidan's in half an hour," he offered, closing the glove compartment back up.

"Thank you, but we're taking her to see someone." I gave him Jake's address.

"No!" Lara shrieked. "I don't want to see him ever again! I hate him! I hate him!"

The driver shook his head as he pulled away from the hotel curb. "Sounds like she needs a new therapist."

"Among other things," I assured him.

Tricia snuggled into Lara's shoulder and whispered, "The

sooner you cooperate with the police, the better off you'll be. Because if my brother suffers any more pain because of what you did, I'll personally escort you to your execution."

"What's your brother got to do with this?" Lara snapped.

Tricia and I looked at each other in disbelief. "Lara, everyone thinks David killed Lisbet. Including the police," I said.

"Why is that my concern?"

"Because he shouldn't be accused of a crime you committed."

Lara yanked her sunglasses off again. I was expecting the evil eye, but she whooped with laughter. Gut-busting laughter. Tricia poked her sharply, but that didn't stop her. "This isn't funny," Tricia protested, poking her again.

"You think I killed Lisbet?" Lara asked, struggling to stop laughing. "Why would I do that?"

"Because she had sex with Jake," Tricia responded, irritated.

"If I killed every slut that dog humped, I'd be a serial killer like no other," Lara sniffed. "And you wouldn't be here," she sniffed at me.

"I didn't sleep with Jake," I said.

"Then why were you coming around, calling all the time?"

"I was trying to figure out if he'd killed Lisbet. And I only called a couple of times."

"All the ugly phone calls about the Web site?"

"Wasn't me."

Lara laughed again. "Wasn't me. I don't need to kill them, I just need to leave him. I was slow in figuring that out, but I finally did."

"Yet you tried to run him over tonight," Tricia pointed out politely.

Lara shrugged disdainfully. "I lost my head. But I stopped at the last second because it seemed too hysterical. More effort than he's worth."

"Still, there's a police detective in the hospital. You need to earn Brownie points wherever you can."

"I have nothing to offer because I did nothing, I know nothing. Lisbet was alive when I took Jake out of there and I didn't see her again."

I didn't want to even lean on a conclusion, much less jump to one. "Took Jake out of where, Lara?"

"The pool house. He and Lisbet were in there, screwing and making one of his movies. I found them, I took him and the camera, and we left."

"What else?" Tricia asked.

"There was some screaming and begging and crying," she admitted and it was pretty easy to figure out which of them did which, "but no killing."

"Jake said no one knew he'd slept with Lisbet," I told her.

"He's lying. Are you shocked?" Lara asked.

"Sounds like he's covering for you," Tricia said.

Lara brightened. "He still cares for me?"

I shook my head. "He thinks you killed her."

"I didn't kill Lisbet and you know it!" Lara screamed at Jake moments later, after Tricia and I had gotten her upstairs to the apartment. It hadn't required nearly the amount of dragging I had anticipated. She'd gained momentum on her own as she'd considered the possibility that Jake was encouraging us to believe he thought she was guilty so we would think she was guilty.

"I never said you did, baby!" Jake cooed, wisely staying on the other side of the living room. He took a step toward Cassady as though to hide behind her, but Cassady stalked away, leaving him to cringe behind a chair.

"You want everyone to believe it was me!" Lara continued. "But I can prove it wasn't!" She yanked the camera bag from my shoulder, almost pulling me off my feet in the process, and shook its contents out onto the couch.

"My film!" Jake sighed, showing more emotion over its return than Lara's. The boy just wasn't very smart when it came to women, because she picked up on it, too.

"You're pathetic," she spat. "You're a terrible filmmaker. And even worse as a lover." She turned to address Tricia, Cassady, and me. "Don't waste your time. He'll give you no satisfaction."

"That's a lie!" Jake protested.

"As a lover or a filmmaker?" Cassady asked.

"Both," Lara answered, stalking into the bedroom. We all followed her, Jake still calling her a liar.

Lara sat down at the computer, slid the disk in, and started loading files. Her hands flew over the keyboard and the mouse. "Who's the real talent here, Jake?" I asked.

"We're a team," Jake croaked.

Lara laughed. "My English is so bad sometimes. Is 'team' the word you use when one person carries the other but gets none of the credit?"

"That's one of its most common usages, yes," I told her.

"I don't have to take this abuse," Jake protested.

"No, you don't," I agreed. "But if you walk out of here, you walk right back to the top of the suspect list."

Jake glared at us for a moment, then plopped down in the chair next to Lara's. He leaned in close to her and she growled something at him in Portuguese. I don't know if he understood it any better than I did, but her tone was quite clear. He sat back up.

Lara clicked open a file. "Watch this. Inside the pool house." On the screen, Jake faced the camera while he hurriedly tucked his shirt into his pants. Lisbet lounged on a divan behind him, taking her time about pulling her dress back on. A bottle of champagne—the bottle?—sat on the occasional table beside her. Jake continued dressing and yelling at the person behind the camera. Lisbet finished sliding into her dress, not seeming terribly bothered by what was going on. She was either really drunk or burned out from all of the emotion of the day. She bent down to pick up her Marc Jacobs pumps and almost lost her balance. Really drunk got my vote.

Jake backed out of the pool house and the camera followed him. He was gesturing and talking a mile a minute, pleading and bargaining. Then the camera fell to the ground and from that angle, caught a bizarre angle of Lara pummeling Jake, Jake taking it for a moment, and then Jake pulling Lara into his arms. Then, unbelievably, he started kissing her and she responded. The kissing got more and more passionate until Lara pushed him away.

"Thank God," Cassady muttered.

But then Lara grabbed the camera, picked it up, and the picture got difficult to understand. Was that the pool or the ground or . . . ? I was lost.

"We're walking away from the pool house here. Going to 'make up.' Because I'm an idiot," Lara explained.

The footage ended. There was an uncomfortable moment of silence while everyone debated what to say next. I was frustrated. The footage showed they left Lisbet alive, but how could they prove one of them didn't go back later? And how could we prove one of them did?

"Beautiful angles, Lara," Jake said respectfully. "Great use of available light."

Tricia rolled her eyes, but Lara turned to Jake with a hint of hope in her eyes. "You really think so?"

"Honey, as soon as we get this other thing figured out, we're taking you to a deprogrammer," Cassady warned. Jake tried to give her a menacing look but Cassady was so past that. "Puh-leez."

"I know 'wordless cinema' is your thing, guys," I said, "but is there any audio on this?"

"Yeah, it's just turned off," Jake explained.

"Can we watch it again—"

"Must we?" moaned Cassady.

"—with the sound?"

Jake leaned over, clicked on a couple of icons, and the footage began to play again, with sound.

"Put down the camera," the onscreen Jake demanded.

"You like everything on film," Lara's voice taunted from behind the camera. "Why not this?"

Lisbet said, "He told me you were only working together, nothing else."

"We're all adults here, there's no need for anyone to get upset or for things to get ugly," onscreen Jake tapdanced. "This shouldn't negatively impact on any of our relationships."

"Forget it, Jake," Lisbet said as she bent down for her shoes. "This shouldn't have happened and your movie isn't going to happen. Just forget it."

"Let's not be hasty. Any of us," Jake pleaded.

"She's done with you, Jake. So am I," Lara replied.

Jake backed out of the pool house. "Wait, Lara, please. I know you're upset, but let's look at this as an artistic experience we can both learn and grow from."

In the real world, Cassady smacked Jake on the back of the head. "There should be a law against you."

On-screen, Jake kept trying. "I made a mistake. But it made me realize what a treasure you are. Why, when I'm living with Godiva, did I have a craving for a Hershey bar? I don't know. I'm weak, I'm stupid," he wheedled.

"Amen, brother," Tricia said. Jake was sinking down in his chair; even he was embarrassed by his conduct. Only Lara was getting any pleasure out of watching him make a fool out of himself.

"I'm so sorry," on-screen Jake said. "What can I do to make you feel better?"

That's when the camera fell—or was thrown down, it seemed now—and Lara started pummeling him. It was hard to understand what Jake was saying as he worked to calm her and pull her into his arms. Especially because there was an odd sound and then voices somewhere else offscreen.

"What's that?" I asked.

We all leaned in as Lara backed it up. "I didn't play it through with the audio before."

She backed up to the point where the camera fell and played it again. She cranked the audio and we all held our breath, listening. We could hear Lara crying and Jake apologizing and something jangling, like wind chimes but not as melodious. Then the other voices. One was indistinct, but Lisbet's was loud and defiant, saying, "I don't care anymore. About any of you." The other person said something and Lisbet repeated, "I don't care!" even more defiantly. Then Lara picked up the camera and she and Jake walked away, leaving Lisbet and the indistinct voice alone in the pool house.

But who was it? I asked Lara to back it up one more time. She did and I closed my eyes to concentrate on just the sound, as blasphemous as Jake and Lara might find that. As I waited for the sound, my own memory of the pool house rushed back. Running up to see Lisbet lying there, wet and dead. Aunt Cynthia walking out with her shoes and the champagne bottle.

I felt ill. The sound came again. That jangling of gold on gold. Ring upon ring of bangles clanging together with every grand wave of her arm. I opened my eyes and found myself staring at an ashen Tricia who looked ready to faint. Jake and Lara had left Lisbet alive in the pool house.

But what if Aunt Cynthia hadn't?

19

Dear Molly, If I'm willing to lie to a man, does that mean I don't care for him as much as I thought I did? Or am I naive to think that any relationship can be completely truthful? This question has tremendous implications for my future in dating, working, and voting, so I'd appreciate an honest answer. Signed, Diogenes's Daughter

Tricia grabbed my hand as we stepped out of the elevator and headed for the door of her parents' apartment. "You sure you're ready for this?"

I'd heard so many lies in the last few days and told enough of them myself that I thought it was time to tell the truth. "Nope."

Tricia actually seemed relieved. "Okay. Me either. So what do we do?"

"I'd say turn and run, but I can't run in these shoes." Of course, I don't think Mr. Blahnik had fleeing in mind when he designed the d'Orsay black satin pumps I was wearing, even if they did have only a two-inch heel. And honestly, running wasn't actually that appealing at the moment. The thought of going into this luncheon and pretending all was unchanged while trying to seek out a way to corner Aunt Cynthia was daunting, but it was enticing, too.

Tricia, Cassady, and I had stayed up all night turning it inside out and upside down, but Aunt Cynthia had maintained her theoretical integrity as a suspect. While Lara and Jake had retired to the bedroom to "discuss their relationship," the three of us had raided Jake's kitchen and, over a midnight supper of cheese and crackers, microwave popcorn, Lucky Charms, and a couple of bottles of Rosemount Estates Shiraz, we laid out what we knew.

Aunt Cynthia had been the last one in the pool house with Lisbet. She'd emerged from the pool house with Lisbet's shoes and a champagne bottle that she could have disposed of well before the police started digging through her trash. She knew the house better than anyone else, so she could have stashed the bottle somewhere no one else would have found it. She was bigger than Lisbet, played tennis three times a week so she was stronger than Lisbet, and had been decidedly more sober than Lisbet.

But why? Why would she have done it?

"*Image vincit omnia*," Tricia had surmised, her eyes brimming with tears. "Aunt Cynthia's not a model of decorum, but even she has her limits. And she loves Davey. Perhaps she felt Lisbet had gone too far, embarrassing herself at the party and then sleeping with Jake. Aunt Cynthia doesn't mind a scene, but she hates a mess. And Lisbet was a mess."

"Aunt Cynthia doesn't strike me as the sort who'll crumple easily, even with Molly's knack for asking the proper question at the improper time," Cassady said. "What's the next step?"

"There's not enough to call Kyle and certainly not enough to tell Detective Cook," I admitted. "Tricia, are you going to the luncheon?"

"More than ever. And you're invited. Both of you. Let my mother try and keep us out."

"What's it going to do to your relationship with your parents if you help nail your aunt for this?" Cassady asked gently.

Tricia spent a moment carefully picking green clovers out of the box of Lucky Charms, then lining them up across her palm. "Nothing worse than what it will do if I know she's guilty and they close ranks around her."

That and the fact that Jake and Lara never emerged from the bedroom led to a discussion of relationships in general and the limits of forgiveness. Which led to my having to call Kyle. I didn't mentioned my suspicion of Aunt Cynthia because I knew it would only infuriate him because I didn't have coherent supporting evidence. Yet. I only told him that Lara had been driving the hit-and-run SUV, and she and Jake were coming in with their lawyer later in the morning to give statements and aid in the investigation as much as they possibly could. Cassady would be with them, but I didn't tell him she was going to spend the morning introducing them to their lawyer, a friend of hers, or that she would have the footage in her pocket; she was going to hold that in reserve until the proper moment. And to buy Tricia and me some time at the luncheon.

The call with Kyle hadn't been as strained as I'd expected. Almost, but not completely. I'd actually considered calling Kyle at work in the hopes that he wouldn't be there yet and I could leave a message with another detective. But that seemed cowardly, so I called him on his cell and didn't ask where he was. He didn't ask where I was either. That and the fact that we'd gone all night without talking didn't bode well for future conversations or for the future itself.

Why was I putting this case between us? Had I sensed his six-month stumbling block? Was I giving him a way out so that I could put the blame on his sense of professionalism instead of my lack of allure? Was I really so into solving this murder that I was making it the most important thing in my life? Or was it just that solving a murder seemed simpler than solving my own life? Maybe too many years of dating in Manhattan had so muted my emotions that I could only handle strong feelings in other people's lives.

The phone conversation had ended with Kyle asking me, "Do I want to know how you found any of this out?"

"Probably not," I answered.

"Do I want to know what else you know?"

"Definitely not. But I will call you soon."

The Pause took hold of the entire conversation and we left it at that, as cold and spiky as it was. I tried not to think about it now, as Tricia and I prepared to plunge into the bosom of her family and pluck out her aunt as a murder suspect.

Nelson answered the door. He was wearing a gorgeous Armani suit, which was apparently his city uniform. "Your parents are receiving guests in the drawing room," Nelson informed Tricia. "Your aunt is in the kitchen, instructing the staff."

"And my brothers?"

"With your parents. Your sister-in-law, as well."

Tricia made a face like the word didn't smell good and as we entered the drawing room, her look grew that much darker. In the drawing room, stationed at Mrs. Vincent's elbow, was Rebecca, wearing a Nanette Lepore multihued embroidered skirt and yellow scalloped sweater, Christian Louboutin yellow patent leather T-strap sandals, and the emerald necklace. With the marble fireplace behind them, flanked by bookcases filled with leather-bound volumes, they looked like they were posing for a portrait artist. Or maybe just posing.

"How nice," Tricia whispered before marching resolutely over to her mother and sister-in-law and kissing them both on the cheek. I followed along, but only said hello.

Mrs. Vincent shook my hand briefly. "Hello, Molly," she said politely.

"Thank you for coming. We appreciate your support," Rebecca said, squeezing my hand like a politician. "I understand you've been trying to help, and it was a nice thought."

I had a couple of not so nice thoughts about that, but out of respect—for Tricia, not for anyone else—I kept them to myself.

"Nice necklace," Tricia complimented. I couldn't have sounded so even and I'd never asked to wear the thing.

Rebecca patted it reverently. "Thank you."

"I thought it would look so nice on her and she's been such an angel through all this." Mrs. Vincent pressed her cheek to Rebecca's. I had to give Rebecca credit, she was playing her part admirably, even though her holier-than-thou attitude was going to send me screaming to the bar in another two minutes.

"So," Tricia asked, "is there an agenda for today?"

If her mother noticed the double question, she managed not to blink. "Cocktails, then lunch, then there will be an opportunity for people to speak to David and offer their support."

On the other side of the room, half a football field away, Mr. Vincent had a son on each side of him and was working the crowd, in political/fund-raising mode. The guests were almost all in formal business attire, suits in respectable colors and cuts, restrained shoes, minimal jewelry. Even the few flashy standouts were flashy only in that deliberate Park Avenue way.

The guest list appeared heavy on the senior Vincents' friends and lighter on the junior end of the spectrum. I didn't know if that was planned or a function of my generation's inability to show up anywhere on time. But I also surmised that one of the purposes of this gathering was to assure the senior Vincents that their friends were familiar with tragedy, too, and were standing by them. Or at least, not shunning them.

"Anything I can do to help?" Tricia offered bravely.

"That awful Crawford girl is here and I understand she's dating a young man at the *Times*. Perhaps you and Molly could talk to her and make sure she's not gathering information for him," Mrs. Vincent said.

"I'll see what I can do," Tricia said.

"We don't have to worry about that with you, do we, Molly?" Mrs. Vincent continued.

"No, ma'am, I'm not dating anyone at the *Times*," I assured her. "In fact, I'm thinking about canceling my subscription. I heard a rumor they hired an old boyfriend of mine, Peter Mulcahey, who doesn't write or behave nearly as well as I do." Mrs. Vincent laughed, but Tricia glanced over at me, wondering if I was deliberately sidestepping the issue of my own article. Which I was.

"Is Aunt Cynthia here?" Tricia asked, making it sound like a casual afterthought.

"Last I knew, she was in the kitchen straightening out the caterer. Go find Regan Crawford, dear, and make sure she's not reading anyone's diary."

"I'm this far from giving Regan the keys to the attic. Just for starters," Tricia told me through clenched teeth as we walked out of the room and down the hallway.

"We looking for her?" I asked.

"Only if she's hiding behind Aunt Cynthia," Tricia

replied. She stopped outside the door to the kitchen, turning to face me. "After Aunt Cynthia agrees to talk to me,
you should be safe for ten minutes. So, excuse yourself to go
to the bathroom. She's staying in the room on the right, just
past the bathroom. See what you can find, then I'll meet you
back in the drawing room and we'll go from there."

What I was hoping to find was the dress Aunt Cynthia
was wearing the night of the party or the robe she had on
poolside or anything else that might have been overlooked
by the police and by Aunt Cynthia herself that might now
yield evidence tying her to Lisbet's death. "On the right.
Got it."

Tricia took a deep breath and pushed open the kitchen
door. The Vincent kitchen made the ones in Viking magazine ads look cramped and dowdy. It was a vast expanse of
gleaming steel, brilliant glass, and sparkling tile. At the moment, it was crowded with white-jacketed hired help filling
trays and preparing plates while Aunt Cynthia argued with a
chef over the amount of dill in the salad dressing.

Her point made, Aunt Cynthia detached herself from the
chef, missing the vicious look he gave her back, and came to
greet us. "Friendly faces!" she exclaimed, hugging Tricia so
enthusiastically that the bangles clanged mightily, seeming
to resound throughout the room. Aunt Cynthia offered me
a kiss on the cheek, which was sufficient since I knew why I
was really there. Followed by a pat on the cheek and one
more chorus of the bangles.

"I hate to interrupt, but I need to talk to you," Tricia told
her. "Could I have a moment?"

"Anything you want," Aunt Cynthia assured her. I followed the two of them as Tricia led the way back down the
hallway to a small sitting room decorated in a hunting
theme that was just this side of precious.

Tricia sat on a brocade loveseat and pulled Aunt Cynthia down beside her. "Molly and I were just discussing, Dad doesn't look at all well. Do you think the stress is too much for him? Should he excuse himself from the meal?"

Aunt Cynthia frowned. "I thought he looked flushed, but I wasn't sure. This has been so hard on him."

I stood up. "I'm sorry. The rest room?" They pointed in unison. "I'll be right back." I slipped out of the room as Aunt Cynthia launched into a recitation of all the ways in which her brother had not been properly caring for his health even before the tragedy and Tricia nodded encouragingly. Funny thing was, Mr. Vincent looked great, but whatever worked.

Out in the hall, I took a moment to get my bearings. Just past the bathroom, on the right. I checked the hallway in both directions to make sure no one was coming and slunk down to the door. There was an awful moment when I thought it was locked, but I gave the knob an extra twist and it opened.

The room was a guest room, with the careful anonymity of a room that has to serve a wide range of people. The sleigh bed and matching dressers were gorgeous, though the ice blue drapes and bedspread were too cool for my taste. But it was the armoire I was interested in.

My heart pounded as I eased open the doors of the armoire, hoping against hope that the multicolored tiered silk dress would be hanging right in the middle. It wasn't. In fact, the armoire was half-filled with men's clothes. Were these Nelson's clothes? How open were they being about their relationship?

I skimmed through the hanging clothes with a growing sense of dread. These weren't Aunt Cynthia's clothes. They were Rebecca's. The men's clothes were Richard's. I rethought the directions Tricia had given me and realized I'd made a stupid mistake. She'd said the room was on the right and she'd said it while she was facing the main entry. I'd gone right with my back to the entry. I was in the wrong room.

Mindful of the limited time, I hurriedly slid the clothes back into place, but one of Rebecca's longer dresses caught on a classic Vuitton satchel on the floor of the armoire. I bent down to unsnag the hem and slide the satchel back into place. When I did, the satchel gave an unmistakable gurgle.

I knelt down and carefully unzipped the satchel. Cradled in a Nautica sweatshirt, the champagne bottle was turned so I could only see part of the back label. Pulling my sleeve down over my hand, I nudged the bottle around until I could see the front label. It was one of the bottles from the party. And the bottom right-hand edge of the label was torn, frayed, and pulled up from the bottle.

I sat back on my heels, light-headed. How had they kept this away from the police? Was Rebecca hiding the bottle for Aunt Cynthia? Had Aunt Cynthia planted it on Rebecca? Or had I been wrong? My heart thudded so hard I could barely hear myself think. Could Rebecca have done this? *Would* Rebecca have done this?

The most pressing question was, should I take the bottle with me or leave it there? I didn't want to contaminate it but I didn't want to lose it either. Where was I going to put it if I took it out of the room? It didn't exactly fit under my skirt, but I couldn't be sure of getting to Tricia without anyone else seeing me first. I stood, the bottle in my hand, still thinking. I turned around and almost stepped on Rebecca's toes.

"Isn't this a surprise," she said with an ugly sneer, her fingers tapping languidly on the emerald necklace.

I kept the bottle pressed to my leg as though it could hide in the folds of my skirt. "I'm sorry, is this your room?" I asked as lightly as possible.

"Why are you in here?" she asked.

"Tricia asked me to get something for Aunt Cynthia and I guess I got the directions confused."

"You're not a very good liar, Molly."

"Actually, I'm an excellent liar. I occasionally surprise myself. You just caught me unprepared. Good lies take time, don't you find?"

"Are you calling me a liar?"

"Not yet."

"Are you planning to?"

"Depends on what you tell me."

"Why should I tell you anything?"

"Because I know what you did to Lisbet."

"Prove it."

A little voice in the back of my mind was screaming and encouraging my mouth to join in. But if I screamed now, there was too much of a chance that things would go awry. I was in her room without permission and holding a bottle that she might have already wiped her fingerprints off. Forget Regan Crawford, I was going to look like the nosy reporter mucking around where I didn't belong.

Rebecca grabbed my arm and pulled it away from my side. "What is that?" she asked, looking at the bottle.

"So you're a good liar, too."

"I've never seen that bottle before."

"Why else would it be in your satchel?"

"Because you put it there. You're planting evidence to make me look guilty because you promised my vicious little sister-in-law that you'd make sure David went free. And you'd do anything for that conniving little brat."

"I had no idea the two of you were so close."

Rebecca smiled. It was the most genuine expression I'd ever seen on her, but it still looked twisted and ill. "So what are you going to do, Molly?"

"Take my chances." I took a step past her, toward the door, but as I did so, she reached into the dresser drawer and brought out a small handgun. Now, I can pick out Jimmy Choos at twenty paces, but all I can tell you about this gun was that it was small and shiny and the ugliest thing I'd ever seen in my life.

"Bad choice," she said, pointing the gun at me. I stopped.

"What the hell are you doing?" I asked, not anxious to be confrontational but not wanting to appear blasé either.

"I told you if you didn't leave this alone, you were going to be next. I've always heard it's easier the second time."

"That's love, not murder," I corrected her.

"We'll see."

The little voice suggested screaming again and I was starting to see the wisdom in that. It must have shown on my face, because Rebecca pulled me close, the gun nestled against my stomach. "Scream and I'll shoot. I'll say there was a struggle after I found you going through my things, planting the bottle and the gun."

"I withdraw my earlier assessment," I said quietly. "You're a fantastic liar."

"Thank you. Now you're going to put the bottle back in the satchel and we're going to take a walk. Throw a few things in the river."

"Like you threw Lisbet in the pool?"

I was expecting her to be angry, but she was proud. "That slut was asking for it. And you know what, it was the smartest thing I've ever done. I was killing myself trying to get back in their good graces, but I kill her and all of a sudden, I'm the best daughter-in-law in the world. They rely on me, they trust me, they believe me. Punching that skank's ticket wound up being my way back in."

"You killed Lisbet to get in good with the Vincents? I don't follow."

"She said she was better than I was, that she didn't have to follow their rules. I tried to go my own way and Richard threw me out. It was all about being a Vincent and what people thought and all that uptight WASP crap. I wasn't good enough."

I wanted to ask how hard she could have been trying when she had wound up in the gossip columns and tabloids on a regular basis, but "That must have been so hard" seemed like a much wiser choice.

"Ripped my heart out. So I decided, I'd beat them at their own game. I'd be a good girl. I had to beg Richard to take me back, but it was worth it. And then David hooks up with Lisbet, who's not only a pig but a slut, and everybody falls all over her. She gets a big party and she gets to wear the emeralds and she makes a fool of herself and nobody bats an eye. I'm so furious I can't sleep and I take a walk by the pool. Aunt Cynthia comes out of the pool house, all disgusted, tells me Lisbet's in there, drunk as a skunk and whoring around. So I go in to talk to her. To warn her, share my experience. Lisbet says to mind my own business. No one's going to tell her how to behave. Especially me."

I stared at her, chilled more by her matter-of-fact recitation of the facts than the facts themselves. She beamed. "Taught her, didn't I?"

"That was worth killing her?" I asked.

"At the time, I was just furious. But it's been incredibly worth it. I'm right where I want to be. Except now, you're in the way."

Glued to my hip, she nudged me back to the armoire. "Pick it up," she commanded, tossing her head toward the satchel. I obediently snagged it and placed the bottle back in its sweatshirt nest. I held it up for her, but she shook her head. "I have my hands full with you and the gun. You carry it."

She took my left arm like she was eight and I was her favorite friend, both arms wrapped around mine so her inner arm hid the gun from view, but not from use. It was pressed against my ribs, right by my heart. I was carrying the satchel in that hand, which made it awkward for us to walk, but gave her control over what I did with it, too. For a raving lunatic, she was pretty smart.

She guided me back to the door. I understood her willingness to shoot me, but still, how did she think she was going to walk me through a foyer full of people and not have anyone notice we had become extraordinarily close?

Because the foyer was empty. Everyone had gone in to be seated for the luncheon. Tricia had probably looked for me in Aunt Cynthia's room and couldn't figure out where I'd gone. Even if I risked screaming now, there was no guarantee in a monster apartment like this that anyone would hear me.

"Rebecca, you're just making it worse," I attempted as we got closer to the foyer. "Stop now and we can work something out."

"I have everything worked out," Rebecca insisted, getting strident. "You're messing it up, but it's going to be fine again, it's going—"

"Rebecca?"

Mrs. Vincent entered the foyer in front of us. Rebecca and I stopped. I could feel the anger pulsing in her body and wondered if she could feel my joy.

"Mrs. Vincent—" I began, but Rebecca pushed the gun more firmly against my side, so I stopped to carefully construct what I was going to say.

"The soup's getting cold. Where have the two of you been?"

"Molly and I need to step out for a moment, Mother. We'll be right back. Start without us."

"How is that going to look?" Mrs. Vincent asked. "It's fine for Molly not to be there, but we're making a statement of family unity and you're spoiling it. Come to the table."

Rebecca propelled me forward. "I said, I'll be right there."

"Rebecca, come to the table at once," Mrs. Vincent repeated. Behind her, Richard and Mr. Vincent were moving into view as they came out of the dining room.

"This is what you wanted, isn't it, Rebecca?" I asked.

"Shut up, Molly."

"To be an indispensable member of the family?"

"Rebecca, in. Now," Mrs. Vincent commanded, imperious finger pointing the way. But Tricia, David, and Aunt Cynthia had come out now and the guests weren't far behind, lured by the scent of trouble in the air.

"Rebecca, explain yourself," Mr. Vincent demanded.

Rebecca was all but dragging me to the door now. Mr. Vincent and Richard were coming for us and, worried that innocent people—besides me—were about to get hurt, I knew I couldn't hesitate any longer. I literally dragged my feet. As we walked past the round table and its rug, I dragged my right foot so the beautifully tapered heel on my shoe caught in the fringe. "Oh, wait!" I exclaimed, "I'm stuck."

It yanked us to a stop. Rebecca leaned to see where I was snagged and I did my plant-and-pivot move, shifting my weight with sufficient force to separate me, Rebecca, the gun, and the satchel and send us all tumbling to the floor.

Screams filled the foyer as people saw the gun. Richard yelled for someone to call 911. Mr. Vincent yelled for calm. Mrs. Vincent yelled for Rebecca to behave herself. Tricia yelled for me to kick Rebecca's ass and Cassady yelled for Tricia to say it again. Rebecca and I scrambled on our hands and knees after the gun. I grabbed it, but Rebecca got up on one knee and stomped on my hand with her stiletto heel. Even as I screamed, I tried to hang onto the gun, but my hand wasn't responding and she yanked it away from me and got to her feet, waving the gun wildly and backing toward the front door.

Richard stepped closer and she leveled the gun at him.

"Don't, Richard," Mr. Vincent advised.

I scooted myself back across the floor until I was close enough to snag the satchel. Rebecca was so focused on Richard that she didn't notice at first; when she did glance down, I froze and she looked right back up at Richard.

"This time, your father has good advice," she told him. "Don't mess with me right now, honey. I'll explain it all later."

I slid my hand into the satchel and wrapped my hand around the neck of the bottle.

"Would someone please explain to me what's going on here?" Mrs. Vincent implored.

"Rebecca killed Lisbet and we have to go dispose of the murder weapon," I explained as I pulled the bottle out and held it up for all to see.

The air pressure in the foyer dropped from all the sudden intakes of breath at the same moment. Rebecca screamed and turned to aim the gun at me, but I swung the champagne bottle low and hard, catching her behind the knees and sweeping her feet out from under her. She fired off one shot as she fell, which sent everyone running for cover. I pounced on her the moment she hit the floor and smacked her hand with the champagne bottle to make sure she let go of the gun. It slid across the floor and people shrank from it as if it were a copperhead.

Tricia was the first one at my side, throwing herself on the ground to pin her sister-in-law's legs down. "Careful, her heels are sharp."

The crowd closed around us as Rebecca continued to writhe and wail, but I wasn't about to get up until the police arrived. I looked up and saw a curvaceous blond on her cell phone. "Are you calling 911?"

She made a face of utter disbelief at me. "Get serious." Someone at the other end of the line answered and she said, "Hi, it's Regan Crawford. Is he in?"

"This is my story!" I protested.

"I don't see you filing it," she said. Then, into the phone, she cooed, "Peter, honey, I have the most amazing story."

Life, love, and murders. Just when you think you have them figured out, they find a way to surprise you.

20

"I hope I never see you again."

Tragically, there were quite a few people in my life that were in a position to be telling me that, but fortunately, the one who was saying it was someone about whom I felt exactly the same. Meeting Detective Darcy Cook had been unpleasant. Getting run down with her had been painful. Saying good-bye to her was delightful.

We were on the sidewalk in front of Kyle's precinct. Detective Myerson had come to retrieve his partner, freshly discharged from the hospital, and go over the paperwork necessary to transfer Rebecca to the care of Suffolk County. Detective Cook was still learning to walk on crutches, but I had no doubt that she would soon be using them as instruments of punishment as well as transportation.

Tricia and Cassady had come along with me, mainly to make sure I actually showed up and spoke to Detective Cook because I would have been perfectly happy to let our relationship languish where it was. But my well-bred buddies had prevailed upon me, convincing me that the gracious gesture would also go far toward mending things with the more important homicide detective in my life.

Assuming they could be mended. I'd pushed Kyle to the

brink and I still wasn't sure if I'd backed off in time or if he'd gone over. I'd actually spoken to Detective Lipscomb more yesterday, in the aftermath of Rebecca's arrest, than I had spoken to Kyle. I'd picked up the phone half a dozen times last night, wanting to call him, then realized I had no idea what to say. This morning, he was standing back and observing as I attempted to mend fences with Detective Cook.

"I understand and I apologize," I told her. Flowers or candy probably would have been too weird, but I wished I had some ceremonial offering other than a handshake. I'd even considered a bottle of champagne, but I didn't think she'd see the humor in it. If I'd handed her an object, she would've been forced to take it, but as I stuck out my hand, I knew there was an excellent chance she was going to just stare at it.

But she shook it. And then she offered her hand to Tricia. "I'm sorry for your family's loss. Losses. But it must help to have such a dedicated friend."

Tricia smiled appreciatively. "Thank you. It does."

"Friends, plural," Cassady corrected, extending her hand.

Detective Cook actually laughed and shook her hand. "Plural."

Detective Myerson gave us all a wave of farewell. "Stay out of trouble. And stay out of Southampton. Please." He began the slow process of getting Detective Cook to the car.

I turned around to face Kyle. He was standing with his hands in his pockets, looking down at the ground. At least he wasn't pinching his lip.

Tricia patted me on the arm. "We're going to walk down to the corner to get a cab. We'll wait for you. Kyle, see you later," she said with a confidence I didn't feel.

"Don't make her cry," Cassady warned him before Tricia led her away.

Kyle's brilliant blue eyes drifted up to meet mine. "Why does she think I'd make you cry?"

"Because I've been my usual calm, unemotional self lately and it wouldn't take much."

His eyes drifted back to the pavement. "You okay?"

"I didn't get shot."

One hand came out of his pocket and ran through his hair. "I know how that goes."

"Kyle, I'm sorry." This isn't where or how I'd planned to say it, but I realized I couldn't wait.

He looked up, surprised. "For what?"

"You want a list?"

He shrugged. "Just tell me if there're any exclusions."

I tried not to smile. "No, I'm sorry for the whole mess."

He let himself smile. "Yeah, but since you turned out to be right, I'll cut you some slack. Just don't plan on using Cook as a personal reference anywhere."

"What about you?"

He squinted thoughtfully and I plunged ahead. "I know it's been six months, a little more, but—"

"Have you been talking to Lipscomb?"

I nodded. He shook his head and I wasn't sure which of his partners frustrated him more at that moment. If I could still be considered a partner in any sense. "This is worth working out," I said when he didn't say anything.

He stepped in close. "Right again."

"Just maintaining my batting average," I said, trying desperately to sound cool, like I hadn't doubted it for a minute.

"You need to leave before I engage in inappropriate public behavior and get in serious trouble." He brushed the back of his hand against my cheek. "Call me when you get to work."

"I'm not being tailed anymore."

"No, but you'll have decided where you want to have dinner."

"I already know where I want dessert."

"Deal." He pressed his finger to my lips and hurried up the stairs.

"Kyle?" I called after him. He stopped and came back down. While we were resolving issues, I had another one to toss on the pile. "Speaking of phone calls. Last week, when you called right as I was leaving, you were going to ask me something and you never did."

He nodded. "I've been busy."

"What was it?"

"Does it matter now?"

"How can I tell when I don't know what it was?"

He shook his head, amused. "I was going to ask you if you wanted to go away for the weekend."

I would have kicked myself if my Blahniks hadn't had such pointed toes. "Did I miss my moment?"

"Not at all. We're just crossing Southampton off the list. We'll talk about it at dinner."

Tricia and Cassady were fidgeting on the corner as I floated up. Cassady's eyebrow slid up to an appreciative angle. "Things back on course with New York's finest?"

"Finest detective or finest friends?" I asked, linking arms with them.

"We were always fine," Tricia protested.

"Liar," I said.

"No, truly," she insisted. "I was furious with you, and rightly so, but we were always fine at the foundation. Well, mostly fine. I honestly can't imagine you making me so angry that I wouldn't be your friend anymore."

Cassady waved her hands in mock distress. "Tricia, please. You know how she loves a challenge. Don't give her one."

I checked my watch. "You two have time for coffee before work?"

"I consider it a medical necessity," Cassady answered.

"I do," Tricia agreed, "but do you? You have an article to write."

"She what?" Cassady answered for me since I was dumbfounded and unable to answer for myself.

"You're not going to let Peter Mulcahey have the last word on this tragedy, are you? Especially since I've instructed my family not to speak to any member of the press except you. Lunch is at one at Aquavit, by the way. Mother, Dad, Richard, Davey, and me."

I looked to Cassady, anxious to share my disbelief. Cassady shook her head. "Let her take charge, Molly. It's her way of grieving."

As we walked down the street, I was profoundly grateful for getting—and taking—a second chance. Seems to me that even when you know how difficult the process will be, some things—falling in love, solving a mystery, making friends—are worth doing again because they give you another opportunity to understand and appreciate the complexities of the human heart. And those lessons, however hard won, help to reassure us that we've done the right thing and life will now fall into place.

For a little while, at least.